W9-AIE-513

RAISING THE DEAD

ROGER L. SIMON

RAISING THE DEAD

A MOSES WINE DETECTIVE NOVEL

VILLARD BOOKS NEW YORK 1988

Library of Congress Cataloging-in-Publication Data
Simon, Roger Lichtenberg.
Raising the dead.
I. Title.
PS3569.I485R35   1988   813'.54   87-40578
ISBN 0-394-56441-3

Manufactured in the United States of America
9   8   7   6   5   4   3   2
First Edition

Book Design: Jessica Shatan

FOR DAVID FREEMAN

THE MESSIAH WILL COME ONLY WHEN HE IS NO LONGER NECESSARY; HE WILL
COME ONLY ON THE DAY AFTER HIS ARRIVAL.
—FRANZ KAFKA,
PARABLES

RAISING THE DEAD

If Spinoza was right and everything is predestined, then there was no point in doing sit-ups. The little paunch that was beginning to creep over my belt was foreordained by a larger power or force, and there was nothing even three hours a day on my slant board could do about it.

It had also been predestined that I would be born in New York, that I would be Jewish, that I would have children, that I would be divorced, that I would be a radical and then not be a radical, that I would be a private detective in Los Angeles, that I would have a variety of cases and finally that I would end up working for the Arabs. Or as Sharif Ali said to Lawrence of Arabia: "It is written, El Lawrence." At least that's what he said in the movie, and that was more than enough for me.

It's just that I never *thought* I would wind up working for the Arabs. I never expected it. It wasn't that I was anti-Arab or anything, at least not consciously. I certainly didn't want to think of myself that way. And normally a political case would start my juices flowing double. That's why I entered this business in the first place. But this time it felt peculiar, as if I were betraying my own people even though the Arabs' cause seemed just and they were willing to pay me well—quite well, in fact.

Chantal Barrault, my French Canadian sometime girlfriend, sometime partner, thought it was funny.

"Big liberal," she said. "An Indian skins his knee and you'd fly to Montana to give him a Band-Aid. But some Jews blow up an innocent Arab and you turn queasy about taking the case."

"I'm not queasy, and we don't know if they did it. It could've—"

"Hel-low! Everybody knows it's the Jewish Defense Squad. Who else could it be?"

"It is, huh? Tell that to the police. They haven't been able to prove anything." My voice sounded oddly shrill. What was I doing, defending the Jewish Defense Squad, of all people? I looked around to see if anybody was listening. We were sitting in the balcony of Greenblatt's Delicatessen on Sunset, perhaps the most assimilated Jewish deli in America, at least the only one I knew that offered a selection of a dozen vintage cabernets and champagnes by the glass to accompany a pastrami on rye. No self-respecting JDS member would've been caught dead there.

Two hours earlier I had been in Orange County at the headquarters of the Arab-American Friendship Association in Fullerton, actually a storefront in a shopping mall between a Wells Fargo bank and a cosmetics store. I had half expected to find threadbare Persian rugs and a portrait of Hafez al-Assad on the wall, but the environment was more contemporary than Greenblatt's—mauve industrial carpets, black high-tech desks and arty sepia prints of Middle Eastern souks on the wall. It might have been a West Hollywood travel agency—"Shop in Downtown Beirut on Our Easy Layaway Plan!"

You wouldn't have guessed that seven weeks before, an explosion had occurred within twenty feet of this very premises when a car bomb blew up a Mazda RX-7 parked out front, resulting in the death and dismemberment of its owner, the Association's president, a lawyer named Joseph Damoor. It had been the first apparent case of the Middle Eastern terrorist war reaching the shores of Southern California. Twenty-four hours before that an elderly Jewish couple on their fiftieth anniversary tour, Stanley and Ethel Eisenbud, had been machine-gunned to death by Arab terrorists at the check-in counter of the Larnaca Airport in Cyprus, half the world away.

Two men were waiting for me: Mr. Said, the Association's short, nervous treasurer, and Dick Terzi, its new president, who looked at me with the smug, self-congratulatory expression of the minor celebrity who expects to be recognized. It turned out he was a disc jockey on one of Orange County's leading easy-listening stations.

"Why do you need me?" I asked them directly after politely turning down their generous offer of an assortment of Danish and halvah. "Aren't the police looking into this?"

"Ah, the police," said Said with the hint of an accent. "What can they know?"

"I'd think in a case like this they'd be making every effort."

"Mr. Wine . . ." Terzi waved his hand in a familiar gesture. "May I call you Moses?"

"Sure."

"Look, this is obviously a delicate matter for all of us. I'm a second-generation Arab-American—Lebanese on my mother's side, Syrian on my father's. You're a Jewish-American . . . also second-generation?"

"Third."

"Religious?"

"Not at all."

"Good, good. . . . Well, I don't think any of us like to see this kind of racial violence here in our country."

"I agree. Antiracism is one of the few causes left worth dying for."

"I can see we're on the same wavelength, Mose."

"I don't think so."

Terzi frowned. "Why not?"

"I hate easy-listening."

The deejay made a show of laughing, but I could see he didn't think it was so funny.

Mr. Said cleared his throat. "Mr. Wine, Mr. Damoor was a great man, a great humanitarian . . . a great force against Arab discrimination in this country. You are no doubt aware we suffer from certain preconceptions at this time. Let me tell you that I myself have spent many extra hours waiting at airports, missed business opportunities, been insulted and—"

"I understand, Mr. Said."

"Mr. Damoor was also my best friend, godfather of my children. He did not deserve to die at the hands of these . . . vigilantes." I could see a tear in his eyes.

"I'm aware of Mr. Damoor's reputation, but I'm still not sure how—"

"The police haven't gotten anywhere, Mose." This was Terzi. "You know how it is—we're dealing with a closed group here. The cops can't even get to first base."

"Why do you think I will?"

"Well, face it." He smiled. "You're one of them."

"The Jewish Defense Squad?"

"Hey, Moses, take it easy. I didn't mean it that way. I know you don't agree with a word they say. We checked you out— otherwise we wouldn't be here, right?" He tapped me on the shoulder and winked. Then he frowned. "You know what those sick bastards did? The next night they stole into Joseph Damoor's backyard and spray-painted 'Revenge for the Victims of Larnaca/Death to Arab Terrorists and All Other Nazi Anti-Semitic Swine!' on the retaining wall of his pool, right where his little girls keep their swimming toys."

I nodded. "I saw it in the paper."

So had Chantal. She reminded me later after I had told her the whole story. She put down her roast beef with Russian dressing and looked at me.

"Moses, don't you realize what this is?"

"What?"

"We've talked about the big international case. This could be it."

"Hmmm . . ." I said.

Chantal shook her head. "You know, sometimes I think you don't really want to make it."

"What's that supposed to mean?"

"You know what it means."

"Right. You think I want to remain this depressed little gum-shoe with a minor-league practice in L.A. when I could be the Melvin Belli of private detection, jetting off to distant ports at the slightest hint of danger."

"Maybe."

"Great. Well, maybe we all live our own lives, huh?" I sat there picking at my tuna-fish sandwich and feeling alienated. In a certain way, Chantal was right. At first, when we had formed our partnership, I had been energized by it. But now, a malaise had set in. I had become sick and tired of my own ambitions. And of other people's too. I drove around the city and all I could see was vacuous lives motivated by self-interest. Even pleasure was gone, unless pleasure could be construed as a bigger swimming pool or a fancier car. The material rush of the eighties was winding down of its own accord, like a carousel going slower and slower until its exuberant carnival music had turned into a discordant dirge.

"So how're you going to do it?" Chantal asked.

"What?"

"Infiltrate the Jewish Defense Squad."

"I haven't the slightest idea. I haven't been inside a synagogue since my Bar Mitzvah."

TWO

"Shalom. You have reached the offices of the Jewish Defense Squad. Please leave your name and phone number at the tone and we will return your call as soon as possible. If you care about the battle concerning Jew hatred, you will call the offices of the American Civil Liberties Union and complain to them in the most vociferous terms: *No Jew* should defend a Nazi under any circumstances. Shalom."

I left a number and the name Mike Greenspan.

Five minutes later I got a call back from a man who identified himself as Howard Melnick. I recognized him immediately as the potbellied, six-foot-tall CPA with the Marine brush cut and the stubby cigars who had been the head of the JDS in Southern California as long as I could remember the organization, the same Howard Melnick I had seen interviewed on television those seven weeks ago telling reporters that no, the JDS did not claim responsibility for the dismemberment of Joseph Damoor, but yes, it certainly applauded the act as a legitimate form of self-defense in the grim war against criminal international terrorism. One thing I had to say for Melnick—he wasn't racked by ambivalence.

I told him I was an unemployed aerospace worker down in L.A. from Seattle, looking for work, and was interested in his organization. He said interested how and I said maybe joining. He said when would you want to do that and I said no time like the present how about now? He said all right and gave me their address, which I already knew.

Ten minutes later I was headed down Fairfax Avenue, L.A.'s Jewish district, that gridlocked melting pot of the pious and postmodern that slices down from the Hollywood Hills past the Farmers' Market and on into the city's black belt. At one time the Jewish Defense Squad had had its offices prominently displayed right on the avenue itself between the Vilna Bakery and a falafel stand. I would see their members then as I drove by, four or five high-school-dropout types lurking by a storefront, overweight, badly dressed and anxiety-ridden, anomalies in the American Jewish world—poor relations. Those days, in the full flush of victory from the Six-Day War and semivictory from the Yom Kippur War, they would congregate ostentatiously behind their office window, parading about and passing secret orders like members of some wacko Bund that got lost in a time warp. But now, judging from their new candy-store-sized digs around the corner on Willoughby, they seemed to have fallen on some-what less upbeat times. Considering all the action in the Middle East and the current religious revival, I wasn't sure why.

Melnick was puffing one of his cigars, standing by the door as if waiting for me, the prime fish of the day, when I got there. Behind him I could see a couple of the present generation of high school dropouts, two extremely short blond guys in yar-mulkes and T-shirts that said "We Get High on Shabbos Can-dles!" leafing through back issues of martial-arts magazines. Above their heads, a large poster advertised the most recent speaking schedule of their international leader, the infamous Rabbi Judah Lipsky. It appeared to be a couple of months old.

"So you're Greenspan, are you?" said Melnick.

"Uhuh. That's me."

"From Seattle, huh?"

"Right."

"Not a lot of Jews up in Seattle . . . oh, no. I take that back. There are a few. Although they wouldn't want to admit it." He laughed and puffed on his cigar. "So, Greenspan, you're think-ing of joining the Jewish Defense Squad. That's a big commit-ment. Not easily done, especially if you're an FBI agent. Half the guys that walk in here are FBI."

"I'm not FBI. I can promise you."

"That's a start. . . . So, out of a job, huh? A victim of dis-crimination?"

"I'm not sure."

"Not sure. Damn straight you're not sure. Listen, Green-span, a lot of educated Jews like you go around thinking you're immune to the anti-Semitic disease, but it's all around you. You think some wisenheimer veepee at Whirlibird Aviation doesn't look at you and think dirty Jew, slimeball kike or what-ever just because you have a Ph.D. from Caltech? Gimme a break, Greenspan. This is the real world out there. And if you think it's filled with the low-fat milk of human kindness, you've got another think coming."

The boys in the back nodded their approval.

"And I've gotta tell you. We don't usually take people in just like that, right off the street. You have to prove your loyalty. How do I know you're even from Seattle?"

"I could show you my ID."

"That could be fake too. . . . Know any people in the Jewish community up there?"

"None that I would trust."

"Haha, I see your point."

"That's one of the reasons I want to move down here. Be around my people."

"Why don't you go all the way? Move to Israel. Everybody else does." He seemed depressed about that.

"I heard a lot of Israelis are moving back here."

"That bunch? Selfish assholes if they're not criminals. . . . Anyway, how about you?" He stared at me, sizing me up like a hunk of kosher beef. "We could put you to the test. You're a little old, you know. How old *are* you? Thirty-five? Forty? In any case, you look in pretty good shape. Ready for something that will really test your mettle right off the bat? Maybe we should put you on cemetery duty."

"Cemetery duty?"

"Guarding the old Jewish cemetery in East L.A. so the beaners, uh, Mexican-Americans to you social humanitarians, don't desecrate the graves of our ancestors. And if you think that's a joke you should take a look at some of the stones over there—covered with piss and Aztec writing."

"Okay, I'll do it."

"Cemetery duty?" He looked surprised.

"Why not?"

"You sure you want to do that?" He frowned, sucking on his cigar. "Okay, well, but I want to warn you. It can get pretty weird over there. A lot of gang warfare. Junkies, low-riders and assorted street creeps. They're a low-self-respect minority."

"I think I can handle myself."

"Glad to hear it. Most Jews come in here acting like they were pussy-whipped at birth. Pass this and you jump to the head of the class. And we could sure use some help. Right, Izzie?"

"Yeah," said the shorter of the two short dropouts, who was now standing up and also studying me with interest. "Me and Moe were gonna go up tonight."

"Izzie and Moe?" I said.

"Right," said Izzie, grinning. "Isador Einstein and Moe Berg —the Prohibition cops. You saw the TV movie?"

"No, but I heard of them."

"They were Jewish." He nodded to his buddy. "That's why we took their names."

"Good idea," I said.

"You want us to pick you up tonight or you pick us up?"

I thought for a second, shrugged. "I don't know my way around so well yet, so why don't you . . ."

"Great. Moe's got an old pink Chevy looks like a regular tacomobile. And it's got plenty of room for the dogs."

"Dogs?"

"The Dobermans."

"Oh."

"So where do we pick you up?"

"I'm supposed to eat tonight with a friend at this place called Canters. You know it?" Every Jew in Los Angeles knew Canters, but I figured it would help if I sounded ignorant. "I'll be in front right after dinner."

"No, no. Not dinnertime. We don't go till late. Around midnight."

"That'll be fine."

The three of them looked at me.

"I'll wait," I said.

I drove back feeling like I had just spent the last half hour traipsing around in the sewers of Paris without rubber boots. I wanted to throw away my shoes and burn my clothes. And then take a long shower, preferably in Lysol. Racist jerks made me crazy, and Jewish racist jerks made me even crazier. I felt somehow personally responsible for their paranoid stupidity. On the other hand, there was something strangely harmless about these guys, innocuous, as if they were part of some dumb after-school club and couldn't have been responsible for anything quite so bold as bombing the headquarters of the Arab-American Friendship Association. Cemetery duty was more their speed. Or getting into shoving matches with particularly pushy members of Jews for Jesus.

When I arrived back at the office, Chantal had a number of news clippings spread out on her desk. She was studying them while glancing up at the TV, which was playing a tape of an old talk show. Joseph Damoor was debating the "Palestinian issue" with a Reform rabbi from Cleveland. Both men looked assured, relaxed, American, far more at home on the golf links or in the TV studio than duking it out in the Negev over fifty miles of arid land. The rabbi, a self-described "neoliberal Freudian," reminded me of the type that officiated at the High Holy Days when I was in high school, the kind that would send the teenage population scurrying for the door as he embarked on a supposedly controversial sermon on racial tolerance at the local country club. By now he was probably more concerned about his stock portfolio or about how to ask the board of trustees for a raise that slightly exceeded their cost-of-living index. A nice man, really, but the kind who made you think religion was about as important to your life as a trip to the Dairy Queen.

Damoor was something different. He had more solidity, convictions. He also had the quiet self-confidence of someone who was going places. He spoke in that low-key witty style so effective on television and dressed in a preppy manner with a perfect Dan Rather cardigan and a haircut just this side of Kennedy shaggy.

"Did you know Damoor was running for office?" said Chantal, leafing through the articles. "A group of businessmen were backing him for the Democratic nomination for Congress. Also he won an award from the B'nai B'rith for fighting prejudice. That's your people, isn't it?"

"Right. My people. Do I go around identifying you with everything French Canadians do in life? You'd make a helluva goalie for the Montreal Canadiens."

"He also went to Rome for an international conference where he met with a group called Peace Now."

"That's the Israeli left."

"I didn't know they had one."

"Who do you think *founded* the country?"

"Hello! You don't have to get defensive!"

"I'm not defensive. I just can't stand it when people make racial assumptions about—"

"I wasn't making a *racial* assumption. I was making a *political statement*—maybe naive, but . . . Look, I'm a French Canadian. We're supposed to be an oppressed minority too. I know this JDS business is making you touchy. They're a nightmare. But just ride it out. When it's over, you'll be the same old semidepressed, freewheeling Moses again." She grinned. "Except you'll be an international hero of peace and justice."

"Is this the guaranteed Chantal Barrault–Nostradamus– Jimmy the Greek prediction?"

"*Absolument.*"

"Great." Not entirely convinced, I sat down in the chair opposite her. It was one of the vinyl fifties retros we'd bought at a used furniture store in Pasadena when we decided to set up the office. It went with the kidney-shaped Formica end tables and the poster of Dick Powell and Claire Trevor in *Murder My Sweet* Chantal had picked up for my birthday at a swap meet in Toluca Lake. I looked over at her. She had a thoughtful expression as she started to go over one of the three-by-five cards we kept, at her suggestion, on each case to make sure we did not overlook anything. This one was a summary of the preliminary ballistics report I got from the Bureau of Alcohol, Tobacco and Firearms. The bomb had apparently taken the roof off Damoor's car and blown it halfway across the parking lot, a bit of explosive overkill.

"Have you seen that little bio I prepared on Rabbi Lipsky?" she said, not even looking up.

"Read it three times," I said, exaggerating by two. Most of it was relatively predictable. Born in Chicago to an Orthodox family in 1936. Formal religious education. Reputation as a firebrand at school. Apparently flirted with the law for a while as well as with journalism, before settling into the rabbinate. Had a series of rabbinical appointments, two of which ended in his being canned for being too militant for the congregation. After the second of these firings in 1964, he seemed to have vanished for about five years, to reappear as the founder of the JDS in New York. The rest was a public history of demagoguery ending, in this country, with his moving to Israel seven years ago. He had been a member of the Knesset since 1983.

"Anything new on the missing five years?" I asked.

"No, but he did spend a year after rabbinical school working for the *Chicago Sun-Times* as a sportswriter."

"Great. Baseball or football?" I looked over at her again. "Whatever happened to the idea of us living together?"

"I thought we were working on a case here."

"We are."

"Well, I think we're having enough trouble doing that to start thinking about getting in deeper at this time, don't you?"

"I don't know. Why not?" I said, getting up and going to her. "Don't you want everything?"

"First of all, I'm not sure *you* really want it. The moment I said yes you'd just change your mind. But more important, I'm worried I'd become like you."

"Freewheeling and semidepressed?" I smiled and put my arm around her waist.

"That plus a certain superior attitude, a sarcastic point of view on life that makes you clever and funny but prevents you from really connecting with other people." She took my arm away. "Now tell me about the Jewish Defense Squad."

"This is beaner heaven around here," said Izzie, whose real name, it turned out, was Sherman Horowitz. I was riding in the back of his Chevy next to the two panting Dobermans as we slid along Brooklyn Avenue, heading east. Moe, slapping a large black industrial flashlight in his hand, was riding shotgun. His name was Irving Horowitz. They were brothers—a Sherman called Izzie and an Irving called Moe.

Out on the street, there was still action in "beaner heaven," assorted Latino types bopping in and out of liquor shops and convenience stores. I sat there, puzzling over why these guys, Fairfax High graduates of the class of '82, were taking me into the fold so easily, if they were that stupid, maybe they *were* that stupid, as we turned off Brooklyn down Eastern Avenue past the New Calvary Cemetery, "Coyishe Gardens," as they described it, toward the old Home of Peace Memorial Park.

"You wouldn't know up in Seattle," said Moe, "but a lotta Jews used to live around here. This was the biggest Jewish community in California."

"Oh, yeah?" I said, doing my best to act the part of a Neanderthal with a prefrontal lobotomy.

"Yeah," said Izzie. "Then they got rich, moved west to Beverly Hills and drove around in German cars. They don't even

remember who they are anymore. They don't keep the Sabbath, won't eat kosher and hardly go to temple except on the
High Holy Days. Boy, are they in for trouble in the next Holocaust."

"Think so?"

Moe turned back to me confidentially. "Some religious people think the Holocaust was God's warning that too many Jews
were acting like gentiles."

"That's a helluva warning."

"Yeah? You should hear what Rabbi Lipsky says—Stop the
car!" Moe tapped his brother, who pulled over while he beamed
his flashlight into the face of a passerby. It was a bent old man
in a straw hat who looked like he was straight off the Sonoran
Desert. Panicking, the man held his hand over his face and
stumbled backward. "Just checking. You never know if it's one
of those greasers with a spray can."

Izzie drove us around the block and turned into a driveway,
parking in front of the chain-link gate of the cemetery. We got
out quickly and slid through a break in the gate where the links
had been cut. "This is where the fuckers get in," said Moe,
shining his light on the gravestone of "Meyer Goldblatt/Devoted
Husband and Father/1906–1969," which had been sprayed turquoise and pink with the zigzag marker of Maravilla, a gang
whose name I recognized as having been around East L.A. for
fifteen years at least. "See, see!" said Moe, leading us behind
a hedge. "If they don't got respect, we gotta teach it to them."
I thought of my son Simon, who was a graffiti artist himself,
and smiled ruefully, wondering what he would say if he showed
up here tonight with his buddies in the KGB, the Kings of
Graffiti Bombing.

We waited behind the hedge. The brothers crouched at the
far end, staring out at the gravestones like a pair of midget

prison guards watching for a break with their growling Dobermans tethered at readiness while I stood a few feet away, arms folded, staring blankly in front of me and feeling somewhere between absurd and ridiculous. Off in the distance I could hear the sound of a Los Lobos record: "By the Light of the Moon." We had stayed there without moving for what seemed like an hour but must have been more like twenty minutes when a half-dozen chicanos who looked more or less like gang members came strolling along the cement path, joking and passing a joint. They walked within ten feet of us, continued on and sat straight down on the extensive family plot of Morris and Esther Shapiro.

The brothers looked at each other and nodded. I wondered what they were up to, because the chicanos didn't have any spray paint and my guess was they had just come there to hang out and smoke dope. I also wondered what the hell I had gotten myself into and what it could conceivably have to do with the assassination of Joseph Damoor.

It was then that one of the chicanos looked up and saw the Dobermans. From the look in his eye I could see he wasn't pleased. He tapped his buddy with the joint, and in a moment all the chicanos were staring out in our direction, none of them looking particularly happy. I glanced over at the brothers, who all of sudden weren't looking particularly happy either. In fact, they looked as if they were about to pee down their collective and fraternal legs. The chicanos, for their part, were beginning to make a rather interesting display of weapons, including two knives, a set of brass knuckles and a steel pipe. Meanwhile, the brothers were trying to decide whether to run, explain themselves or release the dogs, and, from an objective point of view, they were taking entirely too long to make that decision. Just as it appeared one of the Dobermans was going to act of his own accord, I saw the chicano down at the far end, the largest of the group in a cut-off T-shirt that said "Run DMC/ Live at the Palladium," reach under his jeans jacket and pull out a Police Special, which, I knew, did not have to be cocked, and, at the precise moment the Doberman lunged for his compatriots astride the funeral bier of Esther Shapiro, he shot the dog straight in the throat. Its mate, being a sensible animal, yanked itself free of Moe's already trembling hand and hightailed it off into the night.

All this took between three and four seconds, during which time I concluded, if I didn't already know it, that I was in partnership with two rank amateurs whose very inexperience imperiled my own existence, let alone theirs. It was one of those split seconds when a rash act seems the height of discretion, and I, taking advantage of the fact that the chicanos had been watching the other end of the hedge, flew out from my hiding place, kicked the gun out of the shooter's hand and dove for it, retrieving it behind a gravestone and yelling, "Get the fuck out of here!" to my two dense partners, pushing them away with one hand while keeping the chicanos at bay, waving the gun, almost apologetically, in the other. Once we were a hundred feet off, the three of us turned and ran out of the Home of Peace, almost but not quite as fast as the one remaining live Doberman.

"How the fuck didja do that?" said Izzie, his voice quivering with admiration, as I directed his brother toward the nearest on-ramp of the Santa Ana Freeway. The sooner I got these baboons out of East L.A. the safer I'd feel.

"Cambodia," I said. "An elite unit of the Green Berets."

"*You* were Green Beret?" I figured they'd be impressed.

"No, not really. I was attached to them for a while. I just

learned a few things from their martial-arts instructor." Like a good old-fashioned drop kick, I thought.

"*Baruch ha-shem*," said Moe, "We could really use someone like you—now that Gordie's gone."

"Who's Gordie?"

"Gordie Goldenberg. He was our chief asskicker before he made *aliyah*."

"*Aliyah?*"

"*Aliyah*. You know—*aliyah*. I thought you were Jewish. He ascended—emigrated to Israel. Most of our group has done that, to be with Rabbi Lipsky. That's why the JDS is so small now. I mean, a Jew should be in Israel, right? Me'n Izzie'd be there ourselves except our mom's got Alzheimer's."

The blind leading the blind, I thought. But I didn't say that. I said: "So Gordie really knew how to take care of things."

"You ain't kiddin'." This was Izzie. "He knew every karate chop the slopes invented, *baruch ha-shem*."

"How about explosives?"

"That too. Bombs, plastics, ordnance. The works. We called him Cool-Hand Caleb, after Caleb the son of Jephunneh—you know, the dude who was a spy for Moses in Numbers and Deuteronomy."

"Oh, yeah. Sure."

"I've been boning up on my Bible. Reb Lipsky says Torah study is the right arm and shield of the militant Jew."

"I imagine he would. When did this Caleb, uh, Gordie, make *aliyah*?"

"He was going back and forth all the time, but finally . . . six weeks, a month ago." Izzie looked over at his brother for corroboration.

"More or less," he said.

"Any particular reason?" I asked.

Moe suddenly flashed a suspicious look. "What's it to you?" Then he leaned over the backseat toward me as his brother continued westward through the intersection onto the Santa Monica Freeway, and spoke with a bizarre intensity. " 'If I forget thee, O Jerusalem: let my right hand forget her cunning . . . let my tongue cleave to the roof of my mouth: yea, if I prefer not Jerusalem in my mirth.' *That's* the reason!" And he sat back down in his seat again.

And that was all either of them said until we were heading north on Fairfax within a block of Canter's, and that was to ask me directions to my car. I told them to leave me off in front of the deli. At that point I didn't think it advisable they see my car, a BMW 533—a product of a company which, I had been told, once built engines for Messerschmitts—even if it was a 1984 model with an as yet unrepaired dent in the left side. And all the time I was thinking: " . . . Jerusalem in my mirth." Had they been talking with Chantal?

FOUR

G ordie Goldenberg lived with his mother, Tova Baumgarten, a secretary at Temple Shaarei Zedek, and his stepfather, Michael P. Baumgarten, an unemployed mechanical engineer, on the 6400 block of Drexel Avenue near Fairfax. His father, Hirschel Goldenberg, an insurance agent, who had divorced Tova for "religious reasons" eight years ago, had recently died of emphysema. He had a stepsister, Rachel, still living with the parents, who was a freshman at Los Angeles City College in a prenursing program. Gordie himself had graduated from Fairfax High in the class of '84 and then attended Santa Monica City College for a year and a half for an auto mechanics certificate until he dropped out to do "community work."

All this Chantal found out with about an hour of research the following morning before we drove over to the Baumgarten house. Sometimes I was jealous of how easily she could do it, get bureaucrats and employers to expose supposedly confidential information as simply as opening a spigot. She obtained a psychological profile of Gordie from his guidance counselor at Santa Monica CC by saying she was the personnel director of Mark Z. Bloom, the tire and automobile repair chain, and that Gordie had applied for a job. Gordie, something of a charmer, had been close to the heart of this counselor, a woman, who considered it a personal loss that he had dropped out of school. "He fell in love with God," she told Chantal. "Or maybe it was that awful Rabbi Lipsky. . . . But I think it also had something to do with his mother."

"What do you mean?" said Chantal.

"I know I shouldn't be saying this, but he was a little too close to her, if you know what I mean. She's one of those Orthodox-type Jews. I think she even wears a wig. And the stepfather is such a wimp, so . . ."

"So what?"

"Well, you've met Gordie. He's such a handsome boy."

"Are you implying . . . ?"

"Oh, no. Of course not. Nothing nearly so overt. Just, shall we say, an unnatural closeness. Maybe he got trapped in the wrong developmental phase when his father died. You know, in the Freudian sense. But I've already talked too much, and . . ."

While Chantal was on the phone, I was down at Parker Center talking with the detective commander in charge of the Damoor investigation, a beefy black man in a cable-knit sweater named Portland McCormick, who, I knew from police connections, was said to be an old tennis buddy of Mayor Bradley's. He had heard of me too, from Koontz, a homicide commander I had known for years, and was rather amused when I told him I was on the case.

"So the Arabs hired a Jew," he said. "Kind of like the Klan hiring Dick Gregory to investigate Jesse Jackson."

"Kind of like."

He sipped some coffee and observed me with a look that told me I had given him the best story of the week for the boys at Code Ten, the cop bar over on Alvarado. I had at first considered following my usual method of the less contact with the police the better, but something about the international nature of this case warned me otherwise. As if reading my train of thought, McCormick said: "You know, this isn't normal territory for a private eye. The moment there's even the slightest hint of terrorist involvement, the feds are in it up to their asses."

"That's okay. They've got a fat file on me anyway."

"I would imagine. So what can I do for you, Wine?"

"I was wondering how the investigation is proceeding, but I know you won't tell me that, so I'd like to know if you have anything on a JDS kid named Gordie Goldenberg."

"How'd you get *his* name?"

"I can't tell you that. I have my ways of conducting an investigation. Nothing against the law, I can assure you."

"You won't tell me that and you expect me to give *you* information?"

"Let's say I've been hanging around with the JDS."

"Lucky you. Any of it rubbing off?"

"Not so far."

"And you heard Goldenberg left for Israel?"

"I also heard he had some knowledge of martial arts and ballistics."

"Any more?"

"That's it."

"Doesn't sound like the Arabs are getting their money's worth."

"I do my best."

McCormick looked at me a moment, frowned. "We don't know much more than you do."

"FBI cut you out, huh? They enjoy treating cops like they just got out of the second grade. And they're the ones who could use the remedial reading."

The black man half-smiled. I knew I had connected on that one. Maybe not a home run but at least a double. He got up and closed the door. "This doesn't go any further, as they say. . . . We investigated Goldenberg. We investigated all your JDS friends. There weren't many of them. Only about nine. Even in New York they're pretty small. The rest have all gone to Israel by now to be with Rabbi Lipsky. . . . Anyway, Goldenberg." He sat down, folded his hands and looked at me. "Ten o'clock the night before the crime he was patrolling Fairfax Avenue with some friends, making sure black muggers didn't rape Jewish little old ladies. He does that most nights, starting out at Temple Bat Am on Pico and ending up on Santa Monica in the rough-trade district. The day before that he was at his religious school—a yeshiva, I believe you call it—taking classes until six p.m. Between six and ten he says he was studying but doesn't have any witnesses and won't say where he was studying. The morning of the crime itself he was on a plane to Tel Aviv."

"The morning of the crime? Do you know where he is? Are you in contact with the Israeli government?"

"We're not. But I'm sure the FBI is."

"Are they cooperating?"

"What do you think? With all this Iran business you think the Israeli government wants to look like they're harboring a Jewish fugitive who blew up an Arab in the U.S.? Besides, the Israelis are tough. The Mossad kill their own and—"

"They *what*?"

"Come now. This isn't new. They've been doing this for years. I read this book. The first year of Israel's existence the prime minister—what was his name, Ben Gurion—gave orders to set fire to a boatload of guns and killed fifteen of his own people just to keep his own Jewish terrorists in line. Sometimes you've got to eat your own to survive."

I was mulling over this lesson in *Realpolitik* as Chantal and I walked up to the door of the Goldenberg/Baumgarten household. It was of the small Spanish stucco type common to the area, differing from its neighbors only by its unkempt garden and by a mezuzah on the door the size of a small baseball bat. I rang the bell and we waited until a girl in jeans and a pink cotton sweater with streaked hair and a gold *chai* around her neck opened the door. She was a good-looking version of the typical Jewish sorority girls I knew in college, the kind that came from Long Island or Queens, not Scarsdale or Shaker Heights. There wasn't an ounce of the princess about her, and it made me like her right away. It also made me suspect she was dumb.

"Hi," said Chantal, masking the remnants of her Montreal accent and beginning the dialogue we had rehearsed on the way over. "You must be Rachel. I'm Ethel Schwartz, and this is my husband, Edward. We're friends of Gordie's from Temple Bat Am."

"Oh, yeah . . . Gordie?" She said, her face flushing and lighting up as if we had mentioned Bruce Springsteen or Michael J. Fox.

"We're in the Senior Citizens Support Group and he came and lectured one night on the JDS and what they were doing to help the elderly."

"All young Jews'll be old Jews one day," I added with an unctuous laugh. Chantal gave me a look. "Well." I cleared my throat. "We're going for a couple of weeks in Eretz Israel and he told us to look him up when we were over there."

"Oh . . ." Rachel's expression turned distant and thoughtful. "You want to come in for a while?"

"Sure."

We walked into the small house, a jumble of mismatched

furniture and sickly green and yellow shag carpets. Yet there was something decent and homey about it. Family portraits adorned every available shelf and table. In his photos at least, Gordie was as handsome as the guidance counselor had said, a Jewish-Greek god with olive skin, curly black hair and body sculpted by Praxiteles. He did everything but hold a wine amphora. And he was the star of every picture. One portrait showed the whole family, mother and stepsister staring adoringly at him while stepfather, at the back of the frame, grasped the edge of the couch as if he were about to fall out of the picture altogether.

"Sit down. Make yourselves comfortable," said Rachel. "Would you like some coffee? We've got some Oreos. Mother baked some mandelbrot but it's kinda stale."

"No. We're fine," said Chantal. We sat down on a Naugahyde couch beneath a velour portrait of smiling Chasidim dancing around a Torah.

"So you're friends of Gordie's," Rachel repeated.

"Yes. We were wondering how we could find him," I said.

"Oh . . . who? . . . Gordie?" She seemed distracted again.

"In Israel, I mean. We're leaving in a couple of days."

"I don't know if I can . . ."

"He said to ask you for the address."

"He did?" Her eyes glowed, but then she frowned again and ran her hand through her bleach-blond hair. "I don't know."

"It's okay," said Chantal. "We're friends."

"I know, but . . . I don't know."

"Don't know what?" I said. There was no point in being coy about this. Howard Melnick or another of Gordie's JDS buddies could walk in at any moment, and then the game would be over.

"We don't know where he is."

"Is something wrong?" said Chantal, very sympathetically.

"No. I mean we don't know. I'm sure we'll know soon. He's just forgotten to write or call or something."

"But it's almost two months," I said. "Is he usually like that?"

"No. I mean, maybe there's got to be something wrong, but I don't think there is. What could be wrong? Gordie's a hero of the Jewish people. He could save all of us, don't you think? That's what they say. Sometimes, in the middle of the night, he would tell me wonderful stories, like pictures of paradise." She turned glassy-eyed. "Besides, Reb Lipsky says it'll be okay, and—"

"Does Reb Lipsky know where he is?"

"No, he doesn't. That's what's weird. I mean, Reb Lipsky's like a father to Gordie, and when he's in Israel, Gordie doesn't let a day go by without . . . Are you sure you don't want some coffee?"

"So you've tried to find him."

"Sure. My mother has. I mean my stepmother. She's on the phone with Reb Lipsky every day. I mean, every day she can reach him. He's a very busy man with important things to do and—"

The front door opened, and her father and stepmother enterd. They were both carrying groceries. Rachel, the dutiful daughter, rushed up to help them, kissing her father on the cheek; he flinched with embarrassment.

"Parents, this is Mr. and Mrs. . . . ."

"Schwartz," I said, standing.

"They're friends of Gordie's."

"How do you do?" I said, reaching out first to the father and then to the mother, a bosomy woman in a print dress with intense black eyes that were almost exophthalmic. She recoiled as I drew near her.

"Mother doesn't shake hands with men. She's very Orthodox."

"Excuse me," I said, stuffing the offending object in my pocket. "I forgot."

Mrs. Goldenberg smiled at me in a manner that was halfway between concerned and patronizing. "A friend of Gordie's shouldn't forget. How could a friend of Gordie's forget? A friend named Schwartz."

"The Schwartzes are on their way to Israel," Rachel explained. "Maybe they can help us find Gordie."

"They're looking for Gordie?" said the mother, her lips pursing slightly in the position my occupation had long trained me to recognize as intractable paranoid suspicion. It had also trained me to get the hell out as soon as possible.

"Not really," I said, nudging Chantal toward the door. "We're just friends. We just thought we'd make contact."

"And what do you have to contact Gordie about?" she asked.

"You know—Israel," I said. "The Holy Land. What to see. What to do. Where to stay. . . . Nice to meet you." I opened the door and we both slipped out.

FIVE

"Rabbi Judah Lipsky? If I could just get in the room with that bastard, I'd wring his fascist neck!"

"That would be hard with your arthritis, Sonya."

"How do you know what I can do? That's the trouble with people of your generation. You make assumptions about the elderly restricting their options." She pointed a wrinkled finger at me for emphasis. "If you make assumptions about other people, you turn them into what you want them to be. Watch out for that. You're smarter than that. . . . So. You're going to Israel."

I nodded. I was sitting with Aunt Sonya at a side table at Canter's.

"Just don't come back Orthodox on me," she continued.

"Don't worry about it," I said.

"Don't be so cocky. Theism and AIDS are the two most dangerous illnesses in the country today. Didn't you see that article in *New York* magazine? Every Jewish Yuppie in New York's going back to *shul* like lemmings running over a cliff. Besides, don't take this personally, but as they get older, people tend to get panicky and go for simple answers. And nothing, as you know, is simpler than religion."

"The opiate of the masses," I intoned.

"Don't be a wise-ass. . . . Ah, but you'll be all right." She threw up her hands in relief. "You're living with a *shiksa*. They won't touch you over there with a ten-foot pole."

"I'm not living with her."

"You're not? . . . She wants to get married? She wants a certificate of bourgeois legitimacy?"

"No. Nothing like that. She just doesn't want to live with me."

Sonya frowned and shook her head sadly. Beneath her knee-jerk Trotskyite exterior beat the most compassionate heart I knew. Sometimes I thought her political ideals were really a desperate attempt to order the world with love, against all hope and against all reason.

"Look, while I'm away . . ."

"How long're you going for?"

"I don't know yet. It could take a while. Will you look in on Chantal, see how she's doing? Also keep an eye on the boys. Make sure Simon doesn't get in too much trouble with his graffiti and Jacob gets his college applications in on time. He's a smart kid but sometimes his mind wanders."

"Like his father."

"Right." I checked my watch. "I've got to run. I've got an appointment with Howard Melnick."

"The JDS thug?"

I dropped a twenty on the table. "I'll say a prayer for you at the Wall. After all, you never know."

"Don't you dare," she said. I kissed her goodbye and left.

I headed around the corner through the Canter's parking lot toward the JDS offices. It was hard to believe I was actually doing this. Only that morning I had visited the police and the Goldenberg/Baumgarten household to find out what little I knew about the life of Gordie Goldenberg and his curious disappearance on the day of the bombing. When, as a courtesy, I relayed this information to my employers, Terzi became incredibly excited, hung up and called me back ten minutes later.

"I was right, Moses. That's the same kid."

"What kid?" He had never mentioned anyone specific in the first place.

"Ollie North, Jr., with a yarmulke—no offense intended."

"None taken, I assure you."

"He's the one leading the pickets last year outside the Southern California Peace in the Middle East Study Weekend at UC Irvine. They had placards claiming that we were a PLO front and that Joe Damoor was a personal friend of Arafat's."

"Any truth to that?"

"Oh, c'mon, Mose, what're you talking about? I thought you were *anti*racist. Look, you've got to nail that kid. I've been talking to Said. We both think you should get on a plane and go to Israel immediately. We'll pay for everything, however long it takes you. Don't worry about the expense. Stay at the King David or whatever they call that place. This could be great for everybody, Mose. The trail could lead straight to the doorstep of that . . . sonofabitch Lipsky himself!"

"I think *momzer* would be the proper word."

"What?"

"Forget it."

He went on to tell me what a victory against racism this would be. What a defeat for the forces of intolerance. Forget that my evidence was flimsy, barely circumstantial. I *had* to go.

So within a couple of hours, I had booked flight reservations, bought traveler's checks and gone to say goodbye to my kids. Suzanne, my ex, was working on her pottery when I got there. For a while now, she had been creating a series of dinner plates with fetus designs in the center in the style of Judy Chicago. They seemed about ten years out of date, but I usually opted for discretion and didn't say much that could be taken for criticism. Oddly, since I had become involved with Chantal, I had been seeing a lot more of Suzanne. Before she was rarely around, but now, when I came by to help Simon with his science homework or to take both boys to a Laker game, she would be there with a comment and a smile, ready to involve herself in our activities. When I told her I was going to Israel, her expression turned wistful: "We were going to go there. Remember? During the Six-Day War. We were going to volunteer."

I nodded. I remembered.

"Maybe we should have done it."

"I don't think so," I said.

She shrugged: "At least we might have lived authentic lives. At least we might have found something bigger than ourselves, more important than our little egos, our so-called need for self-fulfillment. It never succeeds, does it, that endless questing after the self?" She looked at me with a knowing stare, almost daring me to say I was happy. A dozen years after our divorce, she still had the power to make me feel bad. "Have a nice trip," she said.

Have a nice trip. The words, or were they a curse, still resounded in my head as I climbed the steps to Melnick's apartment. He lived in a small two-bedroom on the second floor above the JDS offices.

"Come in, come in whoever you are," he shouted when I was halfway up the stairs. "We're armed and dangerous, so don't get smart. Who goes there, friend or foe—KKK, FBI, SS, CBS? . . . Ah, it's you, Greenspan," he said, as I reached the landing. The door was wide open and he was holding a bottle aloft. "Just having a little kosher cabernet with my man Sapirstein here." He gestured toward a wiry blond man in a checkered shirt who was calmly leaning against a torn bullfight poster which had been Scotch-taped to the wall. "He always brings me a couple of bottles when he comes in town. . . . Greenspan, the hero of the Home of Peace, meet Sapirstein, the luckiest man in our organization. He's a traveling salesman."

Sapirstein extended his hand. "Ball bearings and rotor blades. Shalom."

"Shalom," I said.

"Well, Greenspan, going back for a little more cemetery duty?" He turned woozily to Sapirstein. "You shoulda seen this boy last night. Knocked off around twelve beaners single-handed, Superjew!"

"Really?" said Sapirstein, studying me. He was dead cold sober.

"Not exactly," I said. "Actually there were about eight of them and all I did was kick one of them and run."

"Come on, don't be so hard on yourself. It's not often you get something to crow about in life." He held out the bottle to me. "How about a little Chateauneuf de Shikkur before you go off?"

"Actually, Howard, I have other plans. You know how I'm between jobs?"

"Sure, sure." He turned to Sapirstein again. "Greenspan got fired up north in a racial-discrimination case. Terrible thing."

"Anyway, I thought I'd take this opportunity to do what I've always wanted to—go to Israel."

"Oh, no. Not another one. Every time I get a good man, he's gone on me. They haven't invented a cure for Alzheimer's, *baruch ha-Shem*, otherwise I'd be here all by myself." He burped.

"I was wondering if you could give me a letter of introduction to Reb Lipsky."

"Reb Lipsky?" Melnick put the bottle down on a Formica coffee table. "I don't think I could do that. I don't think you'd want me to do that."

"Why not?"

"Let's just say Judah and I have had our disagreements."

"What about?"

"I don't think I want to talk about that. And I don't think I know you well enough anyway. But don't worry about it, he's the easiest guy in the world to find. Just go to his headquarters in Jerusalem—the Holocaust Prevention Institute. He'll be there and he'll be glad to see you. I'm sure you two will get along fine." He pronounced the last sentence in funereal tones and sat down, reaching for the wine bottle.

"Greenspan," said Sapirstein, "what company did you say you were with?"

"I didn't."

"Because you may have grounds for a federal antidiscrimination case."

"I don't think so."

"You would know."

The traveling salesman studied me intently, his eyes moving down my face as if he were memorizing the features. He wouldn't stop until he got it all: height, weight, color of eyes, color of hair. He was still watching me from the window as I crossed the parking lot five minutes later toward my car.

Ten minutes after that I was back in my apartment, packing, when Chantal burst in with a bon-voyage bottle of Cristal. We polished it off in under an hour and wound up in bed, making some of the best love we had made in months. But when we were done, I rolled over and stared up at the ceiling with what

Chantal must have interpreted as more than the usual postcoital *tristesse*.

"What's the matter?" she aked.

"It's this trip. It makes me feel strange."

"To the land of your fathers?" She raised an ironic eyebrow. "You should be excited."

"That's the point. I've been everywhere else. Paris, Rome, Tokyo. Even Beijing. There must be some reason I've avoided it."

"Why do you think that was?"

"I don't know." I shrugged. "Pressure? . . . Like when you were a kid and your parents made you visit some distant relative you didn't want to see."

I gave her a kiss, discouraging further talk. There was more I could have said, a lot more. But how could I explain to a gentile two thousand years of pride, self-loathing, confusion, guilt, courage, anger, chauvinism, racism, survival, black humor and pogroms? How could I even explain it to myself? No wonder I steered clear of Israel. I had enough to worry about.

SIX

I arrived in Jerusalem after the kind of eighteen-hour flight that leaves your brains tied to a doorpost. The plane had been crammed twelve abreast with libidinous fraternity kids, Temple groups and about fifty Seventh-Day Adventists from Bakersfield who insisted on singing hymns every hour on the half hour. That coupled with the Chasidim who would get up and pray in the aisles, dovening and chanting at intermittent times depending on where we were in the cosmic scheme of things, made it impossible for a normal adult to sleep more than twenty minutes at a time without intravenous morphine.

Not that I would have done any sleeping anyway. I was brooding the whole way—two passports, one for Michael Greenspan, arranged for me with remarkable rapidity by the Arabs, tucked in my jacket, my own for Moses Wine buried for insurance at the bottom of my suitcase. I was a textbook example of Sartrean bad faith—a Jew working undercover for the Arabs to investigate a Jewish boy on whom I had nothing but the most circumstantial evidence and who may have been no more than an adolescent zealot with an unresolved Oedipal problem in the first place. My plan was to locate Gordie Goldenberg, win his confidence and find out. But I wondered if I had a hidden agenda.

When, at last, the plane taxied into Ben Gurion Airport, everyone started to applaud, some singing "Hatikvah," the national anthem. I could see tears in the eyes of many of the passengers. Indeed, this *was* my first trip to Israel. It should have been inspiring, a stirring emotional return, but inside I felt like Aaron Burr.

Later, when I checked into the King David Hotel and saw the floodlit view of the sixteenth-century walls of the Old City from my room, I started to feel some of that elation. But by then I was too tired even to take a shower and fell like a dead man onto my bed.

The next morning I took a cab over to the Holocaust Prevention Institute. It was on a small tree-lined street called Yellin in what I took to be a lower-middle-class residential area behind the Mahane Yehuda produce market. I crossed an unkempt patio and entered a small, townhouse-sized building made of what I soon learned was the requisite Jerusalem stone. Inside was a mini-museum of contemporary anti-Semitism, walls covered with recent newspaper clippings and cartoons from neo-Nazi parties, White Citizens Councils and similar organizations plus printouts of their latest membership statistics throughout the world. There was also a display of brochures from other groups claiming that Hitler was not dead. It was the kind of stuff that could give you an upset stomach and a migraine within about twenty seconds.

A handful of tourists were eyeballing this bilge under the watch of a tall heavyset man in his sixties who looked like somebody's Uncle Fred. He was tapping his toe and smiling, just dying for someone to ask him a question. I smiled back at him and wandered into the next room, which was temporarily free of tourists, hoping he would follow me in. In a few seconds he was right there.

"Can I help yez?" he said in about as thick a Brooklyn accent as you can find west, or in this case east, of Canarsie.

"Yeah. My name's Mike Greenspan. I'm a member of the JDS in L.A."

"That's great." He continued to tap his toe. "But this isn't the JDS here, y'know. This is the headquarters of the Gevurah Party. That means Power in Hebrew, in case you don't sabe the local idioma. We don't have a JDS in Israel. This *is* a Jewish state—at least it pretends to be."

"So I've heard. That's why I'm here. I'm thinking of making, uh, *aliyah*."

"Hey, that's terrific." His smile turned into a broad avuncular grin. "We can use everybody we can get. I came here myself thirteen years ago and fell in love with the place, sold my trucking business in Sheepshead Bay and never went back. . . . You know Sheepshead Bay?"

"Sure. . . . Howard Melnick told me to come here."

"Howard Melnick, huh? You a friend of Howard's?"

"Uhuh." I suspected I wasn't going to hit a bull's-eye on that one, but I continued. "I'm friends with all the guys—uh, Sapirstein, the Horowitz brothers."

"Izzie and Moe? Their mother's still got, uh . . ."

"Alzheimer's."

"Yeah. Terrible thing. They should bring her here. This place cleared up my emphysema in nothing flat. . . . So what can I do you for?"

"Well, most of all I'd like to meet Reb Lipsky. He's always been a hero of mine."

"You and a lot of people. Want to touch his office door?" He grinned at me, tapping a door right behind him and then turning the handle to show it was locked. "At this very moment he's down in Gaza, leading a demonstration. One of those PLO fucks knifed one of our boys in the market there and those asshole wimps in the government aren't doing a thing about it. But you'll learn more about that later. Anyway, he'll be back tonight. He's speaking in front of the Old City. It's gonna be a madhouse. The Sephardim come out in force anytime the Reb makes an appearance, especially now that there's been a killing." He looked at me and scratched his chin. "Tell you what. My name's Irv Hurwitz. Meet me down by Jaffa Gate, right in front of the Citadel, at six o'clock. I'll take you over and make sure you get a good seat. Maybe meet the reb."

"Hey, thanks a lot."

"Don't mention it. Now I gotta quote Torah to these Jews from Scarsdale. Sometimes the strangest people want to make a contribution." He stared back into the other room, got about halfway, stopped suddenly, cocked his head and then walked back slowly toward me, closing one eye and peering at me as if I were some rare wild animal that had just miraculously appeared from the bush. "L.A., huh? You guys just had a little activity of your own a couple of months ago. Bet you had some mess with the feds." His voice dropped several decibels. "How'd it go?"

"The usual."

"They got any suspects?"

"Nothing definite. They talked to everybody—Sapirstein, Izzie and Moe, Howard, Gordie Goldenberg."

"Gordie?" The name didn't appear to ring a bell, then: "Oh . . . Joshua ben Tsvi!"

"Right. Joshua ben Tsvi." I realized just in time that must be his *nom de guerre*. I mean, why be plain old Gordie when you could have a name straight out of Ecclesiastes? I could hardly blame him.

"I haven't heard anybody call him Gordie in years," said Irv. "Where *is* the kid?"

"I heard he was here."

"Really? That's funny. I hadn't heard that." He looked me over carefully, checking to see if I had anything under my jacket. "Listen, I don't know what you did over there, but over here we're a close-knit organization. We're on our way to getting political power. The reb's already in the Knesset. So no hot-dogging, if you know what I mean. But if you *really* get crazy with your American individuality and want to go off on your own, just remember—democracy is not a Jewish idea. In the glory days of our people, Jews had kings!" He winked and clapped me on the back. "So I'll see ya at six." He started off again. "Greenspan, was it? Mike Greenspan. See, I remember."

I had half a day to kill before my rendezvous with the reb. I left the Holocaust Prevention Institute, heading east on Yellin through the narrow streets behind the market. It was an old neighborhood, familiar, yet strange, with pickle barrels and butcher shops, a kind of odd throwback to the Bronx of the 1950s with added palm trees. But, unlike the Bronx in those days, here everyone was a Jew, or seemed to be, with only an occasional Arab sweeping the streets or pushing a cart. It was at once exhilarating and disconcerting, exhilarating to be a member of a majority, but disconcerting to my sense of reality. Jews weren't supposed to be bus drivers, hard hats, soldiers, hookers or even, for the most part, cops. They were supposed to be doctors, lawyers and CPAs. I wasn't sure whether I liked it, but I knew I wasn't used to it.

I also had the odd sensation I was being followed. It didn't seem likely, and I had no proof, yet it was there nevertheless, a professional instinct.

And then it was gone as I came out on a large commercial street called Hane'evim which led down toward the Old City. Propelled by curiosity, I headed for it as the population balance changed from Eastern European to Arab with sprinklings of Chasidic Jews wearing their furry black hats and long gabardine coats as if the seventy-five-degree temperature were some treacherous lie perpetuated by a conspiracy of atheist meteorologists. I was in East Jerusalem, approaching the Damascus Gate itself, which loomed in front of me, a gateway to the Orient from a grimy picture book, acrid with the smell of decaying garbage.

Crossing a wide footbridge, I plunged through past men who looked like Yasir Arafat clones in checkered kaffiyeh kerchiefs and women masked in purdah out of old Bogart movies, past black-clad Bedouin ladies, bosomy and sullen, and Palestinian kids in shorts and Adidas, into the Byzantine alleyways lined with spice stalls and pita stands and all manner of plastic junk and phony rugs from the four corners of the earth.

And as the Arab bodies pressed upon me, shopping, running, singing, eating, staring at me with hatred or begging me to buy this sandal or that burnoose ("I make you special price, my friend . . . stop"). I felt exposed, Jewish and alone, and I was aware of an emotion I rarely felt at home, not in the bowels of Brownsville, or the barrio of East L.A.: fear. And I wanted to tell them: I'm not the enemy, I'm not the oppressor, I didn't make this deal, I didn't arrange this show. Actually—odd joke —I was working for *them*. But I knew they couldn't understand that. Or it would have been so complicated, so peculiarly embarrassing, to explain it would scarcely have been worth the effort.

So, as if holding on to some atavistic security blanket, I pursued three Chasidim, young boys actually, about twenty, their earlocks and scraggly beards bursting unevenly over virginal skin the color of alabaster, down yet another alley away from the crowd and out of the Muslim Quarter. I followed them around a corner, and the acrid smell began to diminish, the signs on the shops changing from Arabic to Hebrew. We were in the Jewish Quarter. A couple of soldiers, boy and girl, held hands, a pair of Uzis bumping their tight behinds. Young Orthodox women, wearing kerchiefs around their heads and long denim skirts almost to the ground, pushed babies in imported Aprica prams and averted their eyes as we passed. We turned once again through another archway that opened on an immense square. I was in front of the holiest shrine of my people, the Western Wall itself, a military checkpoint blocking my path.

Some joking soldiers inspected our bags for bombs, and the impatient Chasidim hurried through, men on a mission. I stood there staring at it, a giant wall of immense rectangular stones with bunches of men in long black coats, bobbing in front of it like so many mantises with prayer books in their hands. Farther down, smaller clusters of women, determinedly doughty, stood by their section, also clutching prayer books and similarly bobbing. Between them, I could see a table where paper yarmulkes were stacked, waiting for the unprepared. I had started to move toward it when a loud voice stopped me.

"Moses . . . Moses Wine, of all people—*mon semblable, mon frère!*"

I turned to see another frock-coated Chasid standing there. A stocky man with streaks of gray lacing a thick, bushy black beard, he looked like a religious version of Jerry Garcia of the Grateful Dead grinning at me beneath a black hat that was pushed back jauntily over his broad forehead. It took me nearly half a minute to recognize him.

"Max? Max Hirsch? Holy—"

"Don't say Holy Christ around here, Wine! It could get you into trouble."

I laughed, gesturing to his outfit as I walked over to shake his hand. "I didn't recognize you in the—"

"I should've said I couldn't recognize *you* in that monkey suit." He grinned at me. I was wearing a safari jacket. "You look like a Hollywood producer."

"You sure don't look like the guy who was running Cocteau's Kitchen."

"Berkeley's leading lacto-vegetarian restaurant." He laughed. "I remember that time you came after we'd closed, about two in the morning, when your kid was born. You were ravenous!"

"And you made me spaghetti carbonara with vegetarian bacon."

"And you made me godfather of your kid. . . . How is he?"

"Fine. Just fine. . . . The last I heard about you you were arrested."

"For breaking into Edward Teller's office at three in the morning. That was a trip!" He shook his head as if it had been a dozen lifetimes ago. "And what about you? I heard you were a private detective, of all things. Not here on business, I hope."

I hesitated. "No, just touring."

"To see the Western Wall . . . Everyone has to see it once, or a thousand times if they're lucky. Come, follow me this way. Let me be your guide for old times' sake." He lead me past the barrier, handing me one of the paper yarmulkes and saying a few words in Hebrew to a white-bearded old man who started to approach me for charity.

"So you've been through some changes," I said.

"To say the least. I almost died. Something watched over me, I can tell you that."

"What do you mean?"

"It's a strange story. I started out in Brooklyn and ended up in Libya. . . . Now this famous Wall," he nodded in front of us, "was never part of the Temple itself, but part of a platform on which—"

"Wait a minute—Libya? What were you doing in Libya?"

"I'm trying to give you a history lesson, Moses, and—all right, what time is it?" He checked a watch, which I assumed was one of his remaining gestures to temporal reality. "I have a few minutes." We sat down on two of the folding chairs which had been arranged facing the Wall.

"So what happened after Berkeley?" I said, still studying Max's outfit as if it were some Halloween costume he might be wearing temporarily.

"After Berkeley, I went to New York. I was teaching in Bed-Stuy, still fighting the good fight, when they had that strike, remember?"

"The one about too many white teachers in the ghetto?"

"That's right. I got caught in the crunch and got kicked out of the school. I couldn't get a job in a white school either. I was bitter, I can tell you. I went to Europe with a friend. Ibiza. This came to that—we were out of money—and we got involved in a little drug dealing, mostly hash but sometimes, I've got to tell you, a little heroin. Pretty soon we were very successful, running back and forth to North Africa on a regular basis. We had it all, girls, money, the whole thing. I had a connection in Tripoli who was supposedly the brother of some muckety-muck in the government, a friend of Gaddafi's. Anyway, we were getting pretty cocky, and one day, when we were loading up a big shipment in Benghazi, the Libyan secret police arrested us and stuck us in a Tripoli jail without a trial. You can't imagine what it was like—horrible! No sanitation, perverts of all sorts. I fell as low as I could get, physically and spiritually. I had several diseases, including typhus, and was so depressed I hardly spoke to anyone. Twice I tried to commit suicide." He stopped his story and waved to another Chasid who was walking past, carrying his prayer book. "Fortunately, there was this Israeli in the jail, Rumanian by birth. To this day I don't know how he got there. But he was a student of the Kabbalah. You know what that is?"

"I've heard of it."

"Right. Well, in any case, he was studying the *Zohar*, the most important work of the Kabbalah, and every night he would read it to me. Of course, I had been through it all: Zen, Primal Scream, est, guru this and that, whatever. But this was different. It was the work of my own people—a revelation to me. I couldn't get enough of it, studying the En Sof, the God without end, the universe without cause and effect, more complex than Nietzsche. It was as if, wrapping my mind around the mystical thoughts of my ancestors, my spirit was liberated from prison. That man was my first rebbe. And one night, when reciting to me from memory a meditation from Reb Nahman of Bratslav, he told me the door of the cell was open and that I could leave. And it *was* open. Really open. And I left." He looked at me. "I'm sure you don't believe this and think your old friend Max has gone off the deep end and become a religious nut. Personally, I don't know what to make of it myself, but it happened. So I came here—that was thirteen years ago—and studied at a yeshiva. And now I teach there—and give Bar Mitzvahs at the Wall . . . to the children of old hippies like you." He grinned at me slyly the way I remembered him doing when he was the proprietor of the Cocteau's. "So Moses, how're you doing? How do you feel? Who are you?" I stared at him blankly. "Never mind, we'll talk about that later. Listen." He stood. "I have to teach a class at my yeshiva, Derech Chaim. It's all in Hebrew, otherwise I'd ask you to come. What're you doing tomorrow evening, for Shabbat? If you don't have someplace to go on Shabbat in Jerusalem, you're a lost man."

"Then I'm a lost man."

"So you will come to my house. We will sing a *nigun* together. You will meet my family and my friends. I want to hear about what you are doing, your detective work. I don't think I've ever met a detective before."

SEVEN

"What have we gained if we walked out of Hitler's charnel house to become scared shadows in our own land? What have we profited if we escaped the ghettoes of Baghdad and Damascus to be stoned and murdered in our own country by our former oppressors? What have we achieved if we regained Jerusalem and still allow the throne of Islam to sit upon the Temple Mount? The right to call ourselves *humanists* . . . *democrats!*" He hurled the words in English and Hebrew, loudspeaker curses ricocheting off the walls of Mount Zion. "What further humiliations must we suffer from the Sons of Esau? That they outnumber us? They *already* outnumber us in the Galil. And Arabs have babies while Jews have abortions! Must we wait until they are the majority of the Knesset, until an Arab is the Minister of the Interior or *Defense*? Tragedy will be ours if we do not move the Arab jackals out! . . . I want them out . . . out! . . . OUT!" A wild burst of shrill ululation as the Sephardim let out a piercing wail across the Birkat Es Sultan, Sultan's Pools, down to the Valley of Hinnom, the ancient Gehenna where once live babies were thrown into the hot flames by the worshipers of Moloch. Rabbi Judah Lipsky raised his hands to silence them. "Remember . . ." He lowered his voice to a near whisper, turning his attention to the group of American tourists seated in the seats immediately below him. "I say what you think."

A chant started to go up: "Judah ha-Melekh, Judah ha-Melekh," Judah the King, Judah the King, as a heavily perspiring Lipsky leaned forward against the podium, his small-boned body surprisingly frail under the klieg lights.

"But, I must tell you," he continued, "there is a danger even greater than the rabid Arab dog wielding his knife in Gaza. That danger is the same Hellenization that plagued our people in the days of the Maccabees, that same Hellenization that makes Jews adopt every cause but Judaism, that makes Jews, in the interest of so-called enlightenment, see their Torah not as revealed truth but as one other fallible link in man's climb up the ladder of civilization, no more or less than the New Testament or the Rig-Veda. That danger is a society where, as in American Jewish life, materialism runs amok, drunks and half-dressed women dance and give praise to the Lord with African dances, rock music and universal abominations. That danger is, in a word—*assimilation*. And the handmaiden of assimilation is *intermarriage*. And for that reason alone we cannot have the Arabs here. They must go!"

"Judah ha-Melekh, Judah ha-Melekh!"

"One last thing." He raised his hand again, quieting the crowd. "People say I am a racist. I am not a racist. A racist is someone who says that Arabs are fools, that they are such fools they are willing to live in a Jewish state as second-class citizens. No, I respect the Arab. I know he wants this land as much as I do. That's why I'm willing to pay him to leave. The racists are the Peace Now people, the left-liberal, one-world, egalitarian humanists. The coexisters. But I have news for *them:* There is no *Jewish* humanism. There is only humanism. Judaism is divine revelation. Shalom."

Lipsky raised his arms, and the crowd roared back a "Shalom" that shook the Citadel of David as a couple of young bodyguards placed a wrap around Lipsky's shoulders, leading him off the podium much as if he were that other king, James Brown, at the end of a concert. For a moment, he disappeared from sight, but then reemerged fifty feet away from where I was standing with Irv Hurwitz. Hurwitz, sweating with excitement, took me by the arm and led me toward him.

From closer up, Lipsky appeared remarkably intense, his coal-black eyes sunk deep in hollow sockets. His sculpted cheeks were outlined with a full beard, at once Biblical and neatly clipped without earlocks, as if designed to inspire the confidence of both the devout and the patriotic.

"Judah, this is Mike Greenspan . . . the guy I was telling you about. From Los Angeles."

"Uhuh. . . . What's the head count here tonight? Did anybody get a head count? Where's that reporter from the *Palestine Post*? I want to shove this one up his Arab-sucking nose."

"Rosen wasn't here tonight, Judah."

"No, of course not. Why would he be? It's only the biggest event in Israel." Someone handed Lipsky a towel, and we started down the aisle toward a Toyota van, the bodyguards pushing back the Sephardi masses who struggled for a touch of their idol. "I wonder what they'd say if I turned these people loose on the Muslim Quarter. They're all the most liberal journalists in the world until it comes to printing a word about me. Tell that to your ACLU B'nai B'rith. Right, Mr. Los Angeles?"

"Sounds like censorship to me," I said.

"Censorship? Yasir Arafat's on the front page every time he burps, but if I were elected prime minister, they'd do everything in their power not to run it. The only time I make the papers is when I go down three points in the polls."

"I wouldn't worry about it," I said. "The truth is, a hundred years from now, there'll be streets in every corner of this country named after you. The secular politicians like Peres and Shamir will barely be footnotes in the history books."

Lipsky glanced over at me: "Ah, a flatterer."

"Not really. It's what I think."

"Beware of flatterers, I'm told, especially intelligent ones. How long were you with Los Angeles JDS?"

"Not long."

"I can see why. They've got a branch office of the Retarded Citizens Union over there. I had to separate." We came to the van, one of the bodyguards holding the door open for him. He turned and looked at me. "I hear you're a friend of Joshua ben Tsvi."

"A friend. No, I couldn't say that. I came in after him."

"After him?" He frowned. "Then you must have been *very* recent."

"I suppose so. I'm not really from L.A. I'm from Seattle. I just stopped by there on my way here."

"What for?" Lipsky shot back.

"I'm thinking of making *aliyah*."

"Not that. Why'd you stop in Los Angeles?"

"I was out of a job. I wanted to make some contacts—the JDS. You don't get much Jewish content in the Northwest." Lipsky didn't respond. I stared back at him, feeling the peculiar magnetism of charisma. I had felt it before, standing in crowds watching Bobby Kennedy and Billy Graham. It was the same no matter what side of the fence it came from, and it unnerved me. I went on quickly. "It's really amazing being here with you, after reading about you all these years. The honesty of your positions. Most people don't have the guts. The old ghetto mentality is hard to fight."

"I see. . . . And why do you want to make *aliyah*?"

"I started to become conscious of my roots and . . . what else could I do?" I gestured, wondering how well I was lying.

He continued to study me, his black eyes beginning to blink with nervous tension. "Well, this isn't an interrogation. Come on. We'll go get something to eat. See how my deprogrammer is doing."

I followed him into the van with Irv and the two bodyguards, who had Walther automatics in shoulder holsters under their jackets. Irv sat down next to Lipsky, and I took a seat opposite him, between the bodyguards. Behind us was the driver, a squat jowly man in a windbreaker who looked like a Russian Jew.

We pulled out. The rabbi was still watching me as we started to make a circle around the Old City between the Zion Gate and the Church of the Dormition. A sign pointed into the darkness toward the Mount of Olives.

"What's your interest in Joshua ben Tsvi?" he asked.

"I didn't say I had one. I just heard he was over here."

"Oh. This your first trip to Eretz Israel?"

I nodded.

"From Seattle, huh? I grew up in Chicago, near West Rogers Park. My father was a *chazzen*—you know what that is?"

I hesitated a second, trying to dredge up the word from my childhood. "A cantor."

"Good," said Lipsky. "So you really are Jewish. That's a start."

"I grew up back East."

"New York?"

"Connecticut."

"Then you migrated to Seattle and Los Angeles and now here. All Jews have stories. Boaz here grew up in a small village in Iraq where his parents had a successful dairy farm." He nodded toward one of the bodyguards, a musclebound man in his forties with a mottled face like the dark side of the moon. "The mukhti—the Arab headman of the town—didn't like that, and he and two friends came in and shot his father and mother with an AK-47. They shot off half of Boaz's neck too and cut him in the side, but he survived by pretending he was dead. And when the Arabs walked into the next room, he got up, got the family ax and bludgeoned the three of them to death. He crawled out of Iraq on his knees. He's tough. Aren't you, Boaz?" Boaz didn't speak English. For a moment there was a silence as Lipsky stared at me. We pulled up by the Dung Gate. "Not even Boaz knows where Joshua ben Tsvi is. Why'd you say you wanted to locate him?"

"I didn't. I'm not interested in locating him."

"But you knew his name."

"No, I didn't. I only knew him as Gordie Goldenberg. And I didn't really know him. I just heard his name."

"I thought you knew Joshua ben Tsvi," said Irv. "You said ya knew him."

"Not him. I know his stepsister. Rachel. She's a little worried about him. She wanted me to look him up while I was here."

"Let me see your identification," said Lipsky.

"Sure." I reached into my jacket.

"No. Forget it," he said. "Let's go."

We got out and walked through the Dung Gate, approaching another security check on the eastern side of the Wailing Wall. Above us, to the right, I could see the Dome of the Rock and the El Aqsa Mosque outlined against the stars. Below them were the vast excavations of the Temple Mount, an archaeologist's dream. The guards at the checkpoint made a joke in Hebrew, recognizing Lipsky, and we crossed quickly through the barrier. All the time I was wondering: Why is this man taking me? Why does he trust me, even in the slightest? But, I knew, leaders needed acolytes as much as acolytes needed leaders—especially relatively presentable acolytes with shirts buttoned straight and IQs over ninety.

The bodyguards flanked Lipsky, and I followed a few steps behind them as we crossed the vast plaza, only a few lingering Chasidim still dovening the by the Wall, delivering their midnight message to God. Perhaps it was the eerie emptiness, but I was aware of it, for a split second, as a holy place. Almost as quickly, we were through an arch on the other side, turning onto one of the wider alleys called Aqabat El Khaldieh. We were in the twilight zone between the Muslim and Jewish quarters. The streets were empty except for a couple of Arab kids tossing a Wiffle ball off the lip of a Mamluk fountain.

"Twenty years and it's still theirs," muttered Lipsky, as we headed down a set of crumbling concrete stairs. "We're supposed to be the mightly rulers, but you hardly see a Jew out in the Old City after dark." We continued past a small doorway where some white-turbaned men were eating hummous from paper plates and then around a corner across some construction rubble to a steel door.

Lipsky knocked. An eye peered through a slot, and we were admitted into a dimly lit three-story building housing several families. Sepia-skinned men in black hats, white shirts and long black beards wandered about reading prayer books or talking in French while their wives cooked and cleaned and their kids slept on couches and cots. They must have been Moroccan Jews. We climbed to the second floor, where a couple of old men were huddled over looms, weaving.

Lipsky moved between them, surveying the scene impatiently, apparently searching for someone and muttering to himself as if something wasn't up to his expectations.

"Wait here," he said finally, walking past us into a back room and shutting the door behind him.

"Where are we?" I asked Irv.

"Where the rabbi prays weekday mornings," he said proudly. "Yeshiva Torat Cohanim. These men are making priestly raiments according to Talmudic specifications . . . for the sacrifices." He gestured toward the weavers, who looked up at me and smiled.

"Priestly raiments for sacrifices?" I asked.

"For the Third Temple sacrifices. So we can be ready when Moshiach comes. The Messiah." He must've read my expression. "Hey, y'know—it's written. After the Temple is rebuilt, there will be sacrifices. The Messiah will come and the dead will rise from the grave. That's called the End of Days."

"Right. Of course," I said.

Sacrifices. I assumed he meant animal. At least I assumed that's what the Talmud meant. I stood there mulling that over until Lipsky came out of the back room again on a short fuse.

"Can you believe it? He's not here," he snapped at Irv. "That fat shmuck never follows through on anything. He brings them out here, then he leaves them by themselves. Doesn't he realize we're at a crucial point in our work? Sometimes I think half our party never got beyond the eighth grade. I told you— we need a better class of people."

Irv shrugged uncomfortably, probably unsure where he stood in this particular hierarchy. Lipsky turned to me. "Where're you staying?"

"A hotel."

"That must be expensive. I talked to the rebbe here. He says you can stay here, if you want. They'll help you learn how to study too. Some of them speak English. Right now, I have to leave. The man who I was looking for is gone and I want to go to sleep."

"Who's that?"

"Someone."

"Your deprogrammer?"

His eyes started to blink again. "Good to meet you, Greenspan. I hope you enjoy your stay in Israel and decide to make *aliyah*. Most American Jews are used to so much luxury, they come here with good intentions and then they change their mind. Shalom."

"Shalom."

And he headed off down the stairs.

At that point, Irv ushered me out. I said goodbye to him at the front door and took a slow walk around the building, finding nothing. Then I headed back for the hotel, arriving some time after two in the morning still jet-lagged and feeling somewhere between being drugged and hit on the back of the head with a nightstick.

I collapsed on the bed. It gave like a hammock; sleeping on it would probably kill me. I pulled the bed clothes off onto the floor, rolled up in them, and within seconds was asleep, dreaming of men in black hats and beards. They all looked like some grandfather I never had. We were in a kitchen in nineteenth-century Poland and they had bad breath and were trying to make me eat some heavy, cholesterol-laden food. "Beware the End of Days," they were saying, although I knew, even in the dream, that the End of Days was supposed to be a good thing. Just as they were forcing my head down into a bowl of rendered chicken fat, I jumped up and ran past them, out of the house, into a field of wild flowers, like Julie Andrews in *The Sound of Music.*

Ten hours later, I woke up to the conviction that the End of Days was like the withering away of the state, the kind of romantic utopian dream designed to keep all belivers, Orthodox Jews or "scientific" socialists, adhering to the true path. I also woke up to the sound of someone rummaging around in my closet.

Since I had slept on the floor, on the far side of the bed, he must not have seen me when he entered. I reached over and slipped into my undershorts, almost simultaneously jumping up and swinging open the closet door. A wiry man with curly black hair, wearing tight jeans, a violet silk shirt slit to the navel and enough gold chains to choke a Vegas lounge lizard, was standing there with one hand on my suitcase and the other on a long-blade knife. He looked as if he knew how to use it.

"What are you doing here, Mr. Wine?" His accent was an Israeli mix of Levantine and East European.

"I should be asking what *you're* doing here. How'd you know my name?"

"As with most people, it is written in your passport." He extracted my real one out of his pocket. Obviously he hadn't noticed the counterfeit, which was still wedged in my hip pocket.

"I think I'll be having that back, thank you." I moved toward him, but he made a deft flick with his knife, missing my chin by the length of a short hair. "Not bad," I said, after having jumped back a couple of feet. "How'd you know I wanted a shave?"

"What is your occupation? Who are you?"

"I thought you had my passport. You should know."

"An investigator. What kind of investigator?"

"Insurance. You know—fires, accidents, that kind of thing."

"And what are you doing in Israel?"

"Touring. Yesterday I spent a lot of time around the Wall. Today I was thinking of the Holocaust Memorial."

"Tell me the truth," he snapped. "What are you doing in Israel?"

"Hey, I'm a divorced Jewish man. I've never been to the Holy Land. What's so strange about—"

"Don't lie to me." He advanced toward me, and I made a quick retreat around the bed. "Last night you were seen with Rabbi Judah Lipsky entering the Yeshiva Torat Cohanim."

"I'm interested in Reb Lipsky. He's an inspirational leader and—"

"More lies!" He took a swipe at me with the back of his empty hand, sending me flying back into the headboard, nearly bumping over a lamp. "Someone like you is no more interested in Rabbi Lipsky than I am. Is this *interest* why you were sneaking around the back of the yeshiva for twenty minutes after he left?"

"I was lost. I—"

"Bullshit! Now tell me who you are working for or—"

"Now wait a minute. I'm beginning to lose patience." I tried to straighten myself out, feeling a Chinese gong going off in my head. "If you don't get out of here I'm going to have to pho—" But before I got the word out, he had swung his knife and sliced the telephone cable right off the wall.

"Hey, very good. I've never seen anybody do that quite so well."

He smiled. "That is why they call me the Shochet."

"The Slaughterer?" My grammar-school Yiddish was coming back more easily than I had expected. "I bet you specialize in non-kosher meat too." There was a knock on the door. "Ah, thank God, breakfast."

"Breakfast, it is already past noon? It is probably the maid. Tell her to go away."

"No. You tell her."

I pointed to the front door. Frustrated, he turned toward it, and I dove over the bed, barreling past him into the bathroom and locking the door behind me. I pulled the emergency chain the moment I was in there. Then I stared at myself in the mirror. Blood was trickling down over my left eye, raising an ugly red welt where the bastard had slammed me. Just then I heard him running down the corridor. I exhaled slowly. I had seen enough of Slaughterers for one day.

I checked out of the King David Hotel forty-five minutes later. The concierge gave me a peculiar look as I signed my credit-card receipt, studying the swelling gash over my eye. "I got it dovening," I explained to him, but he didn't get it. Then

I left my bag with the bell captain and slipped out an emergency exit near the bar, emerging on a side street down by Herod's Family Tomb. I headed down toward Yemin Moshe, a remodeled housing complex that looked upper-class artsy, then doubled back around the hotel again to the main drag, David HaMelekh. I wasn't sure where I was going, but wherever it was I didn't want the Shochet and his cronies knowing about it. Furthermore, I no longer had my real passport, so checking in at another hotel would prove difficult. And I wasn't so keen on stopping by the embassy for a replacement. At this point, I didn't want some eager beaver in the foreign service plugging my name into the State Department computer just to see if I came up trumps.

I continued on a few blocks and soon was in the central business district again, not far from where I had been the day before. Only now the atmosphere had changed. There were hardly any cars or trucks in the streets, as if the mayor had declared a temporary ban on traffic in order to hold a ten k or a bicycle race. Pedestrians strolled about with loaves of bread under their arms, nodding to each other and smiling. The whole place had a small-town ambience which was vaguely dislocating among the tall buildings. Then I understood. I checked my watch. It was not yet three, but it was already beginning. I turned and headed toward the Old City again. Not even private detectives worked on the Sabbath.

EIGHT

Max Hirsch lived on Misgav Ladach, one of the old streets of the Jewish Quarter that had been so carefully restored after the Six-Day War. I came to it through the square behind the remnants of the Hurva Synagogue, which was the hub of the quarter. Here the feeling of Shabbat was palpably stronger than it was in the city itself. The stores were just closing and the men, wearing freshly laundered white shirts and ornamental yarmulkes, were going home with their wives, who, although they wore no makeup, had similar Oriental ornamentation on their scarfs and blouses. With them were children, scads of children. Although most of them seemed to be of American background, or Anglo-Saxons of some sort, they stared at me in my Hawaiian shirt and faded jeans as if I were an interloper. And although I had done my share of traveling in life, from Andalusia to Manchuria and back, here among my brethren on their festival day I had rarely felt so uncomfortably foreign.

Perhaps it was the very familiarity that created the alienation, all these people who looked like second cousins dressed up like citizens of ancient Judea as if they were about to perform in the Sunday-school Purim play. Max must have sensed my reaction when I came to his door, because he put his hand on my arm and smiled reassuringly. He was dressed in his own Sabbath finery, a rich silk cloak of silver and black stripes with matching slippers and a white yarmulke. "Everybody's on time today. How wonderful! Come in, come in, Shabbat shalom! Hey, what's this?" He looked at my eye. "I thought you weren't working."

"That's another story," I said.

"Really? Well, we'll have to explore that later. All creative work is forbidden on Shabbat. You could go jogging, of course, but planting, building, composing a symphony, detecting—no. So come and meet our friends. We were just debating the ontological proof of the existence of God." He took my arm, leading me across the courtyard of his house.

"The ontological proof?" I said. "I never understood that, even in college."

"Neither did Bertrand Russell." He opened a sandalwood door.

"Before we go in . . ." I stopped. "Has Shabbat officially started yet?"

He shook his head. "Eighteen minutes before sunset."

"Then . . . did you ever hear of someone who calls himself the Shochet?"

"The Slaughterer? I don't believe . . ."

"Curly hair. Wears a lot of gold chains."

"That's not my world, Moses."

"I know, but it's a small country. I just thought . . ."

"Are you in danger?"

"No more than usual."

"Because if you are, you know I'd try to help you any way I could."

"Thanks," I said.

We entered the house. It was of Moorish design and obviously quite old, maybe even hundreds of years, but carefully restored, with whitewashed plaster walls and inlaid tile around the arches. Long shelves filled with volumes of religious books in several languages were interrupted by louvered windows with panoramic views of the Judean Hills and the Wall itself. We continued past them down to the living area, where the other guests were already seated at a long table in front of a fireplace. Three were women, the other a man, a pale, sad-faced black hatter who looked as if he hadn't been in the sun for the last year. Hirsch introduced him first: Shimon DeLeon, a rabbi who spoke only Hebrew and spent most of his time in prison, helping convicts return to the faith. The women were all Americans—Deborah Schatz, a corporate attorney from New York who had a pinched expression and wore no makeup; "Chaya Bracha," a blonde from Colorado who looked like a ski instructor gone religious and also wore no makeup, but didn't need it; and Brenda Weintraub, a theatrical agent from Los Angeles who *did* wear makeup as well as a black designer kerchief from Claude Montana around her head.

"My old friend Moses Wine is a private detective," said Max, handing me a yarmulke as I sat down. I dutifully placed it on my head. "But that hasn't helped him with the ontological proof."

"God is a being than whom no greater or more perfect being can be conceived," said Deborah Schatz, as if she were lecturing Philosophy 101.

"It's clever intellectually, said Max. "But for me it lacks passion . . . faith. In my heart I know God exists, but if I *needed* proof, I would choose the moral proof."

"What's that?" asked Brenda Weintraub, smiling at him with almost childlike eagerness. I remembered how, back in Berkeley, Max was always surrounded by adoring females.

"It's based on the observation that accepted moral behavior is universal." It was Chaya Bracha who answered. "There's no clear reason why, for most people throughout the world, the same actions should engender the same feelings of right and wrong."

"Racial survival," I suggested. "It's more practical not to go around killing each other."

"Perhaps," she said. "But the race could survive behaving immorally. Sometimes even more efficiently. So what reason is there . . . but God?" She half smiled, looking at me with a calm, self-contained expression. "Didn't Dostoevski write, 'If God does not exist, then everything is permitted'?"

Brenda Weintraub shook her head in wonder. "Oh, Chaya, I envy you. You're so amazing . . . a *baal teshuvah*. Don't they say a *baal teshuvah* stands higher than a holy *tzaddik*?"

"What's a *baal teshuvah*?" I asked. It sounded like a sheep dog.

Max laughed. "You're confusing Moses. So many new words at once. *Tzaddik, baal teshuvah* . . . A *baal teshuvah* is a returnee, a secular Jew who has come back to the faith. To some, that makes them holier than holy men, *tzaddikim*, who are already there. Chaya was Joan Feldman of Boulder, Colorado."

"How'd you become Chaya Bracha?" I asked.

"Do you want to know? It's a long story and not that important. What's important is that I am here."

"Chaya lives up in the mountains. Safed . . . the home of the Kabbalah."

"And what brings you down here?"

"I have to help a friend."

Max's wife, Leah, entered from the kitchen with their four children. We must have been close to sunset, because she was carrying the Shabbat candles. The other women stood to join her, placing shawls over their heads and lighting the candles. Leah, a short, homely woman in a gabardine skirt, circled the flame with her hands three times, reaching out over the candles with her fingers perpendicular to her chest. When she was finished, she and the other women placed their hands over their eyes and recited the prayer. I hadn't watched this process in years, since my ex-mother-in-law did it for my children when they were little in order to give them the background that, by implication, their parents were neglecting. It made me feel lonely, empty.

Max blessed each of his children in turn. Then he faced Leah and said for my benefit: "Now I will recite 'A Woman of Valor' from the Proverbs: 'A good wife, who can find?/She is more precious than corals . . .'" He continued in Hebrew while I wondered: How could a man like this marry someone so unattractive? Was he carrying this modesty business a bit far, or did he know something I didn't? She didn't seem very bright either. Maybe the era of liberated women had gotten to him. I found myself staring at Chaya Bracha. In the candlelight, her clear white skin had turned a Rembrandt amber. She would, it seems, have been more suitable. I wondered if she was married. I glanced at her hand for a wedding band, but just then she saw me looking at her, averted her eyes and simultaneously placed her hand in her lap. I couldn't decide whether it was deliberate.

After dinner, Leah brought out a couple of bottles of Crown Royal and the men began to drink—the men plus Brenda Weintraub, who insisted on being included—pounding their fists on the table and singing round after round of Shabbat songs I didn't recognize. Feeling the Scotch, I hummed along anyway, which seemed to please Max.

"You're a Chasid in civilian clothing," he said.

"Not likely."

"Yes, you are. You just don't know it. Where are you staying? What hotel?"

"None. I checked out."

"I see." He studied me a split second before refilling my glass. "I know what we must do. Tonight we must go to the Chasidim of the Reb Arele."

"Yes, Max. Take us," said Brenda Weintraub. "I've always wanted to go."

"You're going to have to sit in the women's section."

"So I'll sit in the women's section," said Brenda. She turned to Chaya. "You'll come, won't you? I'll need you to come."

"Yes, I'll come."

"Remember what we had to go through, in the old days, for a little ecstasy? How we poisoned our bodies?" Max shook his head and leaned in toward me. "Wait until you see this. It makes twenty mikes of windowpane feel like a vitamin pill."

A half hour later, Max, Chaya, Brenda and I left the others and headed across the Old City through East Jerusalem to the run-down streets of the Mea She'arim, the stronghold of Chasidic zealotry. Large numbers of the devout surrounded us, streaming back from the Wall under dim lights that made the whole place redolent of nineteenth-century Poland. I walked with Max, remembering how I had read that all the "good" Jews, the pious ones, had been exterminated during the war, leaving only the tough guys, the militant Israelis and the ambitious assimilated Americans. They must've missed a few, I mused. More than a few. Or perhaps now even the Chasidim were tough.

"Who's the Reb Arele?" I asked Max as we crossed under an arch into the neighborhood itself. It was overcrowded and decrepit the way one imagined an Eastern European slum, and even on the Sabbath, it had the same smell of decaying garbage as the Muslim Quarter.

"One of the leaders of the ultra-orthodox. They don't speak Hebrew because it's too holy and they don't recognize Israel because the Torah says there can be no state until the Messiah comes." He led us through an alley into a broken concrete courtyard with threadbare laundry strung between the windows. A number of pale, scrawny kids with *payess* and wearing white knee socks and yarmulkes with white tassels on top ran about in front of a ritual bathhouse that looked suspiciously unhygienic. After a second, some older people, similarly dressed, came and whisked the children away as if they were being polluted by our apostate presences.

"You know, Moses," said Max, observing my expression, "all this may seem weird to you, but less than two hundred years ago, most of us were like this. Your great-grandparents . . . mine. Maybe they knew something. There." He pointed to a three-story building half of whose windows were boarded up with plywood. "The Reb Arele." He nodded to the side door. I watched as the two women opened it to reveal a set of rickety stairs. They started to climb up, their long dresses revealing not one square centimeter of feminine skin.

"You like her."

"Who?"

"Chaya. I saw you watching her at dinner. You would like perhaps I arrange a match?" He put on a playful Yiddish accent, but he sounded half serious.

"Oh, come on."

"Why not? She's of child-bearing age. Healthy. *Modest.*"

"So I see."

"You're not married, are you? I heard you were divorced."

"Twelve years."

"Well?"

"Arranged marriages aren't exactly my style."

"They're not?" He laughed again. "So we've had such great luck with romantic love, all of us, have we? Maybe we were better off when our families arranged it."

We started for the front door. "What's her background, anyway?"

"Chaya? Ex-rock-and-roller. She quit when her little brother got into heavy drugs."

"That's who she came down here to help? Her little brother?"

"No. He died three years ago. Let's go inside."

We entered a lobby leading into a vast book-lined room halfway between a synagogue and a library. What seemed like a thousand bearded men were crammed inside on benches beneath a giant candle-lit chandelier. Some of them made way, and Max and I slid into a bench near the back. Way up front I could see a tiny, almost elfin man with a wispy white beard, speaking at a podium in front of a dead microphone, which was seemingly the one artifact of the modern world permitted on the premises. I guessed him to be Reb Arele. Everyone was attending him intently as he spoke in a quiet Yiddish drone, clasping his palm over his eyes as if communing with the spirits.

"What's he saying?" I asked.

"He's talking about the Creation according to the Kabbalah. After God created the world, he withdrew."

"Like Nietzsche? God is dead?"

"Not exactly. He contracted." Max glanced over at the next Chasid, who was staring at us, and lowered his voice. "You see, since God is everywhere, in order to create the world, he had to give up His own space."

"So what'd he do?"

"Went into exile, more or less. But His attributes, what the Kabbalists call emanations, continued to fill the shapes, or vessels, of the physical world. But those vessels couldn't contain the divine light. They broke. Holy sparks fell and mixed in with the evil and weakness of earthly existence. The whole cosmos went awry; everything was in exile, *including* God. Creation turned into a catastrophe. And now it is man's duty to repair the world and bring God back."

I looked from the tiny man at the podium back to Max. "And you believe all this?"

"I believe everything and nothing. Sometimes I see it as a metaphor, sometimes the work of brilliant men trying to explain the chaos of the universe before the advent of science. . . . But now even science tells us the universe is chaos when reduced to the smallest particle, so . . ."

Suddenly there was an audible gasp from the audience as Reb Arele stood up, clutching the sides of the podium with his frail hands. He began to whisper into the microphone with an urgency that was almost otherworldly.

"Now what?" I asked.

"He speaks of paradox. He says when the world is in the greatest need of repair is when there is most hope. Now when the secular world has reached a dead end—drugs everywhere, the plague of AIDS, the threat of nuclear annihilation, rampant atheism—perhaps now the Messiah will come. He quotes a nineteenth-century rabbi, Menahem Mendel of Kotzk: 'Before the coming of the Messiah, there will be an age of summers without heat, of winters without cold, and of rabbis without Torah.' "

The Chasidim screamed something in unison.

"They want Moshiach—the Messiah—now," said Max.

"The rabbi says he will come when he comes. Now is the time to welcome the Sabbath bride."

The rabbi sat down. His Chasidim rose as one and began to chant, placing their arms around each other's shoulders and swaying in long lines. The man next to me grasped my shoulder and pulled me with him. I could feel his sweaty palms, smell his body odor. I had a strong urge to leave, but Max, who had his eyes shut and his head pointed toward the ceiling, was in a different world. The Chasidim were singing now. "Come, my friend, to greet the Bride," murmured Max, translating for me, eyes still shut. "Let us meet her, the holy presence." Involuntarily, I turned and looked for the women. They were up above me in a balcony, hidden behind a grille of wire mesh. The Chasidim began to sing louder, stamping their feet and moving out from behind the benches.

I felt myself lifted off the ground, moving with them. We began to form a long, snakelike line, a thousand of us, sliding in and out between the benches, the fervor of the chanting increasing . . . bim bam, bim bim bim bam, bim bim bim bim bim bam. "Let yourself be with them," I heard Max urging. "Forget yourself. Let it happen. Like the old days in Golden Gate Park." So I shut my eyes too. And for a moment I began to feel carried away with it, the music, the movement. I was transported somewhere. Russia? Poland? My great-great-grandfather's *shtetl* two hundred years ago? I was floating in the air like a Chagall character. But then—it must have been an embarrassment, a sense of the ridiculous—my body stiffened again almost as quickly and shut down. I started to drift, looking from Max to the line of dancing men and back again. Again, as on the plane, I felt like a traitor. What was I doing betraying these people, these naive, frightened cousins, who welcomed me in their midst?

"Something wrong?" asked Max.

"It's all right," I said.

But he wasn't convinced. "We'll have to find another way," said Max. He split us away from the line, and we made our way through the crowds of dancing men out of the building. "I'm going to make a project of you."

"To what end?"

"To help you find your identity again. I know this sounds like proselytizing, and we all hate that. But now that Marxism's become a dead end, a modern Jew only *has* three choices." He held the door open and we exited.

"Go ahead, teacher," I forced an uncomfortable smile. "Tell me."

"Okay, you stay with middle-class conformity, which means hedonism, materialism, BMWs, VCRs and all that. You follow modern philosophy to its conclusion and adopt the nihilism of Kafka or Beckett. Or . . . you make a leap of faith and start the road back."

I laughed. "You've got the wrong guy here."

"I know. I'm taking on an impossible task." He grinned mischievously. "Let's say I'm a glutton for punishment. But first we have to find you someplace to stay."

"That's all right. I'll handle it."

"No, no. It seems difficult for you to stay in a hotel, treacherous shall we say. . . . And you'll learn so much more if you stay in a yeshiva." He smiled slyly. "Go native."

"Well, when in Rome . . . Maybe it'll help me find Joshua ben Tsvi."

Max frowned. "I thought you understood there was no working on Shabbat."

"No thinking even?"

"No thinking? Well . . . there are many theories. Erich

Fromm said the Mishnah only intended to forbid work that would change the *physical* world. You probably like *him*. So . . . who are you working for to find this Joshua ben Tsvi?"

I forced a smile. "Now *you're* the one who is breaking the prohibitions."

"You're right. I admit it. I make no claims for being a holy man, Moses. I'm only on the road like the rest of us. And I'm curious. So tell me. Who is it?"

Brenda Weintraub bounded out of the women's entrance with Chaya, bursting with excitement. "What a sight from up there! A Talmudic Busby Berkeley routine! The conga line of all conga lines!"

Max waited for my answer.

"You know how it is," I said. "Psychiatrists, rabbis and private detectives . . . we never reveal our clients."

NINE

I woke up the next morning to the sound of two South Africans dovening. It was six-thirteen and these two sixteen-year-old dudes in "I Surfed the Pipeline" T-shirts and pastel cutoffs were facing the wall, long prayer shawls draped over wide shoulders and neo-punk haircuts, chanting and crying out just like my crazy Uncle Jack, the religious one, did when I was a kid. And all the while they were consulting a prayer book as if it were a training manual for the Explorer Scouts. Once again I almost forgot where I was, not to mention what time it was, and the guttural tones of the pseudo-limey accents strugging with the Hebrew were enough to send my sense of order off into hyperspace.

I sat up on my cot and stared out the window. Outside the gray light was creeping into a half-finished courtyard of concrete and Jerusalem stone. A sign on a door read "Bet Midrash —House of Learning" in English and Hebrew. Then I remembered: the Derech Chaim Yeshiva. Last night, or rather this morning at two, Max had brought me in and waked up the head rabbi. Could they put me up in the *baal teshuvah* dormitory, maybe enroll me in a few courses? They gave me a sheet and blanket and directed me to a room as if it were summer camp. In my jet-lagged stupor, I was much too far gone to complain. And I had to admit I was curious.

I got up and headed for the washroom, stepping quickly around the South Africans lest they become suspicious of a new roommate who was old enough to be their father, and then ducked out of the building. I wanted to go back to Torat Cohanim—the Moroccan yeshiva—to see if I could figure out who Reb Lipsky had been after the other night, the fat shmuck who didn't realize they were at a crucial point in their work. I also figured there was no time like the present. Even if it wasn't yet seven in the morning, I wouldn't be waking anybody up. These folks got up early and prayed late.

Indeed, when I arrived at the Old City yeshiva twenty minutes later, the men were heavily engaged in their prayers, which, it being Shabbat morning, would probably go on for hours, while the women tended to the endless babies. Feeling slightly fraudulent, I had put on Max's yarmulke. I entered the building, smiling to everybody with that look that said I'm-not-a-friend-of-yours-but-don't-worry-I'm-a-friend-of-somebody-else's. It was the same look I had used in high school for crashing parties, and sometimes it worked. At least here it got me up to the second floor past the room, now empty, where the old men had been weaving raiments for the Third Temple, to the door of the back room where Lipsky had gone in search of someone he didn't find.

I waited for a moment by the door, making sure I was alone, no Chasidim, no Slaughterers, before I tried the handle. It was unlocked. The room inside was small, windowless and sparsely furnished. A couple of straight-backed chairs stood against the wall next to a bare end table. It was also so dark, the slight crack I had left when I closed the door behind me providing the only illumination, that I almost tripped over the body on the floor beneath me.

A girl rolled over, banging her feet against the floor and trying to kick. Her legs were bound together at the ankles, her hands tied behind her back. "*Nyet, lo, no, nein,* whatever," she shouted in terror. "Can't you leave me alone? What time is this? What're you trying to do? I told you I'd leave him."

"Hey, calm down. It's okay."

"You're American? She stared up at me. In the dim light I could see a girl about nineteen. She was wearing jeans and a sweatshirt, and her curly blond hair was matted down on her scalp. "Thank God, or I guess I should say *baruch ha-Shem* around here. I've been trying to get by on my high school French, and let me tell you it's bush. The only Hebrew I know is the prayer for the bread. Where I come from, Jews speak English."

"Where *do* you come from?"

"Lawrence, Long Island. The Five Towns." I expected her to smack some gum, but it was clear she didn't have any. "You're not going to hit me, are you?"

"What for?"

"I dunno. I thought these guys were gonna hit me for sure."

"Which guys?"

"The ones who picked me up last night. You're not part of them?" I shook my head. "Hey, then how'd you get in here? You better be careful," she whispered. "This is a Moroccan yeshiva, y'know. I don't want to sound racist, but that's an Oriental culture. They live with violence."

"I'll take my chances." I bolted the door behind me and squatted down to untie her.

"What a way to spend my junior year. . . . Hey, are you from the embassy or what?"

"Let's say I'm just a friend. Now tell me, who picked you up?"

"I don't know who they were." Her legs were free, and she stumbled to her feet. "Can we get out of here, Mr. Wizard? You got in here and everything and . . ." Suddenly she looked as if she were about to faint. "I think I'd like to go to the airport."

I untied her hands and gave her my jacket to wear, simultaneously tearing a piece of fabric off one of the chairs for a scarf. It wasn't much of a disguise, but it made her look enough like a modest Jewish maiden to get us out of there. Two minutes later we were out on the street.

"God, thanks a lot. I don't know whether to run or what."

"Just keep walking," I said. "And don't look back. Now what's going on?"

"You tell me. One minute I'm strolling around the campus

of Hebrew U. The next minute I'm in the backseat of a Toyota barreling toward Gilo. Geez, I don't know what they were so excited about. I wasn't about to sleep with him, not really anyway. Not all the way. I'm not an idiot. A girl can lose her arm nowadays for a little casual sex. I'll stick to my vibrator, thank you very much." I started to laugh. "What's so funny? Hey, can we get something to eat? I'm famished, and all the restaurants are closed for Shabbat. Can you believe this country's Jewish and you can't even get a pisspoor pastrami sandwich?"

"We could go Arab." I pointed up ahead to a hummous joint called Abu Mustafa's which consisted of two wobbly chairs and a table spilling out onto the cobblestones.

The girl and I sat inside, way in the back as a precaution, drinking Turkish coffee and eating sweet rolls. For the first time I got a good look at her. She was pale with dirty-blond hair and wasn't really attractive, more the type you'd call in high school as a third or fourth choice if you absolutely had to have a date and all the other options were taken. But she had more spunk than your average JAP, and someday some Long Island dentist would be very lucky.

But right now the liveliness was wearing off. "I was at this Peace Now rally," she said. "Something about detaining Arab prisoners. I never got it straight. And this guy comes up to me. Not bad-looking, very Middle Eastern. You know—black eyes. He calls himself Yaacov. Asks me for coffee. That went pretty well, so we go out a couple of times. The third time we go to this Israeli movie about the occupation of Lebanon that's got a character based on Abu Nidal and everything and is kinda liberal I guess and he says he has a confession to make. He hopes I don't mind but his name is realy Fouad and he's a Palestinian Arab." She shrugged. "Hey, what was I supposed to say? I didn't want to seem like a racist, and that's what I'm here for anyway, cross-cultural exchange. I mean, I'm not anti-Zionist or anything, but I have no intention of living here. I admit it. I'm spoiled by the American life-stye. So I went out with him again. In fact, that night we went to bed, sort of. I'm always turned on by honesty. But it wasn't easy, let me tell you. Boy, do the Arabs have a lot to learn about safe sex."

"How long was this before you were picked up at Hebrew U?"

"Oh, a month. We were a twosome, if that's what you mean, but I wasn't about to marry him. In fact, I was just trying to figure out how to dump him when . . . Why're you asking me all these questions?"

"Frankly, I'm not sure. Now tell me who picked you up."

"Three guys. I never saw them before. A big, fat blond guy who looked like John Candy and two others. They were wearing yarmulkes and the fringes, you know, *tzitzit*, and came up to me right when I was walking with Fouad. They asked why I was holding hands with an Arab, sort of picked me up between them and half-carried me to their car."

"What'd Fouad do?"

"Nothing . . . ran, sort of. Anyway, they drove me out of Jerusalem, you know, out Derech Hebron."

"I *don't* know."

"That's the big road out of the city. But by the time we were in Talpiot, they had blindfolded me. We ended up in the West Bank someplace, way out in Injun country."

"You mean you weren't here . . . in that yeshiva?"

"Not the first night. We were in this smelly old house, looked like a run-down Arab palace or something with religious quotations on the wall and photographs of great leaders, not just Jewish leaders but all kinds. You know—Sai Baba, John Lennon. The first thing the guy asked me was did I know John

Lennon was assassinated on the seventh day of Chanukah? I don't know why I'm telling you all this. I should be telling the police."

"Maybe it's because I brought you out of Egypt."

"Right." She grinned. "I guess you've got a nice face. Reminds me of my cousin Phil. Lotta guys around here remind me of my cousin Phil. He was my first lover. Anyway, these guys really started in on me, asking me why I was going with an Arab, did I want to injure the Jewish people, didn't I have relatives who died in the Holocaust, really laying a guilt trip. The one of them started to read me the laws of the family from the Talmud while the other played shrink, asking if I was angry at myself or my parents for being Jewish. Maybe they could help me. It was like one of those deprogrammings you read about for the Moonies. But they weren't getting anywhere with me. They were getting frustrated fast, and I thought they were going to hurt me when—"

"Did you get any of their names?"

"No, but the blond one called himself Hosea the Prophet and said when the Messiah came he would be properly recognized. It was then that I thought he was going to hurt me, but some other people came and he cooled off."

"What other people?"

"I don't know. They were in the next room, but boy, were they pissed. I could hear them yelling in English and Hebrew, calling Hosea an idiot, saying he would ruin everything, was destructive to the cause and so on. After they left, the three original guys took me to the yeshiva over here, tied me up and left me. They said they were going to find some friend of theirs and come back, but I never saw them again."

"What friend?"

"I don't know."

"Ever hear of a Gordie Goldenberg or a Joshua ben Tsvi?"

"No, I—"

"Don't move. Just keep talking and pretend I'm here."

"What?"

"Just do as I say. We're being watched."

"How long has *this* been going on? Mickey Mouse on a stick —I thought this was it. Take me to the airport, Mr. Wizard. When this is all over."

"Maybe you'll want to stay. What's your name?"

"Ellen. Ellen Greenspan. . . . Something wrong with that? It's a perfectly average name in the Five Towns. God, there must be fifty Greenspans in the directory."

"No. It's fine. Great name," I said, leaning back against the wall. "Keep talking." I slid down to the level of the table and started duck-walking out the back under the astonished eyes of Abu Mustafa, who was stuffing his face with a jumbo-sized pita.

The man who was watching me had dark skin, short black hair and what looked like a burn scar just under his right ear. He wore a green turtleneck sweater beneath a brown sports jacket with enough of a bulge under his left breast pocket to fit a fairly large shoulder holster. I stood in the doorway of an Arab butcher shop studying him with my body half hidden behind a camel carcass. He was leaning against a vegetable cart and smoking, trying to look nonchalant, when something about Ellen Greenspan's behavior, probably her rigid posture, which, as the truth of her situation was dawning on her, was tending toward catatonic, caught his attention. He glanced to his right and then crossed over toward Abu Mustafa's, peering through the grimy window and noting my absence in a microsecond. He frowned and made another quick glance, this time right *and* left, and headed up the street at a pace just short of a run, turning immediately into an alley behind a leather shop.

I took a breath and plunged after him. He made another turn and broke into a run. I pursued him, and within seconds I was in the middle of the souk, the Arab shopkeepers just beginning to open up for the day, staring out at me between the fat Palestinian housewives with their plastic shopping bags. I pushed past them, moving faster. The crowds were suddenly getting thick. My man dove to his right among some shoppers, and for a moment I lost him.

I then had the disquieting sensation that someone was following *me* and was about to turn back when I caught a glimpse of my man again, heading in the direction of the Wailing Wall, and moved quickly to catch him. But he saw me coming, yelled something in Arabic and ran. I took off after him, following him up a cobblestone ramp past a row of tourist shops selling dime-store religo-crap, Styrofoam Jesuses and olivewood menorahs. Up at the top I could see him at a large ceremonial archway, presenting his identity card to an official in a dark green uniform. He continued on through, and I ran up to the official, simultaneously reaching for my passport and handing it to him. He shook his head, immediately blocking my path.

"You must go Moghrabi Gate or Iron Gate."

"What?"

"Not Mussulman," he said, returning my passport. "Only Mussulman go here. By order of the Waqf."

"What's the Waqf?"

"I not understand."

"What is the Waqf?" I repeated more slowly, glancing past him through the archway at my man, who was rapidly disappearing behind a group of Greek Orthodox nuns.

"I am Waqf," he said, pointing to his outfit, which looked like a sale item from the Banana Republic. "Religious police

Mussulman. You go Moghrabi Gate or Iron Gate. Only way to Noble Enclosure."

The Noble Enclosure. The Iron Gate. What was that about?

I went Iron Gate. It was at the end of the Bab el Hadid and it took me about seven minutes to get there, making only two wrong turns along the way. I went through and came out on the other side in a flat area about the size of two football fields and was immediately approached by two guys in kaffiyehs offering to show me the holy sites and a third trying to sell me postcards. Directly in front of me were the Dome of the Rock and the El Aqsa Mosque. Finally, I was getting the picture. I was at the top of Temple Mount. *That* was what the Arabs called the Noble Enclosure.

I looked around for my man. He was nowhere to be seen, and the immediate vicinity was beginning to fill up with tourists, so I just followed the crowds toward the Dome of the Rock, its ornate facade and golden bronze roof a triumph of Islamic architecture in the pedestrian hodgepodge of modern Israel. Under the scrutiny of two more Waqf guards, I left my shoes near the door and entered. What seemed like hundreds of tourists were streaming toward a set of stairs that descended near the center of the octagonal building. I continued toward them, past a dozen Arab women who kneeled, oblivious behind a rail, praying to Allah.

I saw him halfway down, just beyond a tour group from Leeds. I drifted down with them, hiding myself and listening to their leader, a tweedy British woman with shoulders like a power forward who stood on her toes towering over everyone. "Some call the Foundation Stone the most sacred spot on earth," she was saying. "The Hebrews believe it may be the site of their Holy of Holies, the altar upon which Abraham was supposed to have sacrificed Isaac, which became the most hallowed part, the inner sanctum, of Solomon's Temple. For Islam, it is the very rock from which Mohammed is said to have risen to heaven with his winged horse, drawn on by the Archangel Gabriel." She gestured toward an oddly commonplace granite boulder that jutted out of the earth at the bottom of the stairs. It was worn down and polished in several spots where generations of pilgrims had touched it in the hopes of making contact with some god or other. "Or perhaps it was only the threshing stone for an ancient grain thresher, Ornan the Jebusite."

I caught sight of my man at the back of the stone, breathing hard and staring up at me like a caged animal. He bolted around me, past the British group, and I had moved to catch him when I heard a piercing scream and swung around.

Another man was stumbling toward me, a Chasid. He had a knife in his stomach and blood was oozing from his mouth; he looked like a wounded bull at a corrida. He stopped not more than ten feet from me and gasped, "*Hoserim teshuvah*," and then, in a barely audible whisper, said something like "*nitzutzot*" before he wailed pitifully and pitched forward against the Foundation Stone, grabbing at the guardrail before collapsing to the ground and rolling over on his back, stone dead. I walked over and looked down at him. It was Rabbi DeLeon, Max's friend from our Shabbat dinner, the one who worked with repentant criminals. His already pale face had turned whiter than chalk.

TEN

"It's not forbidden. Jews have prayed in mosques for centuries. Muslims don't put up graven images."

"You're telling me DeLeon was up there to pray?"

"It's possible. Sometimes pious Jews go up there on Shabbat, to be closer to the old Temple. The Arabs know, and I wouldn't be surprised if they . . ." Max gestured halfheartedly. There were tears in his eyes as we stood in the patio of his house, his kids playing obliviously on the concrete in front of us.

"Look, there was this guy following me. I think he was an Arab. At least he had Arab ID. I saw him watching me at Abu Mustafa's and I followed him straight to the Temple Mount. Right to the Foundation Stone. That's where the murder happened. This couldn't all have been accidental."

"Who knows how things happen?"

"You're becoming too mystical for me, Max."

"Too mystical? Perhaps mysticism is only a sophisticated form of observation. But I don't understand. What do you expect me to tell you? That this wouldn't have happened if you hadn't been working on Shabbat?" He smiled wryly. "Why would an Arab have reason to follow you?"

"I'm not sure."

"You must be able to make some guesses. You know who you're working for."

At that moment I knew only too well. I felt heartsick. I looked over at one of his kids, who was pedaling a tricycle around an olive tree.

"You don't have to tell me why you're here," he said. "It's not my business to know."

"What are *hoserim teshuvah*? I think that's the last thing DeLeon said. At least the last thing I understood. After that he said something that sounded like '*nitzutzot*' but it was all a blur."

"*Hoserim teshuvah* are repentant criminals. That was his work, remember? I told you. He took criminals and brought them back to God. It was quite remarkable, really. His success."

"Maybe that had something to do with this."

"At the Dome of the Rock? He spent three days a week at the old Mandate Prison. Nothing ever happened to him there. As for *nitzutzot*, those are the 'holy sparks' I told you about, from the Kabbalah, that remained as vestiges of God's presence on Earth when He withdrew."

"You mean the ones we're supposed to use to repair things and bring Him back?" I didn't mean to sound as cynical as I probably did.

"Moses," said Max, "if you look into your heart, you know who was following you. We all know what we have to, and we are all perfect. We just have to locate that in ourselves."

Just then the piercing wail of a siren broke out.

"Riot police," said Max. "An Arab kills a Jew. It's inevitable. Reb Lipsky will be here within the hour, leading the fray for the television reporters from Tel Aviv. You'll have to excuse me now." He started across the patio. "This could get dangerous, and I have to take care of my children. Perhaps I'll see you at Talmud class tomorrow morning. At the yeshiva." He picked up a tricycle.

"Max," I said, stopping him. "I'm sorry."

"What do you have to be sorry for? I'm the one who should be sorry. You made me the godfather of your child and I shirked the responsibility entirely and went off to be a drug dealer. Shabbat shalom." He opened the door and ushered his kids inside.

I stood there, listening to the escalating sirens and mulling over what Max had said. We all know why we're here. If I looked into my heart, I'd know who was following me. Then I went off to find a phone.

"All hell's breaking loose here!"

"What? I can't hear you. Where are you? This is a terrible connection."

"The King David Hotel."

"What? I thought you checked out of there."

"In the lobby. It's the only place I could use the phone. It's hard to find a phone on Shabbat."

"On what?"

"Never mind. An Arab just killed a Jew in the Dome of the Rock. Put a knife right in his stomach. At least I think he did."

"Did you see it?"

"No, but I was there at the time. I might even have had something to do with it. They're starting to riot in the streets of the Old City."

"What? Are you all right?"

"I'm fine, *baruch ha-Shem*."

"B-what?"

"That's Hebrew for thanks God."

"Thanks God? Hel-low! Are you going religious on me, Moses? You promised me you weren't going to go religious."

"No, I'm not going religious. Now listen, Chantal, I want you to check out our Arab friends, Terzi and Said. I have reason to believe they may have put a man on me."

"Put a man on you? Why would they want to do that? You're working for *them*!"

"Not so loud."

"Are you making any progress, Moses?"

"Not much."

"What about Rabbi Lipsky?"

"I met him, but I didn't find out anything. Not about Gordie either, except that he's called Joshua ben Tsvi. That's all I've got—other than this murder and Ellen Greenspan."

"Ellen Greenspan?"

"I think she might be a link to something. I haven't been able to work much because of Shabbat. It's forbidden."

"What's that got to do with *you*?" She sounded annoyed, or maybe it was the international connection.

"Listen, Chantal, I can't hang around here too long. I don't want the Shochet to see me."

"The what?"

"The Shochet—the Slaughterer. For Kosher meat."

"I can't believe this—you are going religious."

"Just check out Terzi and Said. Okay? Goodbye. I'll call you as soon as I can."

"You're sure you're all right?"

"Yes. I love you."

"Me too. You just don't sound the same. 'Bye."

I hung up and walked out the back of the hotel, standing on the famous terrace overlooking the Old City where Paul Newman dined with Eva Marie Saint in *Exodus*. I remembered watching it as a kid and identifying passionately. I never would've guessed twenty-five years later I'd be standing on the same terrace, listening to the angry chants of my brethren and watching warning flares go off behind the Jaffa Gate and wondering whether I had indeed, in some weird way, been the cause. It seemed so unlikely, and yet . . . At that moment, a sharp headache began pulsing through the side of my skull. It was obvious I didn't know what I was doing and I was clearly operating out of my depth.

But I pushed on, catching an Arab cab in front of the hotel up to the campus of the Hebrew University. Sabbath was winding down, and I hoped the more secular students, their adolescent pheromones set free in the postobservant mating frenzy, would help me find Ellen Greenspan's abductors. They might even give me a clue to the whereabouts of Ellen herself, who had disappeared when I came back to find her after the rabbi's murder.

We drove between the Knesset and the Israel Museum, down to the south end of the campus, where the dormitories were located. I had the driver drop me off by a particularly promising patio where male students were mingling with coeds, some of whom wore short-shorts with halter tops. The cabbie looked as if he were about to drool as I paid him off and I suddenly flashed on rumors I had read about Yasir Arafat being a child molester. Maybe it was part of the culture. Or maybe it was part of any culture to go crazy over seventeen-year-old girls.

I walked over to a kiosk, bought myself an Orange Crush and sat down. Using my best grad-student slouch, I stuck my feet up on another chair and started thumbing through the student daily, trying to look inconspicuous. I spent about a half hour this way, one eye on the students and one eye on the newspaper, scrutinizing the couples and doing my best to decide which ones were Arab-Jewish and which ones were Jewish-Jewish. It wasn't easy, and it made me think how important it was on the battlefield that everybody was wearing a uniform. I was about to give up and devise another approach when two Arab guys about twenty, wearing those checked Palestinian kerchiefs that looked like French bistro napkins, sat down at my table with a couple of bottles of Maccabee beer. I nodded to them and took a few beats before launching in.

"Either of you guys speak English?"

"I speak English," said the taller of the two, an angular fellow in a yellow T-shirt. "I am engineering major. You do not speak English, you have nothing to read. Unless you speak Japanese."

"Great," I said. "I'm, uh, a journalist and I was wondering if—"

"Ah, an American. Who're *you* with? The CIA?"

"What if I were?"

"Where do we sign up? We could use a little spare cash." He translated for his buddy, who guffawed loudly.

"No such luck. Actually I'm with the *Los Angeles Times*." I slipped him one of the business cards I kept for just such occasions.

"Ah, we are going to be in newspaper. To be misquoted most certainly. What is subject? Arab students at Hebrew University study engineering on Israeli scholarship to blow up the Zionist State." He translated this one too for his buddy, who thought it was even funnier.

"No. This time it's interracial romance."

"Ah, dark, mysterious Arab seduces innocent Jewish-American Princess from Larchmont."

"Now you've got it." I had to admit, this guy had a sense of humor. But how had he heard of Larchmont? "I was wondering if you guys had anything to say on the subject."

"What to say? Depends on girl. Some think it dangerous, flirting with Arab, look for thrill. Other think it what you call slumming. Other think they make contribution to world peace. Actually they all racist, but they not know it. . . . Of course, some time you have real girl. Then it different." He paused thoughtfully, then downed the rest of his beer in one swallow.

"You seem to have some experience with the subject. Can I buy you another?" I gestured to the beer.

"So you can write Arab drink Israeli beer at Hebrew University? Break law of Allah?" He was getting a little surly.

"No. I break laws all the time myself. A few of them I'm even ashamed of."

"You keep kosher?"

I laughed. "Not unless they put Tommy's chiliburgers with french fries on the list." And then I thought: Maybe it'd be better for me. After all, keeping kosher wasn't that different from vegetarianism. And most people agreed *that* was good for you. Maybe those rabbis knew something. Maybe there was something in it—the laws of Talmud, a little depth and devotion in my shallow, secular life. But what was I thinking? "So what happens here," I continued to the young engineer, "when an Arab starts going out with a Jewish girl?"

"Starts good, ends bad. No more than that. And if it stay good, crazy Jews come along and try to stop it."

I studied him a second. "That what happened to you? Crazy Jews?"

"No. She left . . . marry doctor in Larchmont."

"Probably for the best."

He looked at me, shrugged. "Hard thing, Arab boy. Arab girl don't fuck, never fuck. Jewish girl fuck quick, real quick. Arab boy think great. I am lucky. I fuck all the time. Have free girl. Be real smart, in driver seat. What Arab boy not know is he fall in love with girl because he never fuck like that before. He not know what fucking do to you, in the heart. He more serious than Jewish girl, more serious than he know himself. Arab boy think he seduce Jewish girl, but it other way around. That what crazy Jews not know. They too stupid to know. But I think they never fuck anyone either. . . . I think I have beer now."

I got up and bought a couple of beers for him and his partner. When I sat down with him again, I asked him, "You know these crazy Jews?"

"Hah, there are many of them. Some of them are even students."

"How about one who looks like John Candy?"

"John Kendy?"

"You like American movies?"

"I love them. I go to them all the time. I like most Jack Nicholson and Pee Wee Herman. He is my favorite—the Pee Wee man."

"Then you must know John Candy. Fat . . . blond . . ." I gestured. "Candy, rhymes with randy. Like something you eat that's bad for your teeth."

"Ah, John Candy. John Candy." Suddenly he frowned and started racing away in Arabic to his buddy, who answered back in staccato bursts. After about a minute of this, he turned back to me and shook his head. "This is very bad man."

"I should imagine. You know where I could find him?"

"I do not know where he lives. I do not know where such people live." He looked insulted.

"I mean where he hangs out . . . where he comes when he wants to kidnap Jewish girls."

"Ah." He fell silent briefly, then went into another conference with his buddy. They seemed to be debating something. "Why do you want to know?" he said finally. "Is this part of your article?"

"The best part."

"All right. We will take you. To Solomon's Cave. Is nightclub where Arab boys pretend to be Jewish. Meet girls after Sabbath. Dance disco to Chasidic band. John Candy always there. They call him Hosea."

"That's right. Hosea."

The two guys' names were Hakim and Yusef, and I left them to be the first in line at Hertz to rent a car after Sabbath ended at six-thirteen. When I drove back in an Isuzu, most of the students had dispersed except for my two, who were still seated at the same table, with a third Arab. He looked about three days late for a shave and ten years too old to be a student. My guess was he was the closest thing they had to a cadre leader and was there to check me out before things got too cozy between us.

"This Mr. Abdul," said Hakim, the one who spoke English. "He come with us."

"Terrific," I said. "Mr. Abdul is always welcome."

We wedged ourself into the tiny Isuzu and started off east again toward the Old City. Immediately, Mr. Abdul lit up a small cigar, staring at me suspiciously and letting the smoke drift in front of my eyes as I drove. Whoever he was, he was not a friendly fellow. I did my best to ignore him, waving the smoke away from my face and fumbling with the radio. We had gone about half a mile when he started talking in a monotone Arabic with the cadence of an experienced interrogator. Hakim turned to me. "Mr. Abdul wants to know if you are a stooge of the Zionist press."

"Not so far."

Hakim reported this, then: "Mr. Abdul wants to know then who you are."

"As I told you. A reporter for the L.A. *Times*."

This was translated quickly. "Mr. Abdul does not believe you."

"If Mr. Abdul does not believe me, I'd like to know who Mr. Abdul is."

"Mr. Abdul is a representative of Hizbullah."

"Hizbullah? The Party of God?" I did my best to avoid slamming on the brakes. The last I'd known of Hizbullah was a television documentary showing them training fourteen-year-olds for suicide missions in South Lebanon.

"Only representative," Hakim assured me.

"Great."

"Everybody deserves representative. Who could deny that, yes?"

"Oh, yes. Nobody. I just didn't realize Hizbullah had representatives in Jerusalem these days."

"Unofficial. . . . Turn there."

I turned down a road near the Sultan's Pools, not far from where Rabbi Lipsky had spoken. We continued around the back of the Old City and then down another street near the excavations of the City of David. We slowed down, and Hakim motioned for me to park by a crumbling wall that looked somewhere near about five thousand years old and probably was. He and Yusef removed their Palestinian kerchiefs and stashed them in the back, adjusting the rearview mirror and making a few passes through their hair with well-worn pocket combs.

"Mr. Abdul will wait in car," Hakim said as he and Yusef climbed out of the vehicle into the already dark night.

"Great," I said. "Somebody's got to watch it."

I followed Hakim and Yusef across a rubble-strewn lot toward another wall where a couple of dozen cars were parked. A light blinked pink and green over a door with the words "Solomon's Cave" scrawled in English and Hebrew in an imitation graffiti style. Although it was still only seven in the evening, I could hear a kind of schmaltzy, up-tempo country music coming from within that sounded like the Butterfield Blues Band playing a Bar Mitzvah. A tall, bearded guy stood at the door, selling admission at fifteen shekels a pop. I paid for my two Arab friends and we entered.

Inside it looked like a Greenwich Village beatnik cave circa 1957 with some layering of the late-sixties psychedelic and even a few postmodern and punk touches thrown in. It was as if several generations of traveling youth had passed through here, emptied out their rucksacks and moved on. The band too was a bizarre assortment of a sixty-year-old tuba player, an overweight violinist, two hippie Chasidim on electric guitar, a saxophone, a bass and a kid on drums who looked about fifteen and had tinted his earlocks green. They segued from "Eleanor Rigby" to "Bei Mir Bist Du Schoen" as the dancers, men *and* women, not touching each other but still dancing, wove back and forth in the now familiar conga line.

When the band finally took a break, the dancers dispersed and sat at tables illuminated by chianti-bottle candles, boys and girls now huddling closely together as if some mysterious house mother had suddenly disappeared. I looked over at Hakim and Yusef, who were tapping their toes and surveying the room, "checking out the local cheese," as we used to say in college. It was then that I noticed Chaya Bracha. She was seated in a corner by herself, looking as modest as the first time I had seen her. Clearly she hadn't come to dance. But what had she come for?

I turned to excuse myself to Hakim and I saw him and Yusef

making for a table of three JAPPY-looking girls in trendy
Benetton sports clothes. I watched, momentarily fascinated, as
they sat down with the girls, identifying themselves as scions
of an eminent Sephardic family in Casablanca, now fallen on
hard times from the unfortunate upsurge in Moroccan anti-
Semitism. When I turned back toward Chaya, she was gone. I
walked over to where she'd been sitting, but I couldn't find her
anywhere, and there was no logical method by which she could
have slipped out. She seemed to have vanished almost magi-
cally.

The band started in again, and several people got up to
dance, this time boys and girls together, as if the religious
prohibition against mixing of the sexes was only for intermittent
observance. Hakim and Yusef got up to dance with two of the
girls, doing some version of the boogaloo in the middle of the
dance floor to "Roll Over, Beethoven" played à la Brooklyn
New Wave with a little Yiddish violin and good old-fashioned
stomp thrown in.

In the midst of the action, John Candy Hosea entered with a
couple of other guys who looked like the Middle East branch of
the Jewish Defense Squad. Snorting and swaggering across the
dance floor, he looked like a combination bouncer and watch-
dog for the WCTU. At length, he took a position at the center
of the floor and stood there, flanked by his two associates,
surveying the scene. I drifted up next to them and stood there
a few minutes before saying anything.

"Whatsa matter? You don't like dancing?" Hosea finally
broke the ice.

"Not this kind of dancing," I said.

"Oh, you like it *real* close."

"No, I wouldn't say that. I know it sounds a little out of it, but I, uh, don't really approve of men and women dancing together."

Hosea stared at me a second, trying to decide if I was gay or religious.

"I guess I shouldn't have come here," I continued, trying to put his mind at ease. "I'm just beginning to study, make a movement back to the faith. And this place is filled with temptation."

"*Baal teshuvah*, huh?"

"Well, I wouldn't go that far. But it sure makes me crazy to see Jewish girls dancing with Arabs."

"Where do you see that?"

"Right here."

"Whaddya mean, right here?"

"Right here, right here." I nodded toward Yusef, who was standing not more than twenty feet away shaking his money maker in the crotch of a blond girl in turquoise toreadors.

Hosea frowned and exhaled, pawing the ground with his foot like a rhinoceros ready to charge. "You sure he's a camel jockey?"

"Not dead sure. Just a suspicion. Somebody ought to talk to that girl."

"You're a good guy, you know it. Concerned. What's your name?"

"Wolfe. Isaiah Wolfe."

"Wolf. Like wild like a wolf?"

"Right. But with an *e*." I could tell it was going to be difficult keeping my identities straight, but there was no way I could call myself Greenspan to the man who had just kidnapped Ellen of the same name.

"I like you, Wolfe with an *e*. . . . I think I'm going to have to check out this camel jockey, see if he's for real. And considering what happened up on the Temple Mount today, I'm not in the mood to be lenient."

Hosea, his two cronies right behind him, strode over to Yusef as I drifted a few feet back, doing my best not to appear as if I had any part in this while keeping close enough not to miss the proceedings. I was afraid I might be wreaking havoc, but from the looks of Yusef, he seemed capable of handling himself.

Hosea asked Yusef a question, but before he could reply, Hosea immediately started barking at him in Hebrew like a drill sergeant at a raw recruit who was about to get twenty years of KP. Yusef couldn't get in a word edgewise. In a few seconds, his sepia complexion started turning a pale magenta. He took a few steps backward. Hakim stopped dancing with his girl and stared at him just as Hosea grabbed Yusef by the shirt and started shoving him toward the door. Yusef shoved back, but Hosea's greater bulk was unstoppable, like a Sherman tank bearing down on a Volkswagen. By now everyone had stopped dancing and several people were shouting in a mixture of languages. I recognized a few words, most of which were curses, as Yusef went flying through the door, a disgruntled Hakim a few feet behind him. They were probably decent guys and I hated to see it happen to them, but under the circumstances, it was unavoidable.

Hosea trotted back toward me, patting his stomach contentedly and indeed looking for all the world like John Candy's stunt double.

"You were right," he said. "Camel jockeys. Two of 'em. How'd you know?"

"Heard 'em talking in a corner. I don't speak Arabic, but I can recognize the smell." The blonde in the toreadors was staring at me quizzically, and I turned away.

"You're a good man, Wolfe. Where're you from?"

"Seattle, by way of L.A. Although I think I'll be staying here for a while."

"What for? *Aliyah?*"

"Been thinking about it. I've been traveling. Friend of mine in L.A. wants me to contact her brother, only I haven't been able to find him."

"Oh, yeah. Who's that?"

"His name's Gordie Goldenberg. Stepsister's Rachel."

Hosea went silent. He stuck his lower lip over his upper and thrust his chin out like a bulldog. "Never heard of him," he said and started off. I decided to let him go.

Just then the band struck up a Yiddish version of "Satisfaction" with the violin in front and I drifted back to watch the action, making sure Hosea didn't leave without my getting another shot at him. I didn't have to wait long. As if guided by some subliminal morality, the dancers had gone back to male-male and female-female, the unspoken androgyny not entirely inappropriate to the ambiguous message of the Mick Jagger tune. Hosea marched in between them like some underage college proctor gone berserk, slapping his thigh and staring directly and closely into the eye of every dark-skinned male to make absolutely certain that beneath the Star of David dangling from a fourteen-karat gold chain the flame of Islam was not burning illicitly inside a swarthy chest. I had the malicious desire to scream: "There is no God but Allah and Mohammed is his Prophet!" but resisted just long enough to stop when a tall, muscular type in a Columbia University sweatshirt, properly incensed with Hosea's crude behavior, slammed him back against a table, dislodging a chianti bottle and several cups of cappuccino. Instantly I made my move, lowering my shoulder and smashing straight into the solar plexus of the mad Mr.

Morningside Heights, sending him flying back against the band-stand, crashing into the violinist, spinning around and ending up spread-eagled over the drums. He tried to pick himself up, but, listing dizzily, tripped over the high-hat again and slumped down against the saxophone stand.

"Good work, Wolfe," said Hosea, hurrying up to me. "Where'd you learn to do that?"

"Martial arts in college."

"Of course, it wasn't necessary. We coulda handled it our-selves, but still . . . Where're you staying?"

"Derech Chaim Yeshiva, at least until I can find that guy."

"Goldenberg?"

"Uhuh."

"What if I told you he goes by another name here?"

"Joshua ben Tsvi?"

"Who told you that?"

"Irv over at the Holocaust Prevention Institute."

"Well, Wolfe." He looked at me a moment, scratching his stomach. Out of the corner of my eye I could see the Columbia student stumbling to his feet. "Maybe I can help you. I'm not sure, but maybe. Anyway, I'll meet you at the entrance to the Wall tomorrow at twelve. Right now, we have more places to go. . . . C'mon *habibi*." He waved to his men and they started out. Then he stopped and turned to me, frowning. "You know, Wolfe, this racial mixing is a very serious matter. The Arabs don't know it, but we are doing them a favor too. Too much of this and, poof, no more Arabs either. No more Jews. No more anybody. Then no one knows *who* he is, you know what I mean?" He walked out the door.

And as he did so, I could see Hakim and Yusef, standing with Mr. Abdul under a streetlamp, watching me.

ELEVEN

"It's a form of forbidden knowledge, Moses. No one is supposed to study Kabbalah before the age of forty, and most people should *never* study it."

I was sitting having coffee with Max at a little outdoor café near the Cardo in the Jewish Quarter, not far from his place. "You mean like those four second-century rabbis?" I said. "The ones whose esoteric studies led them through the gates of Paradise? The first died of depression, the second lost his reason, the third turned apostate and seduced the young. Only one, Rabbi Akiba, was able to enter in peace and come out in peace."

Max smiled. "You've done some homework."

"I'm human. If someone tells me something's forbidden, I'll do anything in my power to find out about it. Besides, that kid from Jo'burg who sleeps in my room snores like a diesel truck. I've got to read *something* to get to sleep."

"You could read detective stories. I read somewhere the Mossad makes their agents read John Le Carré."

"I've been reading Isaiah: 'And it shall come to pass in the end of days that the mountain of God's house shall be set over all other mountains and lifted high above the hills . . .' "

" '. . . and all the nations shall come streaming to it.' " Max completed the stanza.

"Right," I said. "It's gorgeous language. It can make you cry."

"Just the language?"

I laughed. But then I shrugged. I only knew that the previous night, I had left my dormitory room at two o'clock and wandered down to the yeshiva's "House of Learning," where I'd read until dawn. And then this morning, instead of having coffee in the little Arab place across the street, I ate in the dairy kosher restaurant on the corner whose food I detested. "So tell me some more forbidden knowledge." I cleared my throat. "What powers will I have if I study Kaballah?"

"Nothing that will help you find this Joshua ben Tsvi, I'm afraid. How's that coming?"

"I'm not sure. Have you ever heard of someone who goes around calling himself Hosea the Prophet?"

He laughed. "Outside the Book of Revelations, I don't think so."

"Well, I was tracking him down last night, and guess who I saw. Your friend Chaya Bracha."

"Chaya *Bracha*?"

"At a place called Solomon's Cave near the City of David."

"At what time was this?"

"Around seven-thirty."

"Moses, that's not possible. At that time she was with me. At my house. Celebrating Melavveh Malka, the end of Shabbat." He cocked his black hat and peered at me closely. "How much *have* you been reading?"

"Oh, come on! I saw her. She was sitting at a corner table. She must have seen me and left."

He sighed. "Well, you know we all look alike. Jewish people." He grinned and then stopped abruptly. "I'm just concerned for you. You know, sometimes the more atheistical we are to start with . . . when we study these things . . . the more extreme and peculiar our reactions. Some of us have even had hallucinations. But that is not really finding God any more than the use of mescaline or a sensory-deprivation tank."

"I still saw Chaya there."

"Uhuh, well, I suppose it's getting to you too."

"What?"

"The Middle East. You know the old saying 'There are no atheists in foxholes.' Well, this whole place is a foxhole." He smiled mischievously, scrutinizing me through one eye. "You know, Moses, I think I should introduce you to a friend of mine. Rabbi ben Tov. He does mezuzah readings."

"Mezuzah readings? What in the name of . . ." I tried to stop myself from cracking up. "Max, you know I don't have a mezuzah. I *never* had one. They're just, excuse me, dumb, superstitious—"

"—pieces of metal that religious people put on doors. I know. . . . Moses, I'm only offering these things to you. I know you're going to think I'm going off the deep end. I suppose you already think I have, but . . . this Rabbi ben Tov has powers of *some* sort. I don't know what they are exactly, but he seems to know everything about a person before he walks in the door. It's as if he's not part of the material world and is able to see it all clearly without attachment. They say that happens to some when they give up worldly strivings and God becomes the dominant passion in their lives." He smiled his mischievous smile again. "Maybe he can help you with this Hosea."

"Well, he'd better hurry. I'm meeting him at the Wall in about fifteen minutes."

Max laughed. "Not even the greatest Kabbalists could work that quickly. Well, I think you'd better get going."

"Right." I stood, touching the yarmulke which now sat more familiarly on my head. "Oh, I meant to ask you. Any news about your friend DeLeon?"

He shrugged. "On the streets they say the murderer was an Arab from Jannin. Reb Lipsky seems to agree."

"What do you think?"

"I cry, but I take solace. Eternal life is for God alone. But he who believes in Him, who merges himself with His source, also has a *kind* of eternal life."

"I suppose. I'll see you later."

I had an odd feeling on my way over to the Wall, a kind of anxiety, more accurately a moral disquiet. But it wasn't about being employed by the Arabs, anything so quotidian as simple qualms of bad faith. It felt at once more diffuse and deeper. Maybe Max was right. Some kind of change was coming over me. But it made no sense. Was I so weak, so unformed, that a few days in the Holy Land could have this effect? I was feeling a little like a naive character in some dim-witted Shirley MacLaine movie about past lives, as if I had been here before. And maybe I had, at least my genes had. Some peculiar distorted ancestral version of my DNA must have walked down these narrow alleys two thousand years ago. But what did that mean? Was there still some consciousness of that lodged in my chromosomes, dictating my behavior? Did I have a synesthetic memory of the cobblestone, the smell of the camel dung in the gutters? I had no idea. But whatever the case, I was responding on some level that felt vaguely out of my control. I also felt as if I had studied the Kabbalah, although I had never read any of it before, barely knew what it meant, unless Freud and Marx were Kabbalists. And perhaps they were. They certainly wanted to "repair the world" and they certainly were compelled by their own obsessions, given to endless ratiocinations that ended up, often enough, like corkscrews twisted up their own assholes. And like it or not, I knew, for most of my life I had often been the same way.

I doubted, however, that Hosea was troubled by such problems or that he knew much of Freud or Marx, or, for that matter, of anything that took more than thirty seconds of sustained thought, but he *was* standing, as promised, by the entrance of the Wailing Wall when I arrived two minutes early.

He and his friends stood there wordlessly for a moment before he said: "Joshua ben Tsvi sends greetings to his stepsister."

"Great," I said. "Can I see him?"

"What for?"

"She says he's quite a guy."

"I don't think that's possible, Wolfe with an *e*."

"Why's that?"

"Right now he's very busy."

"I don't want to take up much of his time. I'd just like to meet him. Besides, I have a message from his sister."

"What's that?"

"Personal. Sorry."

"What could be personal?"

"Hey, his sister's an eighteen-year-old girl. There's a lot that could be personal."

"Why'd she tell it to you, Wolfe with an *e*?"

"Because I was coming here. Who else could she tell it to?"

It was a pretty lame explanation, but it was enough to fry Hosea's synapses for a second.

"He's not an easy person to meet," he said at length.

"Apparently."

"I don't see him much myself. In fact, it's something of an inconvenience just to get a message through."

"Why's that?"

"Reasons."

"Hmm . . . sounds mysterious."

"Yes, it is. A great mystery. Maybe *the* great mystery."

"Well, I'm willing to take the time."

We fell silent again. Off in the distance, I heard some laughter and singing. Some kid was having his Bar Mitzvah at the Wall and they had just brought over a cake. I remember Max did that, gave Bar Mitzvahs there, and I thought of my own kids for a moment, how I had regarded their Bar Mitzvahs as some kind of second-rate obligation, like paying property taxes. Hosea interrupted my reverie.

"Maybe . . . maybe you will be permitted to see him."

"Oh? Great."

"We can't take you all the way. We're not allowed to."

"Take me as far as you can. If it's far, I'll follow you in my car." I gestured toward the lot outside the Dung Gate, where I had left it for just such an eventuality.

"Impossible. You must come with us."

"Fine. Any way you want it."

We drove out of Jerusalem in an old Renault, Hosea and I in the backseat, his two pals in the front. As we passed the Mount of Olives, right by the old Jewish cemetery from which, it was promised, the dead would rise on the day of the Messiah's arrival, the guy riding shotgun took out a Police Special and rested it on his thigh. In short order we were speeding along a potholed road across arid land that reminded me of the back country around Topanga Canyon through nondescript Arab villages with surly-looking youths loitering on the steps of half-built glass factories and hummous joints. We were entering

what Ellen Greenspan had called Injun country, what I knew
of as the West Bank and what I was sure my companions called
Judea and Samaria.

"See how they live," said Hosea, pointing out an Arab man-
sion at the top of a hill that looked like an oversized cinder-
block bunker. "Fifteen rooms and they still piss in a pot. We
give 'em free health, free schools. Every kid they get we send
them another welfare check and encourage them to have more.
Jews are the biggest shmucks in creation. Maybe that's what
we were chosen for. Chosen to be shmucks."

Just then a kid stood up and threw a rock at our car. It went
skittering across the road a hundred feet behind us. The driver
slammed on the brakes and was about to start around after him
when Hosea stopped him. "Forget it this time. We're late." He
turned to me. "Think that's a joke? One of our settlers died
like that. Rock hit her windshield and she went skidding off the
road into a wall. You can't give the Arab an inch. The only
thing they understand is force. You treat them with loving-
kindness and they think you're simpleminded or weak. Maybe
they're right."

We drove on, past Bethlehem filled with tour buses and the
Etzion Block with its monument to Jewish farmers slaughtered
by the Jordanians in the '48 War. We were climbing higher into
the Judean hills, twisting back and forth, and then descending
again into a more populated area, the Plain of Mamre, on into
Arab Hebron itself, tinderbox of the West Bank.

"Welcome to PLO country," said Hosea as we slowed in a
snarl of automotive and pedestrian traffic. We made a right and
turned down a street which was, if anything, even more
crowded. From the looks of the population outside, we could
have been in Cairo or Amman. The only signs of Jewish life
were some Israeli soldiers, patrolling the sidewalk with Uzis in

front of some shops barricaded by a chain-link fence. Then I noticed a plump Orthodox woman, kerchief covering her head, carrying her groceries with about a half-dozen children in tow. "The old Jewish Quarter," Hosea explained. "Until sixty of us were massacred by the Arabs in '29. The government didn't want us moving back. Could you believe that?"

We pulled into a dirt lot by a bus depot right in the center of the casbah and got out. The guy riding shotgun strapped the Police Special ostentatiously to his hip, and we walked through a group of Arabs playing checkers down an alley to a beautiful old domed building surrounded by heaps of construction rubble. A thin woman in her fifties was up on one of the terraces, hanging laundry. She waved to us and said she would be right down, pinning up a couple of more well-worn sheets before she disappeared. She reemerged at the door in front of us a few seconds later, clutching a box of clothespins.

"What a day," she said. "Never have twelve loads of laundry to do when CBS is coming to interview you. I won't finish the housecleaning either. Come in, come in."

We followed her into the house, which was filled with religious books and children's toys. I could hear at least two of them wailing from the next room.

"What's CBS interviewing you about?"

"The usual. What's a Jewish woman from Borough Park doing in Arab Hebron? Aren't we stealing the land from the Arabs which they stole from us in the first place? It goes on and on. I've been here fifteen years already. I don't know why they're still asking the questions."

"Hanna, this is Isaiah Wolfe," said Hosea. "He says he has a message for Joshua ben Tsvi from his stepsister."

"Oh, yes. Well, he can give it to me."

"It's supposed to be personal."

"I don't think he needs any personal messages at this time." She deposited the clothespins on a table and headed into the next room to pick up one of the crying children. She came back in carrying an infant of about nine months.

"This is Gadi, my twelfth."

"*Your* twelfth?"

"Born when I was fifty-two years old. Would've been my fourteenth, but two died in childbirth. Why should I stop? God says I should procreate, so I have children. The secular Jews have dogs. And let me tell you something, my children cost less than their pets. . . . So what do you want me to tell Joshua?"

"It's a personal message. His stepsister asked me to deliver it to him in private."

"What should be so private when we're among friends?" She studied me carefully. This was one tough woman. She looked like a Mormon pioneer in her kerchief and smock, with a little bit of a right-wing version of Aunt Sonya thrown in.

"I'm just following her wishes," I said.

"I'm sure you are. But we have security concerns here that override those. Does Joshua know you?"

"Not personally. No."

"So I'll tell him you were here and . . . What was the name?"

"Wolfe. Isaiah Wolfe."

"With an *e*," Hosea added.

"Very good. Wolfe with an *e*. Just like the delicatessen in Miami," she said, burping the infant. "You boys have to excuse me now. I've got a lot of work to do." She turned and walked back into the nursery, shutting the door behind her.

"Okay. Let's go," said Hosea. "I gotta get back."

"Go ahead," I said. "I'm going to stay. I want to see Hebron. Isn't this where they have that cave where Abraham is buried? The Tomb of the Patriarchs."

"You want to go, we'll drop you off on the way."

"I think I'll walk."

"Walk? Through that?" He gave me a peculiar look, gesturing through a wire-mesh window toward the souk beneath us. "Somebody gets it in the stomach once a month out there. You got a gun?"

"Nope."

He shook his head. "Okay, suit yourself, *habibi*." He and his friends started for the door. "Hey, what're you waiting for?" he called back to me. "You're not going to invade the lady's privacy, are you? A good Jewish woman. Hanna Klein's a saint like the Biblical matriarchs."

"I have to take a leak, Hosea. Besides, she's a little too old for me."

That managed enough of a laugh to get him out the door.

I walked back into the nursery, where Hanna was changing a diaper beside two cribs and a pair of double-decker beds. "I thought you might need some help," I said.

"I don't believe that, but as long as you're here you might as well wash these out." She handed me a bucket of dirty diapers and pointed toward the bathroom. "So what do you want out of Joshua?"

"I'm not sure, actually. His stepsister's worried about him."

"Tell her not to worry. He's fine. She should know how fine he is."

I nodded and walked into the bathroom. I shook the diapers over the toilet and dumped them in a washbasin. Then I ran water over them. It was a strange sensation, doing it after all these years, but satisfying in a primal way. That was what we were here to do, after all. Eat, shit, sleep and procreate. You didn't have to be a theist to believe that.

"How'd you happen to come here?"

"I was a biology teacher at Bronx Science. One day I was explaining the sonar system in bats—you know, how they navigate in the dark without eyes—and it made no sense so I stopped right in the middle of my class."

"What made no sense?"

"The bats. The design was too complex to be there by accident. It couldn't just be natural selection. Evolution. There had to be a cause." She came to the door with the baby. "I told my husband and we left for Israel the next day. That same day the Yom Kippur War started, the miracle happened, and God returned Judea and Samaria to us just as He had predicted. We had to come here."

"Where *is* your husband?" I asked.

"He died when I was pregnant with Gadi. He was in the Negev fasting, and God took him. The next morning I went into labor."

"That must be hard for you."

"Not at all. I am never depressed. When I get up in the morning, I never ask myself what Hanna wants to do that day. I ask what God wants me to do. Atheists are depressed people. They don't know what they want. . . . After you're finished with that you can leave." She gestured to the washbasin and walked off.

Just then the front door opened and what sounded like a half-dozen kids came running in, screeching and carrying on in a combination of Hebrew and English. Hanna tensed and looked in my direction. Immediately she put the baby in the crib and rushed off toward the door, calling ahead of herself in a sharp-toned Hebrew. A man laughed dismissively in a youthful, open-throated voice. I dropped the diapers and headed out after her.

It was Gordie, all right. Or Joshua, more exactly. He was standing in the middle of the living room in a white cotton gown and purple yarmulke with two little kids climbing on his back and another three grabbing onto his legs. He had a delightful, puckish smile on his face, and his skin was the olive of a Caravaggio with black, almost girlish curls cascading from his head onto the white gown. There was something ageless about him, truly beautiful. I thought of Pan and Dionysus and Tadzio from *Death in Venice.*

Just then he placed the children on the ground and sat on the floor, putting both feet behind his head in the style of an advanced yoga contortionist while placing the fingers of his two hands on forehead and reciting in a high-pitched monotone: "Each person must say, for my sake was the world created. Since the world was created for my sake, I must at all times concern myself with the perfection of the world. Each person will bring to fruition his own godliness. This is what we mean by the coming of the Messiah. And they will beat their swords into plowshares. And their spears into pruning forks. And nation shall not lift up sword against nation, neither will they practice war anymore." Just as suddenly, he uncoiled his legs and jumped to his feet again, picking up the children and spinning around in place, giggling and singing. "Ain't a-gonna be no war no mo' . . . Ain't a-gonna be no war no mo' . . . Ain't a gonna be—" Then he stopped still and stared directly at me, smiling innocently. "We will inscribe on our foreheads a mark of madness. And each time that I look at you and you look at me, we will know we are mad . . . whee!" He put the children down again and started a dervish whirl until he did a cartwheel across the living-room floor. He landed momentarily on his hands and then flipped backward over a coffee table, landing deftly on his feet and springing upward, grinning and laughing uncontrollably, his head swiveling back and forth with that eerie blind randomness of George Shearing or Stevie Wonder at a concert. Then he lay down on the floor and said nothing, his eyes fixed on the ceiling, his mouth half opened and his body as still as a catatonic's.

"Well, Mr. Wolfe, you have succeeded in your mission." Hanna Klein looked at me with cold, judgmental eyes. "Now you can deliver the message from his stepsister."

"That's okay," I said, too stunned to say anything more. I nodded to Hanna and walked out the door.

But I didn't go far. I continued down half a block to a casbah café behind a fruit stand, sat down and ordered a mint tea from a surly Arab in Ray-Ban Wayfarers. It came to me in a grimy glass that looked like a culture medium for tropical diseases, and I peered at it distrustfully while shooing away the flies and waiting for Gordie, trying to make sense of his inexplicable behavior.

I didn't have to wait long. In about five minutes he emerged leading the kids up the street like the very Pied Piper he had quoted. They presented quite a spectacle, this Jewish looney in a white gown guiding a half-dozen Chasidic kids in fringes and *payess* through the casbah of Arab Hebron as if it were the most natural thing in the world. It seemed more than a little risky. And then I remembered: this guy was a martial-arts expert. He could blow up cars. Maybe he had a gun under that gown. Or more.

I watched them go for a moment, then deposited a couple of shekels on the table and hurried to catch up with them.

"Where're you going?" I said, locking step with him.

"We are going to Jesse's Tomb." He started to skip with the kids right behind them. "Would you like to come? Jesse's Tomb is wonderful."

"He is the Son of Jesse," said one of the kids in heavily accented English.

"No, I am not. I told you I am not. King David was the Son of Jesse."

"No, no, no. *You* are Son of Jesse."

He turned to me. "These children are crazy in the head. . . . Come on. Let's run." And they all started running up a steep hill that twisted up a narrow street, the local Arabs paying them no heed as if this were a common, everyday occurrence. I ran alongside Gordie, struggling to keep up. "Some people think I'm crazy too. But I'm not crazy. I'm just happy."

"Why're you happy?"

He stopped and turned to me. "Because everything will be all right. Everybody will be alive and there will be no more pain. No more pain, no more pain." He had started singing. "Soon there will be no more pain, no more pain, no more pain. Soon there will be no more pain, my fair lady."

We came to the top of the hill, where a small settlement had been constructed, beneath an Israeli flag. It consisted of about a half-dozen corrugated-steel mobile homes surrounded by a ten-foot chain-link fence with another two feet of barbed wire on top. In the middle was a small playground with a slide, a couple of swings and a knotty-pine jungle gym that looked as if it had been sent by somebody's rich grandmother back in America. The kids dashed past an Israeli soldier dozing in a guardhouse into the playground while Gordie and I continued on to the ancient tomb. It was nothing more than a few old stones and a crumbling wall in a field of rye grass and wild sumac directly across from the settlement.

Gordie immediately began to pray, standing very close to the frail wall and chanting intensely, almost cleaving to it. Soon tears were streaming down his face, as if the death of the antique patriarch was the personal loss of a close family member. The tears metamorphosed into deep racking sobs, and then, almost as quickly, they stopped again and he faced me with that pure, childlike smile.

"So Rachel has a message for me?" he said, kissing the tomb with the fringe of his vest.

"Sort of," I replied, trying to postpone the moment of truth as long as possible. I was staring at him, wondering how someone with such an incredibly gentle face was capable of planting a car bomb in the engine of Joseph Damoor's Mazda. "She's worried about you."

"She's always worried, my poor sister. When we were little kids, she'd get nervous every time I went out to play ball. She'd think I'd skin my knee or something. Or get in a fight."

"I don't know. I heard you were pretty tough."

"Not now." He laughed. "I don't want to do things like that anymore."

"I'm glad to hear it, because Rachel's worried some people are trying to blame you for the death of Joseph Damoor."

"Who?" He picked up a wild flower and smelled it.

"Joseph Damoor—the president of the Arab-American Friendship Association. The one who got blown up in his car a couple of months ago. The same day you left for Israel. You never heard of him?"

"I don't know. Maybe." He didn't seem very concerned.

"You did demonstrate outside the Southern California Peace in the Middle East Study Weekend at UC Irvine, didn't you?"

"I think so." He frowned, thought back, smiled. "Yes . . . right . . . yes. I remember that." Just then we were surprised by the kids, who jumped out from behind the tomb, dancing around Gordie, singing to him as they laughed and clapped their hands. He blushed a pale rose. "Oh, no. Come on," he said. "I told you—stop." He glanced at me. "Don't tell my sister about this. Or my mother."

"What're they singing?" I said.

"Stupid things. It's too embarrassing to say. You don't speak Hebrew?"

"No."

"I'm lucky."

"Ve sing about the Son of Jesse," blurted one of the kids, who spoke English with a thick Israeli accent.

"Enough Son of Jesse!" said Gordie, who was blushing again. "I told you that is all silliness." He turned to me. "Can you imagine, calling me the Son of Jesse?"

"That should be a compliment. That makes you King David, right?"

"More than that. And it's not a compliment. It's heresy!"

"Am Yisroael, have no fear," All the kids clapped and sang. "Moshiach vill be here zis year! Ve vant Moshiach now! Ve vant Messiah now!"

"Get out of here! Come on! Right now! Go!" He rushed at the kids, shooing them like geese. They ran off down the hill, giggling and laughing. He stood there a moment, staring after them and shaking his head until they were safely back inside the compound fence. "I don't know where they get this idea," he said, walking back toward me. "They and those others. Imagine, they think I am the Messiah. Me? I couldn't pass auto-mechanics school in Los Angeles."

"I don't know what that would have to do with it."

"Children are always in too much of a hurry. How could I be a Messiah? They are *meshugge*. I can't do miracles."

"Does a Messiah have to do miracles?"

"He should have some kind of power." He frowned, thinking. "Not Jesus miracles like walking on water, or the loaves and the fishes. That was all self-aggrandizement, a misuse of Practical Kabbalah, and did nobody any good. And not little visions like I have. They are nothing. But real miracles to cure people, to help people, like the great Rabbi Yochanan. Yes, a Messiah would be able to do that." He frowned again and shivered. "We all want the Messiah. We need him as quickly as possible. Perhaps he will even come soon, *baruch ha-Shem*. But I have no control of myself, of my urges. I am a madman, a child. I am not the Messiah. No way."

TWELVE

ittle visions. Uncontrollable urges? What visions? What urges? What kind of a madman was this? A manic-depressive? A paranoid schizophrenic? An idiot savant? Or was he simply a fake, a poseur hiding behind the sunglasses of madness to deflect any investigation into his true beliefs or background, his actions?

The Messiah of Los Angeles. I half smiled, watching the sun

begin to set across the jumble of television antennas, mosques and minarets that made up the Hebron hills. The Messiah of Fairfax. It would be a peculiar redemption for the Jews indeed if salvation came not from the north, as predicted, or the south, but from the west, the far west. From the Left Coast itself, out of the hot tubs and the sushi bars, the shopping malls and the freeways, would come the anointed one for the final subjugation of evil.

I had spent the rest of the afternoon with Gordie, socializing and making small talk, but I had been unable to find out much of significance. He was living here in this small settlement, working in a dairy and attending the yeshiva over in the larger settlement of Kiryat Arba with the intention of becoming a rabbi. Then he would find a wife, settle down, certainly somewhere here in Judea and Samaria, and have as many children as possible, according to the Biblical injunction. He missed his family and friends back in Los Angeles and hoped they would all eventually make *aliyah*, even the Horowitz brothers once their poor mother had gone over to the other side. I asked what he thought of Reb Lipsky, and not surprisingly he said he was a great man unfairly attacked, a true prophet of Israel who would someday be properly understood by the secular world who unjustly maligned him. Reb Lipsky was his spiritual father. In order not to jeopardize his trust, I stayed clear of more mention of the death of Joseph Damoor or of his coincidental flight from the United States on the day of the bombing.

My approach must have worked, because as the sun continued to set, Gordie invited me to a *mikveh*, a ritual bath. "You take a *mikveh*, don't you, before evening prayer?"

"Oh, yeah. Sure," I said. "Sometimes." Sometimes I even take a margarita and a joint in a Jacuzzi with a French Canadian *shiksa*, I could have added. But I didn't.

He went inside one of the mobile homes and came out with a couple of towels. He handed me one, and I followed him down the hill into the city again, back through the casbah into that tiny, rubble-strewn Jewish Quarter where Hanna Klein now lived. We continued past the old synagogue, which had been recently reconstructed from the 1929 Massacre, down an alley-way where several Jews were headed toward an anonymous doorway. Some were Chasidim, but others seemed more like the old picture-postcard kibbutzniks, their knit yarmulkes the only religious accouterments in otherwise macho, freedom-fighter outfits of khakis, plaid shirts and Nike running shoes. Most of them carried arms, Uzis or pistols on their belts, which they started to take off as they entered the building. And I had thought only women went to a *mikveh.*

The atmosphere inside was surprisingly matter-of-fact, everyone stripping down in a changing room with the familiar odor of chlorine wafting in from the bath itself. Naked, the Chasidim seemed far less exotic, their stringy beards and ear-locks but one odd aspect in conventional male anatomy. One of the kibbutz types came up and made a joke with Gordie in Hebrew.

"He hopes I am not going to have a vision today," he explained to me.

"Do you often have them in a *mikveh?*"

"No, not often." He shrugged. "Except a month ago."

"What happened then?"

"I saw the Ark of the Covenant."

"The Ark of the Covenant," I repeated flatly. "How'd you see that?"

"Here. In the *mikveh.* Floating over all of us."

He finished taking off his clothes and headed for the bath while I disrobed and tried to remember what the Ark was from

Sunday School. I knew it had something to do with Moses and the Ten Commandments, but I had it mixed up with that silly business at the end of *Raiders of the Lost Ark* with the golden horses and the funeral bier that looked like an overdone wedding cake in klieg lights, and its exact significance eluded me.

"But then it wasn't floating," Gordie continued, staring upward as if about to go into another trance. "I found my way in through the double gate, you know, with the arches, beneath the upper stables where nobody has been, and there it was at the end of a dark tunnel. It was so beautiful and splendid. And then an angel came to tell me that if I wished to see this, I must go to the pass and practice."

"The pass?"

"The pass in the mountains. Near where the Ark once rested. Then I can perform the sacrifice." He saw me looking at him strangely, and laughed. "Sometimes I have other kinds of visions. Once I saw my sister losing her virginity. Do not tell anybody. And another time—it was so horrible I can't tell a soul." He stared at me a moment, his eyes fluttering. "They say the Messiah must go alone into the kingdom of impurity to the 'other side'—the *sitra ahra*—and dwell in the realm of an evil god before the world will be saved." He jumped into the bath, dunking his head as if to cleanse himself of these impure thoughts, and then reappeared. "Have you ever had visions?" he asked, smiling.

I noticed the American car before I could answer. It was a Lincoln, and it slid like an intrusive monster in the narrow Middle Eastern street slowly past the slit in the curtained window that overlooked the ritual bath. But even with its size, I might not have paid it much notice had not the face of the man riding shotgun been immediately familiar.

"Do you know a Shochet?" I quickly asked Gordie.

"Yes, of course. Are you hungry? Would you like meat for dinner?"

"No, not any *shochet*. Someone who calls himself the Shochet."

"I don't know what you mean."

"Be right back."

"Is something wrong? You haven't had your *mikveh*."

I didn't answer. By then I was already heading into the changing room again, grabbing for my clothes. I was still buttoning my shirt when I opened the front door and peered out onto the street. The Lincoln was parked about a block down with its nose pointed in the direction of the bathhouse as if waiting for someone to come out. I wasn't sure if it was me or Gordie, but I had to find out.

I waited for a vegetable truck to pass by and cut swiftly behind it through an alley, coming out into the casbah again. Most of the stalls had been shut up for the end of the day, and I slipped between them, moving rapidly to the end of the block. I came up on the back side of the Lincoln and hid behind the tailgate of a pickup, right above a manhole with the old British Mandate seal on it. I was in Palestine and felt it, trying to seem inconspicuous to the stream of passing Arabs on their way home from work. They stared at me suspiciously as I eyed the rear of the Lincoln, memorizing its license plate.

There were four passengers inside, the Shochet and three other men dressed like Levantine lounge lizards in shiny suits, open shirts and dark glasses, the kind of Jewish mafia types I was used to seeing at the falafel stands on Fairfax, but somehow different. I moved closer along the side of the pickup for a better look, smiling at the passersby, then noticed the driver leaning out of the Lincoln and joking with one of the locals in what sounded like fluent Arabic. Perhaps the driver was Sephardic. But even if that accounted for his language abilities, it wouldn't have accounted for the familiarity in this hotbed of racial antagonism. I didn't know what to make of it. Had the Shochet been lying to me, or could this be a mixed group of Jews and Arabs?

I was trying to figure out how to solve this when Gordie came rushing out of the *mikveh* fully dressed, looking up and down the street with a puzzled expression on his face. I imagined he was looking for me, but the guys in the Lincoln didn't know this, and the moment he appeared, the Shochet pointed and tapped the driver on the shoulder. The driver started the car and steered it right past Gordie, going real slowly, while he and his two buddies in the back did a long lookie-loo all up and down the younger man, as if they were memorizing every inch of him. Then the driver gunned the Lincoln,and it backfired twice before skidding across the road, which was about two-thirds dirt and a third asphalt, and then disappearing around the corner onto the main highway.

I walked up to Gordie.

"Are you all right?" he asked. "I was worried."

"Oh, no problem," I explained. "I'm a diabetic and I have to have something sweet to eat every hour or so. I'm okay now."

"I hope it was kosher," he said.

"That's my secret," I said. And he laughed.

We went down to the old synagogue for evening prayer. It was the same mix as in the bathhouse, a few Chasidim interspersed with the religious kibbutzniks I assumed to be the vanguard of the West Bank settlers. I stood there with them, rocking back and forth, pretendng to read the Hebrew in the prayer book and mouthing the prayers as if I knew them. The process seemed excruciatingly long, until an odd change came over me. Even though the words meant nothing, I began to connect to the process, the men swaying, their voices murmuring, sometimes droning, sometimes pleading, sometimes ecstatic. For a moment it seemed as if I belonged there, as if I really understood this. And then in twenty minutes it was over.

I accompanied Gordie back to Hanna Klein's house.

"You're still here," she said, not wildly enthusiastic to see me.

"I told Wolfe you were serving kugel tonight," said Gordie.

"The dinner's off," she said, looking over at him like a stern housemother.

Gordie looked crestfallen.

"Perhaps we should . . ." I began, then I heard a loud Southern voice booming at us from the living room.

"That's the fella. That's the little fella. You're the one, aren't ya? Joshua ben Tsvi!"

A six-foot-four middle-aged man in a Stetson and expensive Italian suit appeared in the door, extending his hand toward us as if we were voters in a rural election. "John Ambrose Kracauer," he said, "humble servant of God and pastor of the First Evangelical Church of Corpus Christi, Texas. Yew may have seen me on TV—*The Modern Redeemer Gospel Hour and Songfest*. If so, don't hold it against me." He laughed and pumped Gordie's hand. "I'm so pleased to meet ya, Mr. ben Tsvi, and to be heah in Hebron, Eretz yiz-rye-ale, just like the good Lord predicted! . . . And who is this gentlemuhn over heah?"

"Isaiah Wolfe," I said.

"Nice Biblical name."

"Yes." I edged into the living room.

"And that's my secretary, Sue Ellen Sizemore."

A cute little number in a beehive hairdo, laden with jewelry, came toward us, extending her hand. John Ambrose blocked her way. "Mustn't-mustn't, Sue Ellen. Hebrews don't shake hands with women." He turned back to us. "I told her on the Concorde, but all those jewels we bought her in Jordan musta got her confused. Bought them from the Bedouins, we did. Plus an authentic Berber tent for our Gospel amusement park back in Corpus Christi. We been makin' a tour of the whole Middle East. Kind of a personal peace mission, if you know what I mean. Plus certain expansions of our ministry—JAKPROD— John Ambrose Kracauer Productions. Which reminds me." He frowned and took Gordie and me aside, backing us into the entryway. "Fellas, I'm in a difficult situation. It took us six hours to get over the Allenby Bridge, and all our bags got left behind in Amman. You know the Ay-rabs. Nothin' gets organized over there, and I'm scheduled to do a live television hookup from the manger in Bethlehem Tuesday. We got nothin' to wear, and worse"—he dropped his voice to a whisper—"I lost all my Grecian Formula. You gentlemuhn must know a local shop where I can procure some before I show my face in public. The way things are now I'm never gonna be able to take my hat off."

"I don't think you can get Grecian Formula in Hebron, John Ambrose," I said, holding back my smile at the edge of a smirk.

"My-my," said the evangelist, his frown deepening. "We will have to do our bidness here very rapidly so I can ascend to Jerusalem and get this situation straightened out. . . . Mrs. Klein, why don't we discuss your proposals *before* dinner? Where is the Rab-eye Lipsky? Will he be joining us?"

"Not at this time."

"A distinguished gentlemuhn of the Lord. His presence would be a great consolation to us. But I think young Mr. ben Tsvi is worthy of our support in any case, as are all you People of the Book. You are the *Chosen* People, after all." He smiled fatuously, walking back into the living room and extending his arms. "Tell us about some of your visions, Mr. ben Tsvi. They would be an inspiration to us. We all know that the 'Great Tribulation' and 'The Rapture' are soon upon us, as Ezekiel himself has prophesied."

"One moment, please, Reverend Kracauer," Hanna said. "Mr. Wolfe will have to leave first."

"He will. What a shame. Delighted to have met you, Mr. Wolfe. I hope we will have the opportunity some other time."

"I'm sure we will," I replied as John Ambrose escorted me out himself.

THIRTEEN

"I think you're all pretty crazy. This religion is a disease."

"You're probably right." Max laughed. We were sitting at the same café again the next morning. It was bright and sunny, tourists filling the plaza waiting for a guide to take them through the Hurva Synagogue across the way.

"Right?" I said. "This kid's sweet, but he's looney tunes. He has visions. Children follow him around saying he's the Messiah. And he may even have killed somebody." Max sat up straight, and I immediately regretted having said anything. It was unprofessional of me to have opened my mouth, and I didn't know why I'd done it except that I was feeling isolated halfway across the world without anyone to talk to, friends, Chantal, my kids. Or maybe I was guilty. Anyway I would have made a lousy secret agent.

"And who would he have killed?"

"Some Arab back in L.A."

"I can see this makes you uncomfortable, so I won't ask you the details."

"Does it bother you that I'm investigating the murder of an Arab?"

Max shrugged. "Do you think I'm a racist? Arabs die too. Besides, I can look at you and tell your political position straight off. Basic internationalist. Sympathy with Zionism but substantially against it. To you the whole thing is a tragedy . . . Hitler killed the Jews, forced them to flee. They came here and now, out of their desperate need to survive, they've turned into mini-despots of their own, perhaps not Nazis but nothing to be proud of."

"Well—"

"Wait. There's more. You don't like the militarism of the state, the economic reliance on arms sales, the aid to South Africa and the contras, the treatment of Palestinian refugees, Ashkenazi prejudice against Sephardim and vice versa, the spying on the U.S., the pervasive fundamentalism, the conservative social structure and the decline of the socialist ideal."

"At least you didn't call me an anti-Semite."

"Because you're not. You just misjudge us—and yourself."

"You mean I don't see what's going on?"

"No, you just understand things too quickly. Maybe we're more like you—at least some of us—than you suppose. You think someone like me takes the Bible as a *literal* document, I who still have the biggest collection of R. Crumm Komix east of Rome?"

"You mean it's only a metaphor," I said, letting the sarcasm drip.

"No. Something more than that. A genuine vision of God seen from the perspective of its time, dictated by men in the language they were capable of understanding to that point." Max put down his coffee and leaned in toward me. "Do you think God is such a limiting thing that it only exists in the vocabulary of the second century? Listen, for all we know, this Messianic Age your young Hebron friend presages may actually be upon us. The prophets said it would come in a time of great turmoil."

"I know," I said, reciting the litany. "Six million Jews exterminated followed by the fulfillment of the two-thousand-year-old dream of the return to the Jewish homeland."

"Well, what could be more tumultuous than that? And all at the same time as the burgeoning of modern science. That could be part of the Messianic Age too, because the Kabbalah teaches us it's God's intention that mankind take responsibility for its own redemption. You know, Moses . . ." He picked up his coffee agan. "Messianism's not quite so far out as it sounds. It's simply the culmination of history in an era of peace under God. It's a wish that can become a reality by all of us agreeing to do it."

"Who's we? Just the Jews or everybody?"

Max laughed. "Somehow I knew you'd ask that question. No, of course not. There is only one God, but there are many ways of worshiping Him. We've always known that. It's all this thrashing about to find God in somebody else's tradition that makes no sense, that alienates us from ourselves. You're

seeing that yourself. You want to come home. There are so
many riches here, it's pointless to consult a Zen master."

"What do you know about the Ark of the Covenant?"

"That's a very big question. What . . ."

"Where is it?"

"Where *is* it?" Max repeated my question, putting his coffee
down and staring at me with an expression that if I hadn't
known better I would have considered darkly suspicious. "It's
disappeared since the destruction of the First Temple. Why do
you want to know?"

"Oh, I'm so high I can't believe it!" We were interrupted by
the intoxicated voice of Brenda Weintraub, the neo-Orthodox
Hollywood agent, who plopped herself down at our table without missing a beat. She was followed by Chaya Bracha, who
held a prayer book in her hand. "He had these *incredible* eyes,"
Brenda continued, "and he told me I'd be married within a year
and my husband is *right here* in Jerusalem at this very moment.
It was amazing, wasn't it, Chaya? He knew my whole family
history—everything about me, including that I was valedicto-
rian of Shaker Heights High School—and he never saw me
before in his *life*."

"Who?" I asked, looking from Brenda, who had undergone
something of a transformation—no makeup, modest smock
dress and monotone kerchief covering every inch of her mane-
like hair—to Chaya Bracha, who stood politely a few feet away,
her skin pure and radiant, looking like a Jewish madonna.

"Rabbi ben Tov. I just had my mezuzah read. You absolutely
have to do it."

"Yes, I've been telling Moses," said Max. "We must get him
in there."

"Well, what about now?" said Brenda. "Let's take him now.
I have to hear what he says to a private detective. That's got to

be extraordinary. By the way, Moses, I've decided to stay here. What about you?"

"I'm not sure. Also, unfortunately, I've got a lot of work to do, and, as I told Max, I don't have a mezuzah."

"We'll help you buy one." She smiled at me and looked down, as if suddenly reminded she would have to behave as a modest maiden if she was to find her intended mate in Jerusalem. "I don't want to seem presumptuous, but this may be your only time to see him. He's leaving for his village in the Negev this afternoon, and I'm sure what he has to say will aide you greatly in your investigation, whatever it is."

"And you might even find out a few interesting things about yourself," said Max, standing, "Come."

Interesting things about myself? I wasn't sure exactly what Max had in mind and I wasn't particularly keen on finding out, but I followed them reluctantly across the square, where I bought a mezuzah Max certified as "kosher" at a religious curio shop. Then the four of us walked up a series of stairs to a small cul-de-sac in that part of the Jewish Quarter that overlooks the Armenian Quarter. Brenda led us to a tiny, decrepit wood door at the very end of the cul-de-sac and gestured for me to knock. I hesitated. I usually had a healthy skepticism of psychics, tarot readers and other assorted New Age rip-off artists, but I was like many people who are adamant in their beliefs—certain doubts about my own certitude lingered just below the surface. And considering how I had been feeling these last couple of days, the strange irrationality that had me running around Jerusalem thinking quasi-mystical thoughts as if sequestered in my own personal jet-lagged sensory deprivation tank, and that this Rabbi ben Tov was a *Jewish* psychic, whatever that meant, with special insights into his own people and capable, no doubt, of revealing the darkest secrets of the hid-

den soul, those repressed fears and failures we most desper-
ately want to conceal from ourselves, I felt particularly
exposed.

So I stood there uneasily a moment, looking at Chaya Bracha
and not wanting to move. She had scarcely said a word since
joining us, but her presence too had given rise to a peculiar
tension in me. This one was from a much earlier part of my
life, almost that preadolescent discomfort you feel when there's
a girl in your class who attracts you but you have no idea how
to approach her. Maybe a foreign student or the quiet one in
the corner who gets all the A's and nobody notices her until
graduation, when she takes off her glasses and shows up in this
incredible dress.

My distraction was not lost on Max, who edged past me,
opening the door and escorting me through into a dank corridor
illuminated only by a single bare bulb of about fifteen watts.
Two men sat at the end. One, whom I assumed was ben Tov,
was an aging rabbi with a mane of white hair sprouting from
his head in wild Einsteinian tufts. He wore a pair of thick
glasses with a heavy metal rim that resembled miner's goggles
and gave him a curiously space-age appearance. Beside him
was a younger Chasid, handsome and swarthy with a thick
black beard which dropped from his chin in a perfectly
sculpted rectangle. The younger man gestured me forward
while simultaneously waving Max off with his other hand.

I walked forward, and ben Tov thrust out his hand for the
mezuzah, examining it impatiently and passing it to me as the
Chasid said something in Hebrew and then, realizing I didn't
understand, translated into English. "He wants only the
scroll."

I fumbled with the mezuzah, extracting the small paper inside it and handing it back to him. The rabbi switched on a

jeweler's lamp, and the Chasid gestured for me to sit down. I sat in a straight-backed chair opposite the rabbi, feeling vaguely anxious, as if I were about to be chastised for some minor infraction, as he pored over the scroll, looking from me back to the paper and up to me again, shaking his head and clucking to himself. Apparently what he was seeing was not very encouraging. Finally, he had a lengthy discussion in Hebrew with the Chasid, who turned to me with a grave expression.

"Do you have eye problems or flat feet?"

"No."

"The feet of the letter *tahv* go off in two directions. See." He pointed to a tiny letter in my scroll illuminated by the jeweler's lamp. "This means you are a man in great conflict. Anguish. He says you are with a woman who is not Jewish, a *goya*. Is this true?"

"Yes."

"This is very bad for your children."

How did he know I had children? "They are from a different woman, my former wife."

"Jewish?"

"Yes."

"They are confused. For your children you must settle this matter. Do you still speak with your former wife?"

"Yes. About the children."

"Do you have a *get*, a Jewish divorce?"

"No. Just a state divorce."

The Chasid relayed this to the older rabbi, who frowned sternly. "This is a great sin. Men who stay with her can be injured. You yourself are bearing a heavy load." Injured? This all seemed like mumbo-jumbo to me, but the accuracy of his observations disturbed me, and I felt myself beginning to sweat. The younger man searched my face a moment. "Do you still have friendly feelings for her?"

"My ex? Sort of. I suppose."

"Perhaps there is hope for reconciliation."

"I don't think so."

"Does she have a man?"

"Not that I know of."

"Did she then? When you were with her?"

"Yes."

His eyes went cold. I could see within their ethical schema that she was a dead woman. He turned to the rabbi, reporting our conversation. He nodded, disappointed, then, in a very cool, brief manner, repeated his instructions to the younger Chasid, who translated. "You must have a *get*. Immediately. Have a *get*. Then have your *goya* convert. Or get rid of her." The rabbi pulled off his goggles as if that were that—my session was over—revealing the gray, almost expressionless eyes of a blind man. He stared at me a moment in a seemingly unfocussed manner, then, apparently as an afterthought, tapped his partner's shoulder and spoke further. "He says intermarriage and assimilation is the root of all your problems," the Chasid continued. "He says you are seeking some kind of solution to a riddle and you will find this all out later when you arrive at it. If there are no races, people will have no identity. They will be lost. Some wish the world to be one, but they are mistaken. If God had wanted the fishes to be like the trees, then he would have made them that way. . . . Is there anything else you would like to know from the rabbi?"

I hesitated. There were a lot of things, but in a way I was afraid of the answers. I thought I'd stick to the case. "Yes. Does he know where the Ark of the Covenant is?"

The Chasid relayed the question. "He says there are many stories. Some say it was hidden under the Temple Mount after the fall of the First Temple."

"Does he know where exactly?"

Ben Tov answered my question without it even being translated. "He says no. Of course not. How should he?"

FOURTEEN

"Hel-low, Moses. You want to sell your BMW? How'm I going to do that?"

"The normal way. Take an ad. Or better still, just put it out on the street with a sign on it. Best offer. Give them three days."

"What? You're *giving* it away. You *love* that car. Something's got to be wrong with you. And I don't even have the pink slip."

"It's in my bottom left desk drawer. Just forge my signature. You know it well enough. And there's nothing wrong with me, Chantal. I just can't, in good conscience, have a German car anymore."

"This is crazy. Moses, you haven't had a problem with your conscience since you got it. World War II was over more than forty years ago."

"I *don't* want to have a long-distance argument with you about the Nazis, okay?"

"Fine by me."

"It's just that I've been doing a little searching. Thinking about my identity. My spiritual roots."

"Your spiritual roots? You used to make fun of people who did that. You're supposed to be on a case. An investigation. Moses, are you being brainwashed by a rabbi or something? You're beginning to sound like a Moonie."

"Don't be ridiculous. Look, this is an expensive phone call. Why don't we just stick to the case?"

"Absolutely. Nothing yet on the Arabs. Terzi denies they've been following you, but that doesn't prove anything. I've been doing some other checking too. I'm still looking into that missing period in Lipsky's life. And our friend Gordie is definitely a strange one. He practices yoga and is something of an escape artist. They say he's some kind of mentalist as well, can read minds and bend spoons like Uri Geller. Or pretends he can. Some people saw him doing it on a Thursday night up at the Magic Castle on Franklin. He evidently put on quite a show."

"It doesn't surprise me."

"You mean you believe *that* too?"

"Spiritual forces. People know things. I just had my mezuzah read, and—"

"Your mezuzah read? What's that mean? You *have* gone off the deep end!"

"No I haven't. I promise you. I'm fine. Perfectly fine." I took a breath. Something told me I was going too far, but I couldn't stop myself. "Look, there's one other thing I wanted to ask you about. I know it sounds weird, but . . . about your own religious background, you've never been very devout, have you?"

"No . . ." Even over six thousand miles she sounded leery.

"I mean, you told me you don't go to confession any more and the Eucharist doesn't mean anything to you."

"Uhunh . . ."

"Would you, uh . . ." I cleared my throat a couple of times. ". . . ever consider looking into . . . ?"

"You want me to *convert*?"

"It's not that difficult."

She hung up.

I stood there a moment in the lobby of the King David Hotel again, watching a group of tourists assemble for an afternoon visit to the Dead Sea and feeling somehow light-headed and disembodied. Was she right? Had I deserted my true self? Was I such a "Zelig" that my whole personality was changing under the influence of religious surroundings? It couldn't be. And yet —it would be a simpler life. In fact, it would be the *only* life that made any sense in this insane world of irrational accident. The rest was just blind will and biological habit, an existential game played by greedy hustlers and French philosophers, nothing but a pleasure principle for the body or the mind, and when that wore out, what? Death and decay. A cruel joke. So why not . . . God?

I left the hotel and walked across the street to the Hertz office where I had rented my car. A skinny bored clerk sat in the back opposite a pale plump girl who stared into a cup of coffee as if it were a kaleidoscope. I cleared my throat several times, hoping to get their attention.

"I was wondering if you could help me. I rented a car with you here the other day and I had a little problem."

The clerk got up and walked over to me with the enthusiasm of a future bureaucrat.

"I was driving around Hebron yesterday and got side-swiped."

"Body injury or injury to car?"

"No, no. No bodily injury. It's just that the bastard took off. I was wondering if you could locate the owner of the vehicle for me." I took out the scrap of paper on which I had written the number of the Lincoln and put it on the counter for him.

"Must see your car first."

"It's, uh, still in Hebron. Inoperative."

"You shouldn't go there," said the sullen girl who stood up and walked over toward us. "You deserve what happens."

"Yeah, you're right. I wish I'd known. The driver was one of those angry Arabs, you know. Real PLO type. He nearly ran me over when I tried to talk to him."

The clerk looked down at the paper. "That Tel Aviv plate. Letters *tahv aleph* mean Tel Aviv."

"Yeah, well, he was still the PLO, I can tell you that. Or Hizbullah or something. He had a kerchief around his face like Genghis Khan. Damn near killed me, and now he wrecked your car. I don't think it's fair that I end up paying for it."

"Give me," said the girl. She took the paper and walked over and made a phone call. I waited a moment, leafing through some travel brochures. I knew that in California the right phone call could give an ID off a license plate in a couple of minutes, but I wasn't sure how it worked here. I didn't know if their computers were up to it, unless they belonged to the Mossad.

It was a while before the girl turned back to me. "This car belongs to Natan Shahar. That is a Jewish name, not Arab."

"Really? That's amazing!" I said, forcing my eyes wide. "Where does he live?"

"Twenty-three Mendelsohn Street in Tel Aviv."

"Great. I'll take care of it," I said and exited before they could say anything or even ask my name.

Two minutes later I was speeding past their storefront in my supposedly damaged Isuzu, up George V to Yafo Street and then out Sderot Weizmann in the direction of Tel Aviv. As I started to descend from the Jerusalem Hills, passing the outlying settlements with the shards of tanks and half-tracks from various wars peering out from behind the scrub pines, a curious thing began to happen. It was as if I were starting to decompress, an actual feeling of lightness occurring as the weight of the ages lifted from my shoulders along with the heavy-handed thump of ominous theology. I actually began to hum. I was Moses Wine again—modern man, atheistical, hedonistic, ambivalent, bebopping along the road of life without stopping to ask too many cosmic questions. I enjoyed the familiar sound of a semi as it whipped past me on the four-lane highway. I felt alert, content.

It was probably this alertness that tipped me off that I was being followed. A Peugeot diesel taxi with no customer had been within a kilometer of my tail since the center of Jerusalem, despite the fact that I had stopped to take a leak only ten minutes out of the city. What confused me was who could be following me. No one knew where I was, and I had so little idea where I was going myself. I was simply pursuing a lead that had, as far as I know, only the flimsiest relevance to the case I was supposed to be solving. Indeed, the case itself, with all its puzzling quasi-mystical overtones, was progressively eluding me. Here I was trying to determine whether this seemingly innocent, slightly mad spoon bender from Los Angeles had actually murdered someone and was now involved in some as yet undefined activity with a female ideologue from Bronx Science and a TV evangelist from Corpus Christi. And what was the role in all this of the infamous Reb Lipsky? Not to mention the Shochet, who, if I remembered my Passover ceremony accurately, "bit the lamb that ate the kid my father bought for two zuzim."

And they called L.A. La-La Land. By comparison to the Middle East, my hometown was as buttoned-down and zipped-up as Zurich.

But none of these ruminations brought me any closer to the mystery of who could be following me in the Peugeot, unless it was a psychic demon sent by Rabbi ben Tov to make sure I got a ritual divorce from my ex-wife. But it seemed to me mezuzah readers tended not to use French cars. They preferred chariots of fire. Or covenant arks.

Whoever he was disappeared the moment I hit the outskirts of Tel Aviv, although I had a lingering suspicion, perhaps it was the glimpse I caught of him talking into a radio, that he was turning me over to somebody. There was little I could do about that, and I continued into the city.

23 Mendelsohn was a four-story apartment house in the middle of a narrow street of decaying Deco buildings. I found it after about a half hour of being stuck in traffic coming down Dizengoff, the city's main street, lined with cafés selling endless varieties of shish kebab and blintzes, a Jewish Europe with no booze but lots to eat. I didn't mind the traffic so much, watching the sea of people parade down the avenue—something as rare as polar bears in L.A.—and it was a relief to see no one was wearing a yarmulke. I realized I still had mine on and was reaching up to remove it when I saw the turn-off to Mendelsohn.

It took another twenty minutes to find a parking place and another fifteen to try to figure out the Hebrew for Shahar among the forty or so names casually scribbled on the building ledger. I felt like a World War II cryptographer, trying to break the Nazi code. I just about had it when I heard a noisy group approaching the building. I ducked into the side corridor just as the Shochet himself arrived with three of his cronies. I watched as they ignored the flimsy-looking cage elevator and climbed the stairs to the fourth floor. Given the size of this small army, I decided to wait. I walked outside, found a decent vantage point in a doorway beside a jewelry shop not more than fifty yards from the Lincoln and checked my watch. It was seven twenty-five in the evening East Mediterranean Time. By the time the Shochet and his crowd emerged, I had memorized every English-language sign in sight and could recite, in order parked, the brand and model of every car within a square block of the nearest intersection. It was ten-fifteen.

One of them was carrying a large brown paper package that under normal circumstances you'd think was somebody's laundry, but this was the Middle East, so you never knew. I considered for a moment breaking into their apartment to see who these jokers were working for—you could bet it wasn't the Chief Rabbi—and why they'd been following me, but I figured I had a better chance of finding out by following them. So as they walked toward the Lincoln, I hurried to the corner and jumped into the Isuzu, banking on being able to catch them before they pulled out of Mendelsohn. The gamble paid off, and I slid in right behind the Lincoln as it turned left onto Ibn Givrol Street. Among the ubiquitous Japanese cars, it was the easiest tail job in town.

Traffic was light, and within a few minutes we were passing the Dov Airport heading into what, according to the map I kept spread on the seat next to me, was apparently North Tel Aviv. It looked like the beginning of the high-rent district, lines of

slightly upscale low-rise apartments spread out in all directions, an odd combination of Miami Beach and Marseilles. But
they continued right on through it, heading north on Highway
Five toward the fancy suburb of Herzilya. But they hadn't gone
another two miles before they turned off the highway back in
the direction of the Mediterranean.

We reached the beach and made another right along a dark
road that snaked along the shore in a vacant area devoid of
people or buildings. All I could see was sand dunes looming in
front of my headlights in the night. I slowed to give the Lincoln
a little room, letting a pickup slide in front of me, then noticed
something peculiar—women, hookers actually, walking along
the dunes in the middle of nowhere. Sometimes singly, sometimes in groups. Every hundred feet or so a car had pulled over
and you could just make out the image of bodies thrashing
around in the backseat or in the sand nearby. It was a red-light
district, and one of the weirdest I had ever seen, as if a com-
mittee of bluenoses had tossed the whole ugly mess out of town
en masse to the sea gulls. And I had come all this way to watch
a group of Tel Aviv sharpies go whoring.

Just then the Lincoln turned in where a quartet of Sephardic
hookers clustered by a lonely telephone pole jutting out of the
sand. They ran over to meet it, sticking their heads through the
side windows. I pulled over a couple of cars away on the other
side of the telephone pole, camouflaging as much as possible
of the little Isuzu behind a clump of what looked like pampas
grass. A girl in a turquoise singlet popped up out of nowhere,
banging on my window. She wore lace Madonna gloves and
looked about fifteen. I ignored her and watched as one by one
the four men got out of the Lincoln and disappeared into the
dunes with the hookers. The girl in the singlet started proposi-

tioning me in Hebrew. When that didn't work, she tried Yiddish.

"I don't speak the language," I said, shrugging in confusion as if I didn't have the slightest idea what she was talking about. She made a circle with her thumb and forefinger, shoving through the index finger of the opposite hand, at the same time thrusting her pelvis forward, belaboring the obvious, but I just shook my head, the naive and bewildered foreigner. She blurted what I assumed was the Hebrew version of "Your mother fucks for pennies!" and walked away in disgust.

I waited a couple of minutes before getting out and strolling over to the Lincoln. I leaned against it briefly, checking out the area, glancing toward the next car and catching a brief glimpse of blonde hair going down on a Chasid, before entering. The brown package was on the floor of the front seat on the passenger side. I hesitated before touching it, a television documentary on the Jerusalem bomb squad flashing through my brain. I dug into my pocket, taking out a small flashlight I carried attached to my key chain. I shined it down at the package, peering closely at it as if I were examining a poisonous fish. On top were written in English the words "Menashe Kandel—Herzylia, Is."

Menashe Kandel, I thought. Not *the* Menashe Kandel, the Israeli movie producer known all over Los Angeles as a kind of billionaire barbarian famous for bringing back the high-rolling style of the old moguls to a business increasingly dominated by junior marketing types acting as face men for conglomerate CEOs. There were a lot of strange rumors about where he got his money.

One of the ends of the package was slightly dog-eared, and I grabbed a pencil from the dashboard and probed gingerly, pulling up the flap centimeter by centimeter. Inside wasn't a bomb, but a stack of newspapers printed on glossy stock. I tugged at the top one. It was *Variety*, the Hollywood trade publication, for July 23, 1987. Beneath it were other issues for the last two weeks. Definitely *the* Menashe Kandel. These goons were probably his people. But why had the so-called filmmaker sent one of his minions snooping around my room at the King David, and why had his man been watching Reb Lipsky at the Yeshiva Torat Cohanim? I doubted he was collecting background for his next movie. But before I had a chance to give it much consideration, someone had his hand on the car door. It was one of the Shochet friends, his face twisted in a postcoital smirk.

That smirk segued from surprise to fury the moment he noticed me. Before he had a chance to act on it, I rammed the door open, slamming it into his stomach. He grabbed for me as I jumped out of the car and started running, pretending to be buttoning up my pants and gesturing as if there were a girl in the car. But this didn't seem to convince him, and he started after me, reaching under his jacket for what I was certain wasn't a candy bar. I dropped dead in my tracks and, with only a slight slipping movement in the sand, ducked down and sprang back up at him, slamming him across the left cheekbone with a right uppercut, by far my best punch. It was enough to send him staggering backward into the car. Then I took off. He started shouting, causing the panicked Chasid to run screaming from his car. I leaped over a dune and rolled down through the sand. By the time I looked back I was halfway to Egypt.

t came as no surprise, an hour later, to see the Shochet's Lincoln already parked in the long driveway of Menashe Kandel's opulent beachfront compound less than two hundred yards up the highway from the four-star Hotel Dan Herzylia. What did come as a surprise was the roughly twenty-five other cars in the driveway, most of them expensive and several of them German, including a couple of Beemers like the silver 533 I was trying to unload. Kandel was clearly having a party. A tape of the score from *Out of Africa* emanated from speakers attached to the large horseshoe of cyprus trees that separated his grounds from the highway.

I was stopped at the front door by a uniformed security guard with a walkie-talkie. I handed him my U.S. passport, Greenspan division, as if it were my invitation. He waved me through after only a cursory check of my photograph and a quick once-over with a metal detector. I entered a sprawling, California-style ranch house that opened out onto the water. The furniture was fifties retro, and most of the walls were decorated with bad modern art or posters for exploitation flics produced by Medo Releasing, the motion-picture company, according to the fine print, of executive producer Menashe Kandel. He apparently had a proclivity for geographical titles, from *Naughty Nurses of*

Naples, with a backdrop that looked suspiciously like Newport Beach in the sixties, to *Surf Killers of Tel Aviv,* evidently shot locally. The crowd itself was a disparate mix of Eurotrash, low-level pop stars and Israeli politicians, with a few local boys who looked like friends of the boss. It reminded me of a party I had attended at the beach house of a well-known record producer on Maui; like that one, it had a casual atmosphere that gave it the feeling of a weekly event, or at least biweekly. The only person not in evidence—except in family pictures of a squat man in his sixties who resembled an aging pit bull terrier in a Hawaiian shirt and Bermudas—was Menashe Kandel himself.

I caught a glimpse of the Shochet and his crew over by the bar. The turkey I had clipped was holding an icy cocktail glass to his cheek while chatting up a starlet type in a Melrose Avenue–style bowling shirt. Trying to stay clear of them, I wandered over toward the food. The sight of someone familiar standing uncomfortably in the corner, nervously feeding his face with potato salad, made me stop. Out of context it took me several seconds to recognize Reb Lipsky's avuncular lieutenant from the Holocaust Prevention Institute, Irv Hurwitz. In about the same time he evidently recognized me. I'm not sure whether he was more pleased or more puzzled to see me, but it was too late to turn around.

"How's the potato salad?" I asked.

"Middling. Greenspan, right?"

"Right."

"Funny meeting you here."

"I was going to say the same thing."

"I got my business. What's *your* business?" He studied me dubiously. "Or have you fallen in with the wrong crowd? You want to hang around with people like this, you didn't have to leave the States."

"I know what you mean. Actually, my second cousin's related to Menashe Kandel. So he told me to give him a call and I ended up at this." I gestured. "I think I've seen enough. You don't look like you're too happy here yourself. What's your excuse?"

"I can't talk about it," he said, gobbling the rest of his potato salad in one gulp.

"Suit yourself," I said, adding the requisite "Shalom," as I nodded to him and strolled off past where a group of the Eurotrash were laughing and dancing together in some approximation of the Swim. I stationed myself behind them, leaning against the wall facing the other way, but keeping one eye on Hurwitz, whose discomfort was, if anything, increasing. He was, indeed, the last person I would've expected to see here. He fumbled with his plate for a moment, started to help himself to another portion of salad, then gave up altogether and walked off.

I followed him as he headed out the rear of the building past a large overchlorinated pool to a white pool house in front of a chain-link fence covered with bougainvillea. He knocked several times on the door. Finally Boaz, Rabbi Lipsky's bodyguard, the one, I remembered, who had bludgeoned three Arabs with an ax, appeared at it, shaking his head and indicating for him to go away. I backed off as Irv slumped off around the pool again, retreating, I assumed, to the potato salad. Inside, someone was cursing a blue streak in Hebrew. This was, as they say, getting interesting.

I reconnoitered the area and spotted a screen window on the far side of the pool house. Keeping my face in the shadows, I carefully climbed up on the fence, straining my neck for a look within. The little house was filled with movie posters and telephones and obviously doubled as Menashe Kandel's office. The man doing the cursing was Kandel himself. He was bare-chested and furious. The man opposite him was Rabbi Judah Lipsky. He didn't look too happy either. But in his usual black coat and tie, he scarcely looked bare-chested.

"Stick to English, huh?" said Lipsky, gesturing toward Boaz.

"What's the matter, rabbi?" said Kandel. "Scared of your own people?"

"I'm not scared of anybody, *Mr. Kandel.*"

"Don't Mr. Kandel me, *Mr. Larson.* And don't tell me that God'll protect you either, you Orthodox *momzer* fuck. I've had enough of that bullshit! I know who you are. You're so special you don't need *me* to solve your *shiksa* problem for you, do you? Now pay up!"

"I told you—you're getting your money. Everything's in place. What's your hurry?"

"You told me that last week. You believe some *goyishe* Christ-waver's gonna save *your* ass and I don't get piss-all from those kikes in Hollywood." The phone rang. Kandel snatched it up. "Kandel here. . . . Right, right. . . . I told you—Rotterdam Arbeidsbank. Forty-five million over twelve months. . . . Debt? Whose debt? . . . What do you mean, collateral? What kind of collateral? . . . Tanks? Who the fuck do you think I am?" He slammed down the phone. "See what I mean—American cocksuckers! They're up to their *pupiks* in those hearings and they still pretend I'm financing movies with used Russian machine guns. You'd think those pricks'd have some brains. All they talk about is grosses. I mean, we're not talking about the Mexican debt here, just a little working capital. I'm not the first Jew who didn't pay his bills in ten minutes. Right, rabbi?" Kandel walked around his desk to within six inches of Lipsky. "If I don't see that money in five days, we're going to have a little kosher meat on our hands."

"Don't threaten me, Kandel. You put a hand on me and you'll have half a million Sephardim on your back!"

"Oh, we're playing King of the Jews here, are we? Just get out. Get out and come back when your boy's done his job, it's all over, and you've got your money—or I'm going to start talking in Hebrew for your goon here!" He nodded over toward Boaz, then pressed a buzzer, barking into an intercom. "Shochet, where's my Shochet? Get my Shochet in here!"

I leaned back into the darkness. At that moment I wasn't interested in seeing his Shochet or anybody else's. The astonishing sight of Kandel and Lipsky together was enough to digest for the moment. I heard some final talk in Hebrew and then some doors opening and shutting, which I figured was Lipsky going and the Shochet coming. After a few beats, I climbed back off the fence and drifted back into the party. Irv Hurwitz was nowhere to be seen; neither, not surprisingly, were Boaz and the rabbi. The party was still in full swing, though. If anything it had grown, as if the overflow from the discotheques up in Herzylia had migrated down for a nightcap. After a while, Kandel himself, still shirtless, made an appearance, working the room like a Mediterranean pasha. Watching him move between groups, I waited for the accidental moment when he was alone. As soon as it happened, I opened my shirt a couple of notches and sidled up to him.

"Mr. Kandel, remember me? . . . Marty, Marty Sugarman. Five years ago. At Fox. I was in Business Affairs when you were selling cable rights. *Surf Killers of Tel Aviv* I think. Right?"

Kandel looked at me blankly. "Oh, yeah. Sure. Marty. How are ya?"

"Great. Great spread you got here."

"Yeah. You a *fresser*? Try the pâté. It's from Citrus on Melrose. I get it shipped in."

"Yeah, I could tell. Look, Menashe, I've got a project I've got to talk to you about."

"Uhuh . . . call my secretary in the morning." He tried to slip away, but I grabbed his arm.

"I know it's not the time, but something magical just happened. It's a Jewish movie and—"

"They don't make money."

"I know. I know. But it's a Singer novel and I know it sounds crazy but I have an old lady in Chicago who'll put a fortune into it if a famous rabbi will bless the project. And there I was having a glass of Kir by your pool and who walks out the door but the great Judah Lipsky himself."

Kandel stared at me.

"If you can deliver him, this lady'll pop for five million in a minute. How long have you known him?"

"I don't know what you're talking about."

"You meet him in the States or what?"

"That wasn't Judah Lipsky you saw there. You're making a mistake."

"Oh, really? I was sure it was."

"I think you've been drinking too much Kir, Mr. . . . Sugarman." And he walked off.

I started after him, then saw the Shochet heading in his direction. I did a quick about-face and headed the other way. Once in the next room, I kept on moving. This clearly was no time for socializing. Besides, there was something about the company that gave me the willies, and as for the food, Ellen Greenspan was right. You couldn't get a pisspoor pastrami sandwich.

spent the rest of the night, or what was left of it, lying awake in my yeshiva bed mulling over the connection between Menashe Kandel and Judah Lipsky. Other than the fact that they both seemed short of money, at least temporarily, and that they were both charismatic assholes, they had about as much in common as a croupier and a nun. As for the money, it was easy to figure how Kandel was short. From my experience, high rollers like that either had enough to buy a medium-sized Central American country or were in hock for the equivalent. They never could stand to be stuck in the middle like the rest of us. But Lipsky? Every year or so he would drop by L.A. and New York to shake the pockets of the local Jewish jingoists, but maybe now, with the Pollard Affair and other such allegations, things were getting a little tighter. And with his ever-widening political ambitions . . .

And what was this *shiksa* problem Kandel had referred to that he had solved for the rabbi? Lipsky had never impressed me as the type who was getting a little on the side, at least not now. He seemed too maniacally possessed for that. But then you never knew. There was a little Gary Hart in all of us. And why had Kandel called him Mr. Larson? And what, if anything, did this have to do with the death of Joseph Damoor?

The whole thing was making me depressed. Whatever my personal ethnic confusions, I didn't want Israel to be a combination of movieland hustlers and racist religious fanatics. And speaking of movies, where did my friend "John Candy," Hosea, fit in all this? If there was a candidate for blowing up an Arab, he seemed far more likely than Gordie. In any case, my next move was to have another run at Gordie himself. But on my way I would stop off in Bethlehem and look in on the Reverend John Ambrose Kracauer. With Kandel and Lipsky he would have made an interesting third for a drag version of the three witches in *Macbeth*.

Bethlehem is less than five miles out of Jerusalem down the Hebron Road, but I was held up by a roadblock—the usual soldiers checking for bombs—and I got there too late to catch the beginning of the reverend's speech. He was standing on a small platform at the gate of the Basilica of the Nativity, an edifice which, its doors and windows barricaded after centuries of holy war, looked more like a fortress than a church. Surrounding the evangelist was a crowd of perhaps five hundred, a mixture of tourists, pilgrims and idly curious Arabs, but Kracauer wasn't addressing his remarks to them. He was facing directly into a mobile television unit for JAKPROD stationed atop a late-model Mercedes bus. And from the looks of his well-coiffed jet-black pompadour, he had found his Grecian Formula.

"Now some folks think the Bible is no more than a history book," he was saying. "Well, it *is* a history book for the past *and* the future, written by God. And just as man is making his way into space with a countdown, there is a countdown in the Bible, and each part of that countdown we call a 'dispensation.' And the final dispensation, which the Bible tells us will come as seven years of global conflagration and chaos, including the invasion of the Holy Land by atheists from the north, which could only mean the Soviet Union, is almost upon us. And we call that final dispensation the Great Tribulation. And this Tribulation leads, inexorably as the Bible has written, to the Battle of Armageddon itself or, in modern terms, to nuclear war."

I edged around the crowd toward Hanna Klein, who was standing with two of her babies near a souvenir stand not far from Sue Ellen Sizemore, who was photographing the reverend with a camera of her own.

"But do not fear, my friends," he continued, "for that will bring the Second Coming of Our Lord Jesus Christ. And do not fear, because all good Christians, plus the many Jews who will convert at that time, as it is prophesied, will be beamed up just before Armageddon to heaven itself and saved by the Lord Himself at the moment known as the Rapture, while the world below is cleansed of sinners—communists, homosexuals and secular humanists—and the new reign of Jesus Christ is proclaimed on earth."

"Nice friends you got here," I said to Hanna. "I didn't know all the Jews were planning on converting."

She gave me a hostile stare and turned away.

"Where's Gordie?" I asked. "I mean Joshua."

"Joshua has gone off to meditate."

"You mean away someplace specific, or is he back in Hebron?"

"Meditation is a private matter."

She took her children and walked away from me around the other side of the souvenir stand. I glanced up at Kracauer, who was now insisting that according to Ezekiel 38 and 9, this Great Tribulation was quite imminent and might even occur while his own ministry was still in "Eretz Yisroale" when I noticed Lipsky's Toyota van pulling in at the back of the crowd. What was this, a fundamentalist convention? The whole gang was here. I headed over in his direction as the van stopped and the rabbi himself got out, flanked by Boaz and the other bodyguard I recognized from the Sultan's Pools. Ignoring a toothless Arab who wanted me to pose for a Polaroid atop a mangy camel, I walked around a tour bus and locked steps with him.

"Shalom, rabbi," I said.

"Oh, Greenspan, isn't it? What're you doing here, going for a walk in the manure pile?" He gestured toward Kracauer.

"I was on my way to Hebron when I saw the crowd. What about you? Here for a debate?"

"There's no point in debating *goyim*, Greenspan. You just use them and spit them out."

"I know what you mean." I smiled. "What're your plans for him?"

"Kracauer? He'll do anything for a little publicity. He's desperate to be the number-one TV preacher in America. But that's not your concern. Have you found your young Mr. Goldenberg yet?"

"Not yet. Any ideas?"

"You'd be better off spending your time at the yeshiva learning. Goldenberg can take care of himself."

"I'm sure he can." We came around the front of the crowd, near where the JAKPROD bus was stationed. "Guess who I ran into last night? Irv Hurwitz. He was at this party at Menashe Kandel's house. I must say it was a surprise to see him there."

Lipsky stopped suddenly and looked at me as his bodyguards surveyed the crowd. "What were *you* doing there?"

"Like I told Irv—Kandel's a friend of my second cousin." I frowned. "He's not exactly the kind of person I came to Israel to meet . . . but I take it you know him."

"What?" Lipsky stared at me, his eyes starting to flutter.

I shrugged. "Hey, Irv said you did. It didn't make sense to me either. He seems like a gangster, with hit men and the whole dirty works. But I figured you were there to convert him. Where'd you meet him?"

"I believe you are mistaken, Mr. Greenspan."

I was about to pursue the question when Hanna Klein came up to the rabbi. She said something in Hebrew and nodded toward Kracauer. Then she looked at me.

"Well, here we are again, Mr. Wolfe."

I half smiled and started to back away.

"Where're you going?"

"Wolfe?" said Lipsky.

"Yes, Wolfe with an *e*. I see you've met."

"*Wolfe* with an *e*?" His eyes started to flutter again, and he barked something in Hebrew.

Before I had a chance to react, Boaz had taken my left wrist, turned it around and affixed it somewhere just below my right ear. Considering how he'd handled the three Arabs when half his neck was blown off, I knew this was no time for an argument.

SEVENTEEN

"Now begin again, Mr. *Greenspan*. You arrived in Israel last Thursday."

I lay on my stomach with my feet bound together and my hands tied behind my back with nylon cord, staring up at the well-covered legs of Hanna Klein.

"Yes, that's correct. That's what I told you."

"But you insisted on identifying yourself to me and to others as Isaiah Wolfe."

"It was a joke."

"You have a curious sense of humor, Mr. Greenspan."

"I know. It's a character flaw. I like to provoke for no reason. A therapist once told me that's how I sabotage all my relationships."

"Was it that kind of sabotage or another sort that led you to appear at the home of Menashe Kandel in Herzylia?"

"I explained it to you. It was all about a relative. Look, I'm sorry. I'm new here. I don't mean to offend."

"Mr. Greenspan, there is no way you could have known to find Reb Lipsky in Herzylia. His itinerary is always kept confidential for security reasons."

"What do you mean, find Reb Lipsky? I didn't even know he was there. The only person I saw was Irv Hurwitz."

"Don't treat me like an imbecile. One night you are in Herzylia, the next day you are in Bethlehem. Where are you getting your information?"

"What information?"

Hanna exhaled slowly and looked over at Boaz, who did not understand a word we were saying.

"Listen, Mr. Greenspan, Wolfe or whatever your name is, you can tell your friends at the Shin Bet to go away. Nothing's going to happen. They can relax. They should know for themselves Rabbi Lipsky would never do anything so stupid."

"What?" I started laughing. "You think *I'm* with the Israeli FBI?"

"What else?"

"I don't even speak Hebrew."

"A perfectly natural cover. They've used far more elaborate than that. Besides, how do we know what you speak?"

"Suppose I were to tell you I was something else entirely different. That I was, for example, a private eye working for the Arab-American Friendship Association in Los Angeles."

"Think of something more believable than that, Mr. Greenspan. Unfortunately, we have seen your type too often before. You are absolutely typical Shin Bet or Mossad."

"What's that?"

"Secular, supposedly idealistic—reporters, professors, even lawyers and doctors. Of course, then there are others of a totally different kind." She shook her head in disgust. "What a pass we have come to when Jews are forced to spy upon Jews."

"Maybe they have a good reason."

"Yes. The betrayal of God."

She stared at me with contempt before leaving me to stew. Boaz sat in a chair opposite me, watching me as if I were a close relative of Abu Nidal. So I was a Mossad agent. I had to smile. I remembered when I read *Exodus* years ago, as a teen-age romantic, I wondered if they had come to me in the middle of the night asking me to help my people on some life-threat-ening mission I would have cooperated. And now here I was, lying on a dirt floor in the old quarter of Hebron, paying the price of membership without ever having had a chance to de-cide.

Meanwhile, something had been interrupted. Or at least in my Shin Bet/Mossad capacity they wanted me to think that. But what was it, and why? Apparently Reb Lipsky and Kra-cauer were involved, probably Gordie as well, and possibly Menashe Kandel, at least peripherally. And certainly Hanna Klein knew about it. But the names didn't add up to enough and I didn't have enough time to think it over, because Hanna returned momentarily, this time accompanied by my good friend "John Candy," better known as Hosea.

"That's him, all right," said Candy, looking down at me as if I were the last cockroach that had just sneaked out from under his refrigerator. "He'll talk or I'll turn his kidneys into Play-doh."

"All right," she said. "Where is he?"

"Where's who?"

"Joshua ben Tsvi."

"Gordie? How'm I supposed to know? You just told me he was off meditating."

Candy snorted and prodded me with his foot.

"All right," said Hanna. "Who are you working with—the other members?"

"The other members of *what*?"

"This is no time for being bashful, Mr. Greenspan. You know what I'm talking about. I'm sure you don't have to go back to your *computer* to give us a list."

"Look, I told you. You've got the wrong guy. I'm about as much a Shin Bet agent as I am a Moose or a Knight of Columbus. I don't know *what* you're talking about!"

"She's talking about the Jewish Desk, weasel-face. The biggest collection of traitors to their own people this side of the finks at the Warsaw Ghetto. What do you *think* she's talking about?"

"I never heard of a Jewish Desk."

Candy glanced over at Hanna, who nodded almost imperceptibly. He bent down and lifted me up by the collar, pulling me halfway off the floor, and then bashed me across the forehead with a wheelhouse right that sent me flying backward into the wall. It felt as if I had just been hit by a steel wrecking ball.

"Now are you going to tell us who's in it?"

"I don't have the slightest—"

This time Hosea kicked me in the stomach. Then he came at me with his elbow, ramming me just above the eye and banging my head against the wall again with twice the force. When I came to, the inside of my head was ringing like the gong at a Zen monastery. I felt blood trickling down my left cheek.

"I regret using the brutal methods of your pathetic trade," said Hanna. "But according to Hosea you have been tracking us for some time. Apparently you arranged for the escape of a young woman, also curiously named Greenspan, we were attempting to deprogram from her shameful liaison with an Arab. Fortunately, she is now back under our supervision."

"Hey, watcha apologizin' for?" said Hosea. "We're only followin' the Biblical injunction of an eye for an eye." He cocked his arm again.

"Wait a minute. Wait. I don't know a thing," I managed to say, rolling my jaw back and forth to see if it was broken. "I promise."

"No. Leave him," said Hanna. "His own *guilt* will make him change his mind."

"I'll be back, asshole!" said Hosea.

He gave me a last whack in the kidneys before they disappeared through the door.

I closed my eyes and concentrated on my breathing to avoid the pain. I had been reduced from trying to figure things out to trying to survive. I was throbbing in six places. After a while, I guessed it was about fifteen minutes, it reduced to around four. Four horrendous ones, but still four. At that point, I opened my eyes again. Boaz, who had been sitting in the same chair the whole time, hadn't moved an inch from his post, but the line of the sun had moved approximately three feet across the floor, cutting me now right across the nape of my neck. It felt searingly hot, penetrating my skin to the bone as a pair of flies played tag around my left ear.

I looked up at Boaz and smiled, waiting for some semblance of a human connection, but I didn't get one. I imagined after what happened to him back home in Iraq, my recent japes looked like no more than a little after-school fun. But I smiled again anyway, this time succeeding in eliciting something in the rough vicinity of a nod. Then I said, "Hanna." He stared at me as if I were speaking Chinese, but I repeated it, this time flapping my fingers and thumb together like a mouth talking. I kept at it a couple of minutes, and Boaz finally got the picture that I wanted to talk. It took him another couple of minutes to decide whether he had the authority to leave me alone and go find Hanna. I kept alternately smiling and nodding to encourage him. Finally he got up and backed out of the room, shutting the door and bolting it behind him.

I immediately started shimmying across the floor, scraping my pants against the hard dirt. I reached the wall and hiked

myself up to examine the arched window. It had a simple sliding lock and crossed sash bars. I was able to open the lock with
my teeth and push up on the bar with my forehead. The frame
flew off the casing with a sudden squeak. I slid as quietly as I
could out the window onto a flat roof of scorchingly hot tar and
rolled over to the edge. Bad luck. It was about fifty feet straight
down onto a construction site of broken granite and rock. I
rolled over the other side. Worse luck. An alley filled with
broken glass and garbage. A steel ladder attached to the wall
descended straight to the ground, but only a madman or an
aerialist would try to negotiate that with his hands and feet
bound. I was lying there wondering what to do and when Boaz
would return with his grappling-hook arms, or possibly Hosea
with his eager boots, when I heard what sounded like a giggle
coming from the far end of the alley.

One of Gordie's kid friends raced around the corner and
jumped behind some empty vegetable crates. He must've been
playing the local variant of hide-and-seek or ringalevio, and he
was crouching low, peering around some rotting lettuce.

"Psst!" I said. "Up here!" The kid looked up, puzzled. "I'm
Gordie . . . Joshua's friend. Remember me?" He stared at me
a second, then nodded. "Hide up here and I'll distract them."
I pointed my chin toward the ladder, and the kid grinned, getting the idea. He hurried over and skampered up, making the
roof just as his pals came racing around the corner and down
the alley out of sight.

He smiled triumphantly, then walked over to me with a
smile. "You all tied up," he said.

"Yeah. I've been playing a game with Boaz."

"Boaz play game?" I remembered this one's accent from my
previous visit. He was staring at my face, which I assumed was
covered with cuts and bruises.

"Yeah. It's an Iraqi game. Very tough. He was teaching me."

"I never heard Iraqi game."

"Very rare. The children of the caliphs of Baghdad used to play it. During the Thousand and One Nights. They used to tie up their friends, beat them up and leave them in strange places until somebody found them. Kind of sadistic, if you ask me, but you know those Shiites. . . . I think he forgot I'm up here. Maybe you could help me out." I held up my wrists toward him. The boy studied me gravely. I could see he was vacillating. "And at the same time you could make yourself twenty shekels."

"You pay?"

"That's the idea."

"Okay," he said and kneeled down, starting to untie my arms. "This on very tight. Boaz know good knots. Is that right English, knots?"

"Right. Very good." I wished he would hurry up.

"This double square-type knot with rope made of strong and durable synthetic material."

"Uhuh." Inside, I could hear several sets of feet climbing the stairs. "Couldn't you do it a little faster?"

"My fingers tire. What hurry? This interesting."

"Yeah, fascinating. But get a move on, huh? It's pretty hot up here and I've got kind of a sun allergy. You know—allergy, sickness. Just do it, if you want your money!"

He gave me a strange look but managed to slip the knot just as I heard Boaz shouting inside the room. I stuffed some cash in his hand, then hurried to untie my feet and rolled over past the perplexed boy, hiding against the wall. He was even more perplexed, open-mouthed even, when I jumped up the moment Boaz and Hosea, loaded for bear, came flying through the window and gave Hosea a decidedly satisfying swift kick in the groin and wheeled around and let Boaz have a solid chop in his Adam's apple. Then I slid over the side and skipped down the ladder three steps at a time, not even bothering with the last six as I leaped into the alley and ran off into the Hebron casbah without so much as a glance back at my pursuers.

Twenty minutes later I was on the Arab bus heading back for Jerusalem, half acknowledging the curious stares of my neighbors while surreptitiously peering under my seat for mysterious packages even though I remembered reading that Arab buses were far more safe than Israeli. No one usually wanted to bomb them. But I seemed to be developing a Middle Eastern mindset.

EIGHTEEN

"Menashe Kandel is friends with Judah Lipsky?"

"I wouldn't say friends. Lipsky owes him for something. He solved his *shiksa* problem, whatever that is. If he doesn't pay up, Kandel promised to turn the rabbi into so much kosher meat. Of course, then he'd have to deal with Lipsky, who claims he's got half the Iraqi Jews lined up for a Holy War."

Max laughed as I winced while his wife applied hydrogen peroxide to a wide cut above my left eye.

"You know, Moses, this is exciting stuff for us religious people. The high point of my day is usually going to the Wall to lay *tefillin*."

"I don't know. Everyone around here seems to live a pretty dramatic existence. Maybe too dramatic. What about your friend DeLeon, palling around with *hoserim teshuvah* and then winding up with a knife in his back?"

"No. Not that way," said someone sharply. It was Chaya Bracha, who was standing in the kitchen doorway, watching us. "Tape it together. Otherwise he'll need stitches." She walked over and kneeled down next to Rachel, taking the scissors from her hand and cutting a length of gauze, which she taped above my eye, tugging the wound together as she pressed it down.

"I thought you were a rock-and-roller in your past life," I said.

She smiled. "I was around a lot of bar fights. You look like you were in a big one."

"Yeah, Lipsky's people thought I was in the Mossad or Shin Bet or something." I gingerly touched the other wound on my cheek. "They've got a helluvan idea of how to treat the government."

"The government doesn't always treat them so well," said Max. "Besides, you weren't always exactly sympathetic to the CIA as I remember, Moses. What'd they want to know?"

"They wanted to know what happened to the kid I was looking for."

"I thought you found him."

"He's disappeared again. From everybody, evidently. Or at least they want me to think that. Assuming they really believe I'm working for the government, maybe they're trying to send a message, set up deniability for somebody. Maybe Lipsky."

"What do they say the boy's doing?" asked Chaya.

"Meditating."

"This is good," said Max.

"Somehow I figured you'd say that."

"What do you think his meditation will lead to?"

"How should I know? Spiritual enlightenment. Isn't that what meditation is supposed to lead to? 'May the words of my mouth and the meditations of my heart be acceptable . . .' "

"Definitely a Reform background," said Max.

"What'd you expect?"

Max shrugged and walked off, picking up a prayer book and heading off in a corner to doven. It was dusk, and in the distance I could hear others praying, groups of male voices murmuring at walls, seeking salvation. I sat there as Chaya swabbed and taped the second wound. She did it with a gentle competence that relaxed me for a moment. My mind drifted back to Gordie. Did I ever have visions, I remembered he asked me. I hadn't had a chance to answer, but I knew if I had had visions I might have been afraid of them. I usually clung to my rationality like a security blanket, but Gordie ran from his as if it were a curse, into the arms of God. There could be a comfort in dreams. And yet one's visions could be so powerful they could become an excuse for murder. Manson had them on one hand and Buddha on the other. And the original Moses. He had a vision of this Promised Land he was never able to reach. That was the problem with visions. They were so often better than the reality.

"Gordie told me he had a . . . you know . . . dream that an angel came to him and said he had to go to a pass and practice. A pass in the mountains."

Chaya nodded as if I were saying something perfectly reasonable. "Practice for what?" she asked.

"To see the Ark of the Covenant."

"That could take practice," she said, frowning and calling out something in Hebrew to Max, who looked up at us. He closed his prayer book and walked over.

"Moses says this boy wants to see the Ark of the Covenant."

"Call him Joshua," I said.

"Joshua."

"That would be very difficult to do, since no one knows where it is," said Max.

"I thought it was hidden under the Temple Mount."

"So they say. Of course, as you know, that is under Muslim religious control. There would be no way to find out without excavating directly below their mosques."

"That would take a while," I said.

"Yes, and be rather impossible under present conditions. . . . Of course, there are those who have tried other methods."

"Like explosives?"

Max nodded. "But they usually are trying to destroy the mosques themselves, El Aqsa or the Dome of the Rock, which is not really a mosque. A few years ago an ex–air force pilot— a war hero actually—even had a plan to blow it up with an F-15. And then there were some crazy Americans who walked backward facing the sun, prayed to Abraham and John Lennon and tried to do it with three sticks of gelignite and a box of safety matches. It was rather a scandal and made some people say that all the nutcases here were born in the States. . . . You know, Moses, there are also many who say it is God's will that we retake the Mount. To do nothing about it is a sin." He looked at me carefully, studying my reaction. "And then there are those who say it is not even necessary to retake the Mount. It is only necessary to prove that the Ark is there. That would prove God's covenant with Moses was real, that the Ten Commandments were real and the Oral Law was real and that we *are* the Chosen People."

"What about you?"

Max shrugged. "For me it is impossible to know God's plan beyond what He has revealed to us."

But not to Gordie, I thought. Evidently with Gordie He made a special deal. "Where did the Ark *rest*?"

"Rest? I don't know what you mean."

"Neither do I. Except he said something about this pass being near where the Ark rested."

Chaya pursed her lips, apparently making some kind of connection. She said something in Hebrew to Max, and he answered her briefly. They then launched into a discussion of a half-dozen exchanges, obviously a disagreement of some sort, which was finally resolved when Chaya turned to me: "They say that the Ark of the Covenant rested for a while at Shiloh . . . after Joshua conquered the tribes and united the land."

"Joshua? At Shiloh? I suppose that could be where he's practicing for his . . . "

"Or meditating," she said. "Unfortunately, there are many passes near Shiloh. I doubt you would be able to find him, especially since you don't speak Hebrew—or Arabic. No one around there speaks English, except for an occasional tour guide at the old sites."

"How far is this place?"

Max and Chaya looked at each other before he answered. "Thirty, forty miles. Nothing is far here."

"I think I'll take a run up there."

"Now?" said Max, frowning. "You'll get lost in the dark. It's all winding roads. Arab villages. Why don't you wait until morning?"

"I don't know how much time I have, if this kid's planning to do something crazy."

"But you won't be able to find him at night anyway. And if he's as dangerous as you say he is, if he *did* kill that Arab, it could be quite risky. Anyway, in the morning—I cannot do it —but perhaps Chaya will ride up with you. She knows the area. And she speaks both languages. Besides, I'm sure you will find her much better company than me." He smiled slyly.

I looked over at Chaya, who smiled also, saying, "I have a cousin in a *moshav* near there. It gives me an excuse to visit. We could leave at dawn and be at the pass by seven or eight."

"And," said Max, "we're having a little going-away party for Brenda Weintraub tonight. She's flying back to L.A. tomorrow. We'd all be disappointed if you didn't attend."

I'd thought Brenda Weintraub was staying in Jerusalem to look for a husband. Perhaps she was cutting it short for the fall television season.

Max left to purchase some extra wine and Crown Royal while Chaya went off into the kitchen to help Rachel prepare some desserts. I stood at the window, staring out across the plaza below at the Wall. Although it was now dark, a couple of dozen Chasidim where still visible praying before those vast rectangular stones that formed the last remaining remnants of their former Temple. The Jews were worshiping a *retaining wall*, I thought. What a cosmic joke. But scarcely unique. All across the globe it was the same. Catholics kneeling before the Virgin, Iranians praising Allah, Saudis praising a different Allah, Americans genuflecting to capitalism, Russians worshiping Marx and Japanese singing to the prosperity of their company

—a whole big world huddled together terrified in their caves the same way they were ten thousand years ago.

But was I immune? There was something that felt warm and womblike here in Max's apartment, the familiar smells from the kitchen, the soft enveloping furniture whose comfort generations of affluent suburban life could not erase. Even the curves of the sculptured walls themselves were consoling. And yet I felt a vague disquiet, a disquiet which later increased as the party progressed, as if I were in the middle of a dumb show, a staged event. And I kept wondering for whose benefit it was being staged, mine or theirs.

"The trouble with you secular Jews," said Max, pouring me a glass of Crown Royal sufficient to put away Mean Joe Green, "is that you don't know how to hold your liquor. You've become so obsessed with health you've forgotten how to have fun. You're the *real* Puritans."

He downed his glass and waited for me to follow suit. Like a good fraternity boy, I emptied mine and held the glass upside down to show there wasn't a drop of Scotch left. It was my second one, and it wasn't long before I felt the alcohol build up in my calf arteries. Chasidic music was playing, and I half walked, half stumbled to where a crowd had gathered around Brenda, who had been drinking herself and was dancing her farewell, waving a silk scarf over her head like one of the Sabine women.

"You like that?" said Chaya, who had come up behind me.

"Not bad."

"I've seen better." She had a discreetly playful smile on her face and was standing with her shoulder touching mine.

"Really?" I said. "When you were on stage did you do things

like that—wave a scarf like Mick Jagger and toss it out to some horny bastard in the audience?"

"I might have." She laughed. "I don't remember."

"You don't *remember*?"

"Well . . . I do remember kicking off my heels when some guy in the first row began to stroke my feet." She wiggled the toes of her shoes, which were of the schoolmarmish lace-up variety. "That was interesting."

"I should imagine."

"Of course, here things are much more powerful."

"Are they?"

"Oh, yes. Ever since I became *baal teshuvah* the intensity of my erotic feelings has grown much stronger."

"But you don't act on them."

"I do what I wish." She looked at me, gauging my reaction. "When I have to."

"And when do you have to?"

"God created our bodies for pleasure. I'm sure He didn't intend for us to deny ourselves."

"But only when we're married, right?"

"True. But what is marriage? And who is a spouse? You remember the Song of Songs—'O that thou wert as my brother, that sucked the breasts of my mother! when I should find thee without, I would kiss thee.' "

"I remember 'Thy breasts are like young roes that are twins, which feed among the lilies.' "

"What about 'Make haste, my beloved, and be thou like to a roe or to a young hart upon the mountain of spices'?"

"That's quite a line. Is it poetry or an invitation?"

"I thought it was a metaphor." She smiled in amusement. "I'm looking forward to our trip," she added. "If you're not in *too* much of a hurry, I know some interesting hiking trails along the way where there are meadows with wild flowers that grow up to the waist. Or perhaps we could take the coast route."

Then she walked off, leaving me with a great deal to think about. Perhaps more than I wanted. What was going on here—an abrupt personality change, a showing of true colors, or something else again, something I never would have predicted?

The party ended early to give Brenda an opportunity to get back to her room at the Hotel LaRomme and pack. Max brought some pillows, and Rachel made a bed for me on the couch so I could leave early with Chaya. Then everyone said good night and I lay there in the darkness, unable to sleep, staring up at the ceiling and trying to remember more of the Song of Songs. I recalled being caught reading it behind my desk in Sunday school by a junior rabbi, who insisted its earthiness was entirely symbolic. The verses made me think of Chantal and made me feel a bit guilty about whatever thoughts I had about Chaya. But not that guilty. Chantal had hung up on me, after all. And as for Chaya, what had I done? And what was I likely to do? Not much, I was thinking, when she appeared in the living room in her nightgown, ostensibly to get a glass of milk.

"Trouble sleeping?" I asked.

She nodded. The response did not surprise me.

She came and sat beside me on the couch.

"Why don't we go to your room?" I suggested.

She nodded again, and I stood, following her down the short corridor to what appeared to be a guest bedroom. She shut the door behind us. I wrapped my arms around her, holding her to me and feeling the sleek curve of her back, thinking too bad this isn't going to last but at least I don't have to worry about safe sex, as I pushed her back hard against the wall and grabbed her handbag. She lunged for it, but I shoved her back harder again and opened it. Inside was a .22 caliber small-bore automatic, some ammunition and a government-issue transmitter with an LED read-out. I zipped it all up and threw it back on the bed as she stood there staring at me.

"Look," I said, "I don't care whether you guys are with the Mossad, the Shin Bet or who. It's all the same to me. I just hate being made a fool of—by you and by my supposedly good old friend Max Hirsch, the born-again rabbi. So the next time he wants to meet me 'by accident' in front of the Wall or any other place, or the next time one of his fellow operatives is murdered trying to tell me information so I will pass it to him while he pretends to give me religious instruction, tell him I won't remember his name. Tell him I won't remember the name of the godfather of my children either."

And with that I walked out the door.

NINETEEN

"So you've heard of the Jewish Desk, Mr. Wine."

"Hanna Klein told me something about it."

The man who identified himself as Yitzhak half smiled. He was in his middle sixties, barrel-chested, in a short-sleeved khaki shirt, with thick, furry eyebrows, gray eyes and serial numbers tattooed on his left arm. I was sitting across a table from him in a basement room of the building still known as the Russian Compound, headquarters of many of the law enforcement agencies, overt and covert, of the land of Israel.

Ten minutes before I had been picked up on the highway heading north toward Shiloh. That had not surprised me. What had surprised me was the extent of the operation and its rapidity. Only twenty minutes after I left Max's, a souped-up police-type Dodge Charger, a Toyota Land Cruiser, and a helicopter converged simultaneously on my puny little Isuzu at the exact moment it came over a hill about a mile outside the rat's-nest town of Shufat on the outskirts of Jerusalem. The helicopter hovered overhead until I climbed into the Charger. I was escorted back through the empty streets to my subterranean destination.

"Then you are not surprised we have such a branch," he continued. His accent was Eastern European, with that slight overlay of Oxbridge that foreigners often affect to show their disdain, or at least distaste, for the more slovenly American language.

"No, not really. You have to have a way of keeping tabs on your own zealots. I was just disappointed to see an old friend of mine was part of it."

"You feel betrayed."

"I'd say so."

The man called Yitzhak studied me awhile before continuing. "Well, in any case, we are sorry to have brought you here so abruptly. But, of course, you have no real reason to complain, because you yourself are here in our country on clandestine business of your own, not as a tourist or as a young Jewish man eager to avail himself of the opportunity to immigrate under the Law of the Return. A pity, because there is a great deal here for you, and you will never see it." He shrugged. "Anyway, we are fully aware of your activities."

"I wouldn't doubt it."

"Including the name and address of your employers, the reason for your visit and so forth." He offered me a Gauloise and I shook my head. He took one himself, and I found myself staring at the numbers on his arm, wondering what camp he had been in, as he lit the cigarette. "A certain amount of congratulations are in order. Not a great deal, but some." He exhaled. "You may be pleased to know that we have already been in contact with U.S. authorities about the return of *their* citizen Gordon Goldenberg in connection with the ballistic assassination of the Arab-American Joseph Damoor. As soon as this young man is in our hands, which I expect will be any moment, he will be returned to them forthwith. I am sure also that your employers"—he looked down at a file—"Mr. Said and Mr. Terzi will be equally pleased and you will be generously rewarded."

"Suppose he didn't do it?"

"Goldenberg?" He twisted his head and smiled at the absurdity. "Why would that be?"

"I don't know. Call it Kabbalistic intuition."

"Yes, your friend Mr. Hirsch told us of your attraction to Kabbalah. That old flirtation with secret knowledge. Frankly" —he nodded toward the file—"it did not surprise me. It may interest you to know that my brother, a rabbi and scholar of Kabbalah who was brought to Treblinka with me, thought he could transcend the ovens by reciting the hidden tetragrammaton of God a thousand times. He was incinerated within a week. Some others of us who were atheists escaped to fight in the Resistance and spent the rest of the war blowing up Nazi troop trains. I hope you would like to think of yourself as one of those who would have fought."

"Yes."

"In any case, your fighting days in this episode are over. It is now twelve-thirty A.M. We are asking that you leave the state of Israel within twelve hours. For your convenience a reservation has been made in your name on the eleven-A.M. flight from Ben Gurion Airport to Los Angeles. We have also reserved a room for you tonight at the King David Hotel, with which we understand you are familiar." He stood. "I hope, Mr. Wine, that your next visit to the country of your ancestors will not have to be so hurried and that you come with an open heart and an open mind. Remember too that we, like you, are still an idealistic people. But in order to remain idealistic, we must first be able to survive. And as the poet Glatstein has written, 'Dead men don't praise God.' " He walked over to the door with a slight limp and opened it. "And now, if you will excuse me, my long-suffering wife has a habit of waiting up for me. I would like to be able to go home and go to bed."

"I understand. I won't ask you why you want me out of the country so quickly, because I'm sure you won't tell me. But would you mind answering one question? Suppose Gordie was acting under the orders of Rabbi Judah Lipsky?"

"Mr. Wine. Rabbi Lipsky, reprehensible as we may find him, is above all a politician, a member of the Knesset and the leader of a political party with an election coming up in very short order. What possible reason would he have to order the murder of an Arab-American on American soil, risk apprehension and have his cause—not to say his public career—discredited forever?"

"A *shiksa* problem?"

This time Yitzhak didn't even smile. "Rabbi Lipsky has been

married for seventeen years. In his position, he wouldn't touch another woman, let alone a *shiksa*. Moreover, everywhere he goes, he is constantly surrounded by the ultradevout, who would sooner flay themselves with hot irons than so much as look at a gentile woman. So if, for some unknown reason, he got the peculiar idea in his head, the only time he could meet such a person would be in the shower. Perhaps it is you who has the *shiksa* problem. Good night, Mr. Wine."

A young soldier who spoke only Hebrew was waiting for me outside with an airplane ticket and my fully packed suitcase from the yeshiva. He opened the door of the Charger and drove me back to the King David, where he escorted me to the front desk and said a few words to the concierge, who immediately signaled for a bellboy.

I took the opportunity to wander around the lobby. Although it was late, there were several people seated in the various sofas and easy chairs—a group of well-dressed women, a man by himself in a Panama hat, two Japanese businessmen and a pair of young dudes in Hawaiian shirts. I wondered which ones had been put there to watch me. The earliest test would have been to head into the men's room and see who followed, but the soldier was still there, so instead I walked over toward the bell captain's desk, where the hotel events of the day were listed on a black felt board. I had missed the lecture on Old City excavations presented by a company called Dig for a Day and the tour of the Massada for UNESCO doctors, but the "Michael Silverman Bar Mitzvah Reception—Congratulations to Mr. and Mrs. Arthur Silverman of Short Hills, New Jersey" might still be in progress if the starting time of nine o'clock was any indication. Indeed, I could hear the muffled strains of "Moon River" drifting in from the patio. After about a dozen rounds of "Hava NaGila" with the requisite hora, that was just the kind of nauseating tune to accompany a Short Hills Bar Mitzvah boy as he danced stiffly with his mother.

At that moment the bellboy came up with my suitcase to take me to my room, but I took the suitcase from him and opened it right there, taking out a tie and returning him the case along with a twenty-shekel note. I told him to go ahead without me— I'd be up later. Then I put on the tie and headed for the Bar Mitzvah, catching a reflected glimpse of the man in the Panama hat rising from his chair as I pushed through the revolving door out onto the patio.

The party took up most of the outside of the hotel. I had half expected to find one of those grotesque fifties affairs out of *Good-bye Columbus* with a chopped-liver statue of the Bar Mitzvah boy surrounded by half-eaten matzo balls and maybe a dill pickle stuck by some local wise guy right between the statue's legs, but although there was a huge tent erected alongside the pool as well as a Glenn Miller–size bandstand and a portable parquet dance floor, the whole affair reeked of second- or third-generation good taste, as American as apple pie with just a piquant whiff of the ethnic.

Things were just starting to break up, and a few people from other hotels were drifting over toward the parking valets, who were stationed at the far side of the tent. But there were at least a hundred assorted relatives and friends left, and I mingled with them, oddly enough feeling the most at home I had since I'd come to Israel. I had a brief conversation with a woman named Eleanor Sheckman who swore she knew me from paddle tennis at the Short Hills Country Club and another with a guy in a Don Johnson jacket who thought the Dow had peaked at 2600 and was getting into silver. Then I heard a short man in a tux, who must have been Mr. Arthur Silverman himself, complaining that he had to clean out all the rentals from the Hertz garages in both Tel Aviv *and* Jerusalem just because his wife suddenly decided to end her ten-year feud with her second cousins from Milwaukee. It was a shame I was going to give these friendly people the scare of their lives, but at least it would give them something to talk about when they got home. In fact, if I did it right, they'd be dining out on it for years.

I looked over at the man in the Panama hat, staring straight at him until he had to turn away. Then I backed rapidly through the dance floor, detouring behind the bandstand and picking up a trumpet case that was lying beside a set of drums. Before anybody could notice, I carried the case around a group of dancers and slid it under the blue-and-white cloths of one of the party tables. Then I went looking for Eleanor. I found her over by the bar, ordering a Bloody Mary. I stood about twenty feet away and waited until she looked in my direction. Then I frowned and beckoned to her. She walked over, sipping her drink.

"I don't want to freak you out," I said in a low voice, "But I just saw something a little bizarre."

"Really?" She gave me an interested look, as if I had something else in mind.

"Not that." I grinned quickly. "Maybe later. . . . Look, I'm probably paranoid but I was standing over near the fence there when I saw this guy—he looked dark, you know, Arab or something—slip out from behind that tree and stash a small suitcase under a table near the dance floor. Then he disappeared off behind the tennis court someplace."

"Which table?" She suddenly looked alarmed.

"I think it was that one." I pointed.

She bent over and looked underneath. "Ohmigod!" she said.

"Amazing, huh? The last thing we need is something like this at Michael's Bar Mitzvah."

"Right, right." She started clenching her fists.

"With the cousins reconciled for the first time in ten years."
I shook my head. "Can you imagine? What do you think we
should do? . . . Wait a minute. I've got it." I drew her to me
and whispered. "You go inside and quietly tell the concierge
what happened. I think I read they have a special police force
for dealing with things like this. I'll stay here and keep an eye
on things, make sure no one hurts themselves by accident, you
know."

"Okay." I could see her counting to herself to keep from
panicking before she nodded and walked swiftly back into the
hotel.

I waited a couple of minutes before taking a slow walk myself
in the direction of the hotel. I entered by a different entrance
and followed the sign to my left down the steps to the men's
room. I nodded to the attendant and immediately walked into
one of the stalls, locking it behind me, unbuttoning my pants
and sitting down as if to take a nice long shit while positioning
myself with a good view of the door through a stall crack. It
wasn't more than fifteen seconds before the man in the Panama
hat came in. He walked over to the sink and began to wash his
hands, slowly, one at a time, finger by finger. Then he took off
his hat, got a comb from the attendant and started to run it
through his thinning hair. Strand by strand. Every few seconds
he glanced over in my direction, and I moaned softly, a man
with a serious constipation problem.

It seemed like a long time (I was beginning to wonder
whether Eleanor had actually carried out the required task),
but probably wasn't much more than five minutes, when I finally heard the screaming siren of the Jerusalem bomb squad
wailing down David ha-Melekh and screeching to a halt in front
of the hotel. The attendant bolted from the bathroom as if he

were remembering when the Irgun blew up part of the King David in '46. The now hatless man in the Panama debated for a moment what to do, glanced over at my stall, at which point I groaned extra loudly, and then he hurriedly grabbed his hat and dashed out after the attendant.

I pulled up my pants, stood up on the toilet seat, opened the opaque wire-glass window above me and hoisted myself out onto the street. I emerged on the sidewalk, fifty yards down from where a trio of sappers were unloading an antidetonation robot from the bomb-squad jeep as the Silverman Bar Mitzvah crowd looked on in fascination and horror. A couple of policemen were urging people to stand back in Hebrew as some Good Samaritan translated into English. I drifted down toward the parking valets, who themselves were totally transfixed by the events.

"The Toyota," I told the nearest valet, who was staring off at the robot, which was just then being deposited on the now-empty dance floor and guided in the direction of the table.

"Ticket?"

"Uh . . . I don't know. I think I lost it in the middle of all this." I gestured.

"What color?" he snapped impatiently.

"Green."

"We have no green. Yellow or blue."

"Blue. That was it. Blue. How could I forget?"

He glared at me.

"Why don't you just give me the keys and tell me where it is? I don't want to interrupt you." I nodded toward the robot, which was now extracting the trumpet case from under the table.

The valet grabbed a set of keys and thrust them at me, pointing up the street. "End Emile Botta."

I handed him a twenty and split. Out of the corner of my eye I could just see the robot flipping open the case, revealing a gleaming trumpet. I heard one of the sappers shouting a long curse in Hebrew, probably something to do with the questionable background of somebody's mother.

I didn't wait around for a translation, but continued straight on past Eleanor Sheckman, who was staring after me with a baffled expression. I waved to her and kept going. Within thirty seconds I was inside the blue Toyota Corolla speeding as fast and as far as possible from the King David Hotel. When I reached Rehov Yafo, I turned off on a side street and parked, quickly relieving an old Citroën of its license plates and placing those on my new Toyota. Then I scraped the Hertz decal off the windshield and drove off into the night. I was almost to the outskirts of the city, just past the East Jerusalem YMCA aiming for the road to Shiloh, when I changed my mind and made a U-turn. There was something I should do first, but I knew from here on in vacillation was not the order of the day. Two minutes after the sappers found the trumpet, there was probably someone up in my room, reporting my absence to the Shin Bet. From then on in, I'd be one of the least popular people in Israel. This was not a country that saw bomb scares as a practical joke.

TWENTY

I broke into Rabbi Judah Lipsky's office at the Holocaust Prevention Institute at exactly two-sixteen in the morning. Considering the man could have been a top-ten target for half the members of a *Who's Who of World Terrorism*, getting in wasn't all that difficult. It was simply a matter of climbing over the exterior wall and prying open a small window above a display of California synagogue swastikas. The door to Lipsky's office itself, which old Irv had so graciously identified for me a few days before, was then easily accessible with my trusty American Express card. I didn't leave home without it.

In fact, it was so easy, I immediately started wondering if I could possibly find anything of interest. And what was I looking for? Some connection, a smoking gun that would link Menashe Kandel and Rabbi Judah Lipsky in some sinister plot. But to do what? Blow up the Temple Mount? That scarcely seemed Kandel's territory, unless he wanted the global rights to the film version of World War III. And as for Lipsky, the man called Yitzhak made a certain amount of sense. The rabbi was first and foremost a politician, albeit clearly of the demagogic kind, and, like most politicians, he was ninety-five percent air and five percent dare. He wasn't about to risk Armageddon for his beliefs, or even for a few votes. That was more the meat of messianic Christers like the Reverend John Ambrose Kracauer with their vision of Jews as the shock troops of some theistic nuclear war, miraculously "Raptured" to their salvation on the lining of an atomic cloud. But even the good Dr. K. seemed more interested in outflanking his media competitors back home for the ultraright piece of the fundamentalist pie than in creating a conflagration in which, heavens-to-Betsy, real people might get hurt in an international stampede of extremist loonies rushing from Mecca or God knows where to rescue a rock. No, this all seemed to stem from a different agenda. But what?

I knew I didn't have much time, and I had to make an educated guess among the stacks of files, boxes and bins piled about the room in seemingly random order. Papers were strewn about the desk, and books in Hebrew and English were stacked to the ceiling in the corners. It wasn't the workplace of an orderly mind, and in an odd way I sympathized, or at least identified, but I gambled on the obvious and chose the bottom drawer, the only locked one, of the file cabinet, working it with the screwdriver I had lifted from the tool bag in the trunk of the Toyota.

It had a heavy-duty door-type latch and deadbolt and I was getting nowhere working methodically, so I grabbed a paperweight from Lipsky's desk, pushed the screwdriver deeper into the mechanism behind the lock and banged down hard on the end with the weight. It made a horrible racket, but something was dislodged and the drawer slid open. I flicked on the lamp and looked in.

At first glance, it seemed like a total waste of time. The drawer was stacked high with the most useless form of Lipskyana, photos of the rabbi, paperbacks of his books, newsletters of the Gevurah Party with the usual warnings about the Arab population crisis and the dangers of miscegenation. The bottom was worse—unused stationery and envelopes, going back to the rabbi's days back in the States with the Jewish Defense Squad as well as political screeds written at the time, attacks on Jews who spent more energy defending blacks than their own kind mixed with denunciations of antiwar activists as communist dupes. Scanning this bilge was making me so hot under the collar I almost missed the most important thing when it fell out in front of me. I stared straight at it for about fifteen seconds before even thinking to pick it up.

It was a personal photograph in one of those folded cardboard frames of a blond girl in a bikini who was almost beautiful but not quite. She was standing on a beach and waving to the camera with a friendly, almost naive smile. The words "Forever yours . . . S" were scrawled across the top in red ink. Slipped in with the photo was a yellowed newspaper clipping from the *Long Beach Press Telegram* dated June 4, 1969. The headline read: "Actress Leaps to Death."

Most of the article had been torn off, but I started to read what I could. Suzi DelVecchio, a "part-time actress and waitress," had jumped to her death from the Harbor Island Bridge near San Pedro the previous day. There was no suicide note, and her most recent "professional activity" was listed as *Naughty Nurses of Naples*, produced by Menashe Kandel. That certainly rang a bell, but nowhere near as loud as the door banging in front of me.

Irv Hurwitz was standing there in his pajamas, holding an Uzi. The spectacle might have been comical if his demeanor hadn't been so distinctly deadly.

"Fuckin' Greenspan. The traitor asshole. You want me to shoot first or call the police?"

"I think you'd better call the police."

"I figured you'd say that. You *are* the police, you Shin Bet creep."

"Right, right, I am the Shin Bet," I said, stalling for time and letting the photo ball back into the drawer. The good thing about an Uzi was that it inspired improvisation. "You don't want the death of a Shin Bet agent on your hands. It wouldn't be so great for your organization."

"What would be great'd be to pull one of you vultures in and prove you been spyin' on us once and for all. The rebbe'd have a field day with that in front of those *goyim* in the Knesset."

"Trouble is I don't really work for the Shin Bet."

"So what? Then you work for the Mossad. It's the same deck with different cards."

"Not them either. . . . You're not going to believe this, but . . . " I exhaled, shrugged. "Howard Melnick sent me here."

"*Howard* sent you?"

"Yeah. He's concerned Gevurah is trying to destroy the JDS in a power play. I told him it wasn't true, but he insisted I come here anyway and check it out."

"That's the biggest load of crap I've ever heard!"

I had to admit it sounded that way to me too, but I pressed on anyway. "That's why I'm here tonight." I gestured toward the files. "For a last look around. Naturally I didn't find anything, and I'm going back tomorrow. Here's my ticket." I reached into my pocket and waved it at him. "See. My name isn't even Greenspan," I added, as if that meant anything.

He stared at me, his finger edging closer to the trigger. For a moment I thought he was going to blow me into the next room, all over the posters from the White Citizens Council, and I started to consider my physical options, such as they were, but something about his expression, a slight ambivalence, maybe, as if he were in the middle of an internal debate, made me hesitate.

My patience was rewarded when he lowered his weapon. "All right," he said. "Get outta here. But be on that plane tomorrow or I'm personally gonna track you down and shove this Uzi up your ass and pull the trigger until I plaster your Arab-loving butt to the ceiling! And if you ever do *anything* to hurt my rebbe, even that's gonna be too good for you!"

I took the message and got out of there fast.

Now I was really confused. "Arab-loving butt"—did he know who I was too, or had paranoia taken over entirely? And if he did, why had he let me go? Or was he also Shin Bet, another member of the Jewish Desk planted to keep an eye on Reb Lipsky from the very middle of his operation, even to sleeping in his headquarters? But why didn't he then just turn me in, pick up the phone and call the Russian Compound and save everybody a lot of aggravation? Why *had* he let me go?

At three in the morning, the conundrum was too much for me. I needed some sleep in a decent bed, no matter what. Otherwise I was useless. I drove over to the Jerusalem Hilton and checked in for a couple of hours, knowing even that was pushing the edge of the envelope as far as the authorities were concerned. Then I went upstairs and placed a long-distance call to Chantal. Fortunately I caught her before she went out to dinner.

"Are you talking to me?" I asked.

"Maybe. As long as I don't have to hear about converting."

"Don't worry about it."

"Well, that's an improvement."

"It's about the only thing that is. At the moment I've been kicked out of the country."

"What do you mean?"

"I don't have time to explain. And I don't even know if I could. Right now I need you to find out anything you can about the suicide of an actress named Suzi DelVecchio. There's an article about it in the *Long Beach Press Telegram* for June 4, 1969. I could only read the first couple of paragraphs. Somebody tore off the rest. Probably Lipsky. Call me back in two hours."

"How can I do that? It's after six here. The libraries are closed."

"Drive down there or something. Use your initiative. This is an emergency!"

"Moses, are you all right?"

"*Baruch ha-Shem.*"

"Hel-*low*. I thought we were done with that mumbo-jumbo!"

"Okay, okay. *Allah akbar.* Call me back. Right now I gotta get some sleep before I get arrested."

"Moses, wait."

"What?"

"Joseph Damoor was supposed to be in Israel last week."

"How'd you find *that* out?"

"Remember that Peace Now conference in Rome? I've been reading the transcripts. They invited him."

"You're brilliant. . . . I miss you."

"Finally."

"Good night."

"Good evening."

I hung up, and the next thing I remember was the phone ringing again in what felt like ten seconds later. I didn't have to reach for it, because my hand hadn't left the hook, even though it was five-thirty on the dot.

"Chantal?"

"I'm down at the *Press Telegram* morgue. You certainly picked a weird one here."

"Tell me."

"What do you know?" she asked.

"Actress jumps to death. Appeared in Menashe Kandel flick. That's about it. Who was she?"

"Catholic girl, aged twenty-two, parents dead."

"What's so strange about that?"

"Nothing. It's the husband."

"What about him?"

"He disappeared."

"Who was he?"

"That's the point. Nobody knows. There was a follow-up story in the paper a week later. 'Actress Has No Funeral' was the headline. It said that although actress Suzi DelVecchio had been legally married in Nevada in May 1967 and never divorced, no one turned up to claim the body and no one could locate the husband, although police in two states made a serious attempt to track him down. But they didn't have a home address, occupation, nothing. In fact, the social security number listed on his marriage license belonged to a dead man."

"That old dodge. Does it give this guy's name?"

"Yes. James Larson."

James Larson. *Mr. Larson.* I rubbed my eyes and sat up straight in bed. That was the name Kandel had called Lipsky the other night when they were squaring off against each other. Could it be? That would make the rabbi the missing husband. It seemed crazy, but there was the girl's picture. And it all had happened right at the end of the sixties, his famous "missing period."

"Moses, are you there? Hello? . . . The girl was three months pregnant too, if that makes any difference."

"That's a helluva *shiksa* problem."

"*Shiksa* problem? You know I think that's a vile, racist term."

"You're right. But it's colorful."

"What is this?"

"I'll explain later. Right now, I gotta get out of here. You've outdone yourself. I miss you more than ever. 'Bye."

I hung up and pulled myself out of bed, throwing myself under a cold shower and dressing in three minutes flat, staring in the mirror at the rings which were forming around my eyes just below my bandage. A purplish shiner decorated my left check. I finished dressing, went down and paid my bill. Then I inveigled a cup of black coffee out of the waitress fifteen minutes before the dining room opened, gulping it down with a stale roll. When I got out of there, it was twelve minutes to six. With any luck, I could catch Lipsky while he was still at morning prayer.

TWENTY-ONE

About thirty men had gathered to doven in the tiny synagogue inside the Yeshiva Torat Cohanim. They were heavily draped in fringed prayer shawls, some covering their heads almost like monks, which made me think of Obi Wan Kenobi. I entered and stood at the door, my skullcap firmly in place.

Lipsky was up in front, leading the prayers, as Irv had proudly informed me was his weekday habit, his anthracite eyes darting about beneath the fluttering eyelids. Boaz and the other bodyguard were there too, their muscular arms laced with leather phylacteries which gave them the appearance of bit players in *Road Warrior*. But I didn't let that stop me from walking straight up to Lipsky and addressing him directly.

"I want to talk to you, Lipsky. Now."

"This is a holy place," he replied. "Get out or I'll call the police."

"Will you . . . Mr. Larson?"

Everyone turned around. Boaz and his partner started to approach, but Lipsky warned them off with a look.

"Are you going to come outside or would you rather I announce everything right here? Some of these people must speak a passable English."

Lipsky studied me coolly, his expression betraying no apparent trepidation. As the others watched he slowly unwrapped his prayer shawl, kissed the fringes and folded it. Then he nodded to me and opened the door. I followed him out.

"What do you want?" said the rabbi as we reached the end of the cul-de-sac that stood next to the yeshiva. "Whoever you are, I'm certain you didn't come here to recite accusations that have no basis in fact and of which I am equally certain you have no proof whatsoever."

"I want to know what Gordie Goldenberg has to do with all this."

"All what?"

"James Larson. Suzi DelVecchio. The whole sordid mess from '69."

"What're you talking about? Gordie Goldenberg was barely *born* in 1969."

"Where is he?"

"I don't have the slightest idea."

"I want him stopped."

"Whatever Gordie Goldenberg is or is not going to do is no concern of mine. And if it were, I wouldn't be able to stop him anyway. So if you will excuse, Mr., uh, Greenspan . . . " He started off but I held his arm.

"Look, either you tell me where Gordie is or I'm going straight to the offices of the *Jerusalem Post*—or the *Palestine Post* as you call it—and tell them everything I know."

He laughed. "They wouldn't print it."

"Why not?"

"You don't know, do you?" He stared at me, smirking contemptuously.

I wondered myself when he started off again. I didn't waste any time, grabbing him around the neck and gagging him while pulling him through a half-open door and slamming it shut with my foot. "All right, Lipsky. Let's do this the direct way!" I backed him up against the inside wall, simultaneously shoving my knee in his groin and pushing his chin up with my palm until his neck started to quiver and he gasped. "Now where's Gordie?" I let up with my hand just enough to give his jaw some movement but not enough for him to scream for help. "Come on. Nothing would give me greater pleasure than to tear your fascist, racist balls off!"

He sucked air through his nose and gasped again. "Near Shiloh," he said.

"I know that. Where near Shiloh?" I pushed my knee directly into his left testicle and bore down.

"Somewhere in the Wadi el Haramiye . . . the Pass of the Thieves . . . I'm not sure."

"You'd better not be lying to me, Lipsky, or I'll personally plant a bomb in your van during your next anti-Arab rally!" Then I let go of him and walked out, barely resisting the impulse to crush every bone in his body. When I hit the street, I broke into a dead run. I figured I had about fifteen seconds before he sicked his dogs on me. And unless I took drastic steps, one way or the other they'd be with me the rest of the way.

TWENTY-TWO

"First customer of the day. I make you special price. Where you from? New York?"

"Los Angeles." I was standing opposite a sleepy shopkeeper in the Old City souk who had just rolled up his metal door after I knocked a half-dozen times.

"Los Angellus, Cal-ee-four-nia," he said. "Special price Los Angellus, Cal-ee-four-nia. Here fine Bedouin coat. Not like other in Old City, done in factory by phony stamping machine. This antique from ancient Sinai. Original stitching. Priceless."

"I don't want it."

"How much you want to pay?"

"I told you, all I want is a regular thing Palestinians wear on the street."

"What you want *that* for?"

"That's what I want. Do you want to sell it to me or don't you?"

"I get up early morning get you *that*? How a man supposed to live?"

"Look, just sell it to me or I'm going someplace else."

The shopkeeper shuffled disgruntledly back into his stall and came out with an ordinary-looking cotton cloak and red-checked Palestinian kaffiyeh.

"Put it on me." He looked at me strangely, but I waved a fifty-dollar bill past him and he quickly changed his mind, slipping my arms through the sleeves, then adjusting the kaffiyeh on my head and securing it with a braided belt.

He handed me a mirror to examine myself. "You look just like PLO terrorist," he said. "Haha, just kidding. . . . Cost one hundred dollars."

I gave him a fifty and left, heading across the Muslim Quarter for the Damascus Gate. I had come full circle—a Jew hired by the Arabs to infiltrate the Jews now forced to dress as an Arab in order to avoid apprehension by his own people, whether in the Mossad or the ultra-Orthodox or both. It was an identity crisis of more or less Byzantine proportions and more than a little nerveracking as well, as if I were a guest at some real-time costume party at which the exposed losers would be shot at dawn.

I nodded to several passersby who greeted me in Arabic as I

approached my car, which was parked in the dirt lot near the Arab bus terminal across from the gate. Besides changing its license, I had already scuffed it up and added some garish crepe-paper decorations to the antenna and rear-window shelf in the chicano style that was similar to the Arabs'. It was unfortunate I couldn't take the time to get the whole body painted before I set out for Shiloh and the Pass of the Thieves, but whatever I could do would have to suffice. I slipped on a pair of sunglasses under my kaffiyeh and checked my reflection again in the rearview mirror. Only about an inch of skin was visible between the kerchief and the glass, and I had to admit it was a macho image. Then I started the car and pulled out. Whether it was sheer orneriness or a dimly awakening suspicion of the truth, I knew I had to get to Gordie Goldenberg before the Shin Bet or anybody else could stop me.

As I had the night before, I headed out of Jerusalem on the Nablus Road, north into Samaria, passing through Ramallah with its gardens and the Arab village of Beitin near the austere Jewish settlement of Beit-El where Jacob dreamed he saw the ladder. It wasn't until I was approaching Shiloh itself that I saw the roadblock that I assumed had been erected in my honor. Two soldiers were standing by a half-track parked in the middle of the road, stopping cars as they came in either direction.

I pulled over immediately onto a dirt road and rambled on about a quarter of a mile until I was out of sight before stopping. I had no idea where these side roads went, and the wadi itself, from what I could tell on the map, was only accessible from the main highway. But to go on from here by car would be fruitless. I found a turn-off near a couple of tamarisk trees and parked behind them, locking up and hoping no one would notice; even if anyone did, on Middle Eastern time tables, he wouldn't be in too much of a hurry to report it.

From there I sat out on foot. It was eight o'clock in the morning and already beastly hot. I came out on the main road and set off in the direction of the roadblock. Within a few minutes I was walking up toward a couple of Israeli soldiers who looked in their late teens. I hoped they didn't speak Arabic. I put my head down as I stepped slowly toward the barricade. They stared at me suspiciously, and I wondered if I was going to be asked for an identity card. I didn't have enough experience as a colonial to know whether the best plan was to nod obsequiously or to hold my head high like a haughty rebel. But as I came around the side of the half-track, they just looked at me and laughed, one of them tossing a cigarette butt near my feet and making a joke in Hebrew that I was sure had racial overtones. Look at that dumb Arab who just bought himself a new bathrobe. It made me angry, but I continued on. It was a weird world we lived in.

I bypassed the ruins of the Fountains of Shiloh, where some gray-haired American women were getting an early start, listening to a guide speculate about where Joshua had erected the Tabernacle for the Ark, and headed on to the pass after a more modern Joshua.

I reached it ten minutes later. A bridge about seventy-five feet long crossed a gorge labeled the Wadi el-Haramiye in Arabic, Hebrew and Roman letters. A path ran down the opposite side into the wadi itself, which was a dry riverbed cutting through some sharp sandstone outcroppings; it looked not unlike a Southwestern arroyo. I was about to cross over to it when I saw Boaz and his partner, a harelipped man with a burn scar who reminded me of a Sephardic version of the degenerate killers who ran with Peter O'Toole at the end of *Lawrence of Arabia*. They were leaning against an old Renault parked at the top entrance to the path and watching as I approached. I didn't doubt they were waiting for me. I also didn't doubt these dudes spoke a pretty fair Arabic. The question was whether to walk right past them or to look for an alternate route. But since any evasive action was likely to provoke suspicion and since the most important thing was to encourage the belief that I hadn't yet arrived, I chose the direct route and walked straight at them.

They watched me step for step as I crossed. Almost instinctively, I glared back at them. When I reached their side of the bridge, I stopped not more than ten feet away from them. The two men checked me out carefully. I stared at them and hissed, trying to deflect suspicion by seizing the high ground of racial antagonism. Then I said, "Hah tuey ahy phnah," making up a dialect on the spot and raising my hand in a gesture of disgust as if they were deliberately blocking my way. The partner looked incensed and for a moment I thought he was going to strike me, but Boaz restrained him, they had more important tasks, and I continued off down the path into the wadi, my disguise intact. I didn't look back up until I reached the dry riverbed. They hadn't moved.

I walked along the bottom for a while, checking the various tributaries and caves. The area was large, not half so extensive as the Grand Canyon or even Bryce, but big enough that it made me not too optimistic about finding Gordie. I trudged on anyway. Soon the sun was straight overhead, the light-colored rocks of the pass turning the arroyo into a reflective furnace. My shirt and back were covered with sweat, the dampness even soaking through my new Arab cloak. I stumbled a couple of times and realized I was beginning to feel dehydrated and slightly dizzy. But I continued.

An hour later I still hadn't found Gordie. It was all starting to overwhelm me—the heat, the lack of water, the exhaustion, disorientation. My head began to swim. Maybe Gordie wasn't here after all. I felt angry, angry at myself and then at Lipsky and then finally at Max. It was an anger that swept back to the Berkeley days and then forward to this arroyo and then back to the Wailing Wall again. My son's godfather. I saw his hand extended in greeting, duping an old friend, his coterie of Orthodox agents with its own born-again Jewish Mata Hari to lure me. Not to mention Rabbi DeLeon and his *hoserim teshuvah*, reminding me of *nitzutzot*, holy sparks, as he plunged to his death. What were holy sparks, anyway? It was all a theistic shell game as far as I could tell. The whole thing was making me sick, figuratively and literally.

An intense wave of nausea came over me, and I slumped under a shady ledge to rest. The head that formerly was swimming now was throbbing, my brain pulsating in dizzying waves I hadn't experienced since experimenting with mushrooms years ago. Holy sparks, I thought. That was what I needed, a little divine intervention. Maybe if I stared at the rocks long enough I would see them, the godly presences supposedly hidden in all things, just waiting for release.

I folded my legs in the only meditation position I knew, the lotus, and took a cleansing breath to clear my mind. Then I looked straight ahead of me, but I didn't know what to chant. "Om" seemed somehow inadequate for the *En Sof*, the so-called God behind God, the God "without limit" who had contracted in order to give us the space to exist. So I said simply "One," feeling my pulse rate slow and my eyes dilate as I looked directly at the cliff across the riverbed, staring at it to see if I could perceive the holy sparks glowing within the ageless sandstone face.

What I saw was two climbing ropes hanging from a clamp attached to a ledge halfway up the cliff. If I hadn't been concentrating so intensely I doubt I would have seen them, because their color was almost the same as the rock's. A curve in the cliff led around the corner through a narrow canyon lined with cactus, and I got up and started to follow it. I was partway down when I saw a cave. It was about sixty feet in length and oval-shaped, and I could just see inside where a sleeping bag, a Coleman lantern, more ropes and pitons and some books had been stacked beside a model of some sort. I was about to enter when I was grabbed hard from behind and yanked backward.

"Joshua! It's me!" I said, just managing to rip the kaffiyeh from my head before I was wrestled to the ground.

"You, Wolfe?" He jumped back, flushed with embarrassment. "Oh, no. I didn't realize. I apologize. I beg your pardon. I'm so sorry. Are you all right?"

"I'm fine. Don't worry."

He looked me over carefully to make certain I wasn't just being polite and was actually in one piece. Then he wrinkled his brow, puzzled. "Why're you dressed like the son of Isau?"

"To get through to see you."

"Who would want to stop you?"

"Several people, I think."

"Why would they want to do that?"

"I'm not completely sure. . . . Have you got some water in there?" I gestured into the cave.

"Come. Please." He led me inside, still staring back at me as he went into the corner for a clay pot and poured me a cup of water. I grank it greedily. "I saw you there meditating," he said.

"Yes, I don't do that often."

"You should. Of course, when you do it, you should wear phylacteries and a *tallis*, as it is written." He nodded toward his, which were folded neatly on the floor with his books. "That way God will hear your prayers."

"I think He heard me." I smiled. "At least I got some water."

Gordie laughed. "Do you want some more? How about something to eat?" He pointed to a box of fruit. "I'm sorry if I hurt you. You are a good person, Wolfe. I can see it. I'm young and I cannot see many things, but I recognize that."

"How do you do it?"

"I don't know. I look in their eyes and I know it. That's all. Also I saw you with the children. You were good to them."

"You were too, Joshua."

"I love to be with them more than anything. To make them laugh. Play funny games."

"I used to like to do that with my children when they were little."

"You have children? I would love to meet your children."

"Perhaps you will."

"I would tell them what a *good* father they have, that they must honor you. I want so much to be a father someday, help my children grow up. You must teach me then, Wolfe, what to do. A life of helping others is the only life worth living, wouldn't you agree?"

"I suppose so. Although I can't say I always do it."

"Who does? We are only men, after all. Are you sure you don't want something to eat?"

"No. But I wouldn't mind some more water."

Gordie smiled again, and I watched as he went to pour me another cup. There was something truly decent about him, a throwback to another time when people's values were more important than their achievements or their beauty. It was also clear he was a little nuts, maybe more than a little. And it made me wonder whether in our cold, materialistic age only the crazy had the potential for righteousness. Or had it always been that way?

"I am so glad you have come here to celebrate with me," he said. "Tomorrow is the Ninth of Av and the end of lamentation."

"The end?"

"Yes. You know, the Ninth of Av, the day on which the First and Second Temples were destroyed. It has always been such a sad day for us, full of grief, but tomorrow will be different."

"Why's that?"

"Because we begin the Third Temple," he said, smiling shyly and passing me the cup.

"How's that going to happen? Buildings already exist on the Temple Mount."

"They will be destroyed, as it is written."

"By whom? God?"

"Yes, of course. Sooner or later God would destroy them. But it is better that we help. It would please Him. Then the people would end their suffering sooner and, as they say, the Messiah would come speedily in our days."

"And who is going to do this? You?"

"I will do my part," he said, continuing to smile at me as if he took a personal pleasure in my enjoyment of the water. And I wondered what he meant. Did he have help? Who would it be? And for what? "I am prepared," he continued. "It is my mission in life. Do you have a mission in life?"

"I'm not sure. No one has told me yet. How long have you known this was your mission?"

"Many years. I mean, many years for me." He laughed. "Six. It was the day before my Bar Mitzvah."

"God came to you then?"

"He comes to all of us, if we listen. He will come to you too, Wolfe. Maybe sooner than you expect." He sat down on a stool-sized rock and took off his shoe, shaking it to remove a pebble.

"How'd He come to you?" I asked, leaning against the wall opposite him while casually scanning the cave for weapons. I didn't see any.

"In a vision," he answered. "I had gone to see *Raiders of the Lost Ark.*"

"*That's* where your vision came from?"

"No. Not from the *movie.*" He laughed again, noticing my incredulous expression. "It came later. But I guess in a way it started there. My father had taken me. For my Bar Mitzvah."

"Your stepfather?"

"No. My real father. He thought I'd like it because it was about the Jews and the Nazis, but I told him it was silly and walked out."

"What'd he do?"

"Nothing. I wanted him to argue with me, but he didn't. He was always trying to make up to me after he left my mother because she was too Orthodox. So I just left *him* and ran away. All the way from the Cinerama Dome to Fairfax. And I ended up in the offices of the JDS."

"And that's where you had your vision?"

"No. I was still waiting for my father to come and get me. But when he came and saw where I was, he just turned around and walked away. I never saw him again. Perhaps that was *his* mission, to leave me there, because that day was the Ninth of Av too and religious people were filling the *shul* down the street. Howard Melnick took me there. I had never seen such passion, such love of God. People were crying for the destruction of the Temple, throwing themselves to the ground, weeping and pulling at their clothes."

Gordie stood and shook his head, filmy tears of memory glistening in his eyes. "And then," he continued, "that Ninth of Av before my Bar Mitzvah, I saw Rabbi Lipsky for the first time, and when he stepped in front of the congregation it came to me like a fireball in the mind—the splendor of the New Temple to come, more beautiful than anything I had imagined, than anything I had seen in a museum or in a movie. I knew right then that this was a message from God, that it was my mission to help."

"And you told Rabbi Lipsky about the vision?"

"Yes, yes. That very night. When Howard Melnick introduced me. Since then I have been practicing." He gestured to the ropes and pitons on the floor.

"And now you're going to do this all by yourself?"

"It's God's will." He looked over at me and smiled again. "Besides, it only takes one—and it's easier that way."

"Suppose I tried to stop you?"

"Why should you do that?"

"I don't know. Pretend it's my mission."

"Well, it would be impossible for you." He laughed. "How would you do it? Would you kill me? You could not catch me and tie me up." As if by way of demonstration, he sprang past me, executing a perfect dive-and-roll and ending up at the mouth of the cave, his arms extended. "You see—I *have* been practicing. Besides gymnastics, I studied mountaineering, self-defense and magical escapes." He took a piece of rope and twirled it in the air, making a knot at the end.

"Gordie . . . suppose this isn't all what you think it is, suppose people are trying to use you . . . exploit your visions?"

"I don't understand."

"That whether they believe or not, they have other reasons for wanting you to continue, reasons that are murky, maybe even evil."

"What difference would that make? If others are doing something or allowing me to do something, then that is *their* mission." He tossed the rope into a corner.

"And you're acting alone," I repeated, watching as he walked over and unzipped a rucksack. "That's very brave of you, courageous. But there's something *I* don't understand. Why isn't Rabbi Lipsky helping? You'd think he of all people would want to participate in the coming of the Third Temple. That must be very disappointing for you."

Gordie shrugged, slipping his phylacteries into the rucksack, but I detected the first hint of defensiveness.

"Unless, of course, he felt you could do this by yourself, he encouraged you in your holy work but did not feel, somehow, that in his position as a rabbi he should be personally involved . . . or Hanna Klein either. Is that possible?"

"Rabbi Lipsky is a great man," he said slowly.

"I know. I know. A very great man. A leader of our people. A king really . . . yes, a king." I stopped and studied Gordie, who suddenly had become quit tense. Some way or other I was going to stop this kid, but I wasn't yet certain how or whether the time was right. There were too many pieces missing. I walked over to him and looked down at his rucksack. I could see what seemed like detailed architectural plans folded on the floor underneath it, but I still saw no sign of weapons anywhere. It didn't make sense. He wasn't doing this by hand. "Are you *sure* you're working alone? It seems so . . . overwhelming."

He looked away. "I have some help," he said reluctantly. "Someone has been helping me."

"Who's that?"

"I cannot say."

"Well . . . I'd be willing to help you too, if you needed it. Perhaps that's *my* mission." I smiled shyly. "Of course if you don't trust me . . . "

Gordie stared at me, I looked straight back at him.

"I've never been much of a Jew," I said. "I grew up almost an atheist. But being here in this country, I don't know, it's hard to escape it. I'm not sure if it's in the air or in the trees or what it is, but if there were anything I could do to make things better for my people, anything at all to bring them some kind of rest, some peace, finally, after so many generations, I would do it. . . . Besides, how could I have found you in this giant canyon? It must have been part of God's plan." I looked away. I didn't mind putting on an act when it was necessary. But with this kid, somehow, it turned my stomach . . . and then, who knew, maybe it wasn't entirely an act.

TWENTY-THREE

I never thought that I would be the one to blow up the Dome of the Rock. I was not by nature a terrorist and had no wish to become one. A "freedom fighter," perhaps, although that term had been so debased recently it should have been banned from the language. Anyway, one man's "freedom fighter" was another man's "terrorist." It all depended on the cause. In this case the Temple Mount had been unfairly denied my people for a long time, since the year 70 to be exact, when the Romans, in a fit of imperial frenzy, burned and trashed the Jewish marvel of the ancient world. And now here I was, an unlikely candidate in a long parade to help resurrect it. Part of me found it surprisingly easy, even oddly titillating, to play the role.

Actually that particular detonation was not my precise assignment. Gordie had another plan, which he still would not reveal to me in its entirety and for which I was but a spear carrier, an aide who would help him transport the five packets of military plastic, RDX, molded in the style of IRA-type delayed-action bombs, required for our task. These explosives we had obtained later that day from a one-eyed man named Yoel in a farmhouse outside the Arab village of Jaba, a man who, it turned out, was a *hoser teshuvah*, a supposedly repentant criminal released from prison under the religious recognizance of the now-deceased Rabbi DeLeon, whose associations I knew well. In return for nine thousand dollars in cash, this Yoel also provided us with some French commercial explosives —Nitrotex and Gomme L—as well as detonator caps, delayed-action fuses and the clockwork egg timers used, he repeated, although Gordie was already quite familiar with them, by the Baader-Meinhof gang.

We waited with this arsenal in the stable of the farmhouse, not talking, eating pita and olives given us by Yoel, while I wondered where Gordie had obtained the nine thousand and why the Shin Bet hadn't swooped down on him already, at this point swooped down on us. Unless my association with him now protected me. Or unless, strange thought, they never intended to touch him in the first place. I also wondered who was coming to pick us up.

Gordie spat out his last olive pit and stooped over to examine the weaponry, counting the detonator caps that he had already counted three times before. Then, slowly, carefully, he started loading the packets of plastic into a Maccabee Beer case, smoothing them and separating each one with sheets of cardboard. He then closed the case, sealed it with masking tape and started to wrap the detonating devices, stashing most of them in a vegetable gunny sack which had the words "Perishables—Handle with Care" printed on it in English and Hebrew.

"Suppose someone gets hurt," I said when he had finished.

"No one will get hurt. Only God should take a life." He looked up at me with that face of his, as innocent as a Botticelli. "I promise you. The way I am doing this, no one can get hurt."

Except you, I thought. You are a dead man, or, more exactly, a dead boy. It's only a question of when, now. Why don't you know it?

I realized John Ambrose Kracauer knew it when, a few minutes later, I heard a car rumbling down the dirt road that led to the farm and went to the window. Outside the television van for JAKPROD was pulling to a halt with Sue Ellen Sizemore leaning out the window, panning the area with a video camera, recording everything for posterity or, at least, the next episode of *The Modern Redeemer Gospel Hour*. At that precise moment, Rabbi Lipsky's words echoed in my mind ("He'll do anything for a little publicity. He's desperate to be the number-one TV preacher") and I knew too well the source of Gordie's money and of his "help."

Kracauer himself betrayed only the slightest flicker of surprise when he saw me, carrying one of the cases into his vehicle a few minutes later. "Well, well, Brother Wolfe," he said, "joining our young prophet of God, Mr. ben Tsvi here, in his holy work?"

"I'm trying," I said, adding, "Thank you so much for financing our project. I don't know how we would have been able to do it without you."

He tapped me ever so lightly on the back as I slid my cargo on top of Gordie's into the van refrigerator. "I can feel the presence in your endeavors," said the evangelist, shutting the door for me. He then slid the van door shut and nodded to his driver, who pulled out, heading rapidly back to the paved road into Jerusalem, while Sue Ellen, at Kracauer's instructions, aimed her JVC camcorder at Gordie, who was sitting behind her directly adjacent to the reverend and well positioned for a two-shot.

"I'm interested in a *last* interview with you, Joshua . . . that is, before Miss Sizemore and I abandon the Holy Land with such reluctance for our more mundane home in Corpus Christi. I hope you won't feel offended, Mr. Wolfe."

Kracauer turned toward me, but the word "last" in his initial dialogue with Joshua had resonated with such ominous ambiguity that I was facing the other way and said simply, "What?"

"No matter," said the reverend, who had no intention of being deterred from getting his money's worth. He signaled Sue Ellen to roll the camcorder. "Joshua, as a young prophet of the Hebrew nation who has been, as you have told us, called by God, would you tell our viewers whether you believe we will see Armageddon in our lifetime?"

"Armageddon? I don't know." Gordie frowned, uncomfortable with the questions as well as with the video camera zooming in on him. "I want Messiah . . . what we call Moshiach."

"Yes, yes. Of course, you do. But tell me this." He took a

three-by-five card out of his jacket. "Who do you think said, 'It can't be too long now. Ezekiel says that fire and brimstone will be rained upon the enemies of God's people. That must mean they'll be destroyed by nuclear weapons'?"

He looked at Gordie, who shook his head in bafflement.

"Why, that was President Ronald Reagan himself, in the year of Our Lord nineteen hundred and seventy-one," said Kracauer, smiling broadly as he faced straight into the lens. "And in the year nineteen hundred and eighty he told the audience of Reverend Jimmy Bakker's very own PTL show, which has been so maligned, 'We *may be* the generation that sees Armageddon.' So what do you think of that, Mr. Joshua ben Tsvi? We all have a role to play in God's inevitable plan, even the President. Wouldn't you agree?" He was milking the kid right up to the last minute.

"Yes, yes we do," said Gordie.

"And what do you think the role is for all the good people watching our *Modern Redeemer Hour* . . . for all those charismatics and pentecostalists out there who are, of course, the deep, deep friends of the Hebrew people? How can they partake in God's plan in which you are sacrificing yourself so bravely? Why through *contributions*, Mr. ben Tsvi, wouldn't you agree? In fact, we could say their contributions will *bring on* Armageddon, *bring on* the Rapture, now couldn't we?"

I guess we could, I thought, in a remote sense. At least in that way John Ambrose Kracauer wasn't a liar. But he was certainly a killer. Because there was no way he would leave Gordie alive after all this to recount somewhere, sometime, however discreet and well-intentioned he was, the reverend's supporting role in his activities. That would leave Kracauer with difficulties that would, by comparison, send Jim and

Tammy Bakker back to the bush leagues of evangelical scandal. No, Gordie had to go. And as for me, the junior messiah's humble assistant, there was no doubt I was also *de trop*.

But as we drove into the city and I could see the streams of Orthodox making their way to the Western Wall on the eve of the Ninth of Av, I knew that Gordie would be the least of the reverend's problems. The way I saw it, there wasn't *anybody* who knew about that boy who wanted him to come out of this as a sentient human being. Except maybe his mother and his sister. And maybe me. Basically, it was all Stephen Spielberg's fault. If *Raiders* had been a more realistic movie, hadn't seemed "silly" to Gordie as he had told me back in the cave, then he wouldn't have run out on his father right in the middle of it that evening six years ago before his Bar Mitzvah and wound up in the arms of Rabbi Lipsky, seeing visions of future temples, and I wouldn't be trapped here in Jerusalem with a kid who had no choice but to commit suicide if he didn't accidentally start World War III first. And I wouldn't have the Reverend John Ambrose Kracauer staring at me, wondering whether he had to have me taken care of individually or could trust me to be crazy enough to join Gordie on a one-way trip to my maker. Spinoza *was* right. There *was* no point in doing sit-ups. Everything *is* predestined.

But right now, like it or not, in a state of exhaustion that was beginning to verge on the drastic, I had a world of destiny to alter—and the first part of it was to ditch my friend from Corpus Christi.

"Where do we leave the van?" I asked Gordie, in my best tense, conspiratorial tones but loud enough to be sure the reverend could hear it.

"Near the Tomb of Zechariah. When it's completely dark, I

throw up the rope and climb over the Eastern Wall just beyond the excavations. It is so high no one has tried it. So they'll never suspect."

"And then I follow."

"If you can. After I hoist the boxes. By the time anyone sees us, it'll be too late. We'll be on top. I know the way down through the stables where they keep the Ark."

"Okay. That sounds fine." I glanced over at Kracauer, who was half smiling to himself, seemingly satisfied. The plan was truly lunatic. And if I was going along with it, I had to be certifiable as well.

"The Tomb of Zechariah," he said, turning back to Gordie. "I am pleased you have not changed such an appropriate choice. It was Zechariah' own prophetic visions of the coming Messiah that brought the children of Israel back to rebuild Jerusalem in the days of Darius the Persian. . . . Andrew," Kracauer said to his driver, "bring us to the Tomb of Zechariah, as I told you. There, unfortunately, Miss Sizemore and I will have to say goodbye and Godspeed before we repair to the airport. I know your mission will prosper, but our flight to Dallas leaves much too soon for us to see the results. However, you may rest assured, Joshua ben Tsvi, as a prophecy of the Armageddon to come, your last interview will appear on twenty-seven syndicated cable channels of American TV our very next broadcast this Thursday." Interspersed with an appeal for funds and newsclips of your head being blown off, he might have added.

"Wait a minute," I said. "Could you just pull over a second?" The reverend looked at me. "I beg your pardon, sir, but I've, uh, got to relieve myself."

Kracauer frowned. "Couldn't you wait, Mr. Wolfe? We've

almost arrived." We were approaching the corner of St. George and Shmuel Hanavi, near the Mea She'arim.

"I, uh, it's kind of an emergency. I guess I'm . . . a little nervous."

"That's understandable," said Sue Ellen Sizemore.

"Yeah, I, uh, it's pretty intense . . . and I don't want to dirty up your car." I smiled weakly. Kracauer stared at me, and I shrugged. "It's kind of embarrassing," I said, "for a grown man."

"Just be quick. Andrew, accompany Mr. Wolfe. Make sure he doesn't get . . . lost."

We pulled over by an empty lot across from a religious curio shop on Shivetei Israel. I got out of the van with Andrew, a beefy blond in a Texas A&M warm-up jacket. The shop was closed, and I smiled politely at my keeper and headed around the corner of Mea She'arim Street, continuing straight through the gates of the Chasidic stronghold itself.

"You gonna take a piss in *here*?" said Andrew, clearly repelled by the sea of sweaty, bearded types in fur hats and dark winter coats streaming at us on their way to the Wall.

"They *do* piss," I said. "In fact, I remember seeing a urinal right in there." I pointed to the headquarters of the Reb Arele, walking slowly toward it, knowing that Andrew, suspicious of its decrepit facade and peculiar, dank odors, would lag behind.

I was right. I was inside the building a good fifty feet ahead of him and made straight for the stairs that led up toward the Bet Midrash, the House of Study, on the second floor, where a couple of dozen men ranging up into their nineties were poring over Talmudic texts in the dim light. They looked up, almost too puzzled to react, as I crossed directly through them, acting as if I were absolutely positive where I was going, luring Andrew after me. I came out on a corridor and turned a corner where a dull youth was swabbing the floor with ammonia. I hesitated a second, trying to decide which way to go, and Andrew came around the corner and clasped me by the arm.

"I think you're trying to give me the slip, wise guy."

"No way. I'm just looking for a place to take a leak."

"I thought you knew one. Come on." He clamped down hard on my wrist and started yanking. He had a helluva grip, but I resisted. Suddenly, his eyes dilated. "Let's go, Jewboy," he said, reaching for the handle of what looked like a pistol under his warm-up. Before it was halfway out, I grabbed the kid's disinfectant with my free hand and hurled the chemical in Andrew's face. As the driver cried out in anguish, I kneed him in the groin and let him have as hard a karate chop as I could muster under the circumstances. His knees buckled, and he dropped the gun as he crumpled to the floor. The wide-eyed young Chasid held his hand to his mouth in amazement as if he were getting a sneak look at one of those violent movies he was forever forbidden to see. "Bad guy," I said, winking at him and stuffing the pistol under my shirt. "Wash his eyes out with gentle soap and water when he comes to. He'll be all right." Then I ruffled the kid's hair and headed off down the back stairs without the slightest idea whether he'd understood a word I'd said.

I came out on the rear side of the building and got lost for a moment in the endless maze of Mea She'arim until I came out on the street again where the van was parked. No one was around. The vehicle was empty. They must have gone off looking for me, as I had hoped. I climbed inside and opened the refrigerator. Over half the explosives had disappeared, including all the plastic. Damm it, I thought—Gordie. My plan had misfired. When Kracauer and his lady friend got nervous and left, the kid must've grabbed as much of his arsenal as he could handle and split. I wasn't going to give him the chance to come back for the rest. I checked the area again—still empty—attached one of the short fuses to a small container of the Gomme L and lit it. Then I jumped out of the van and ran fifty feet away, waving and shouting to make sure no one approached. Just then Kracauer came running toward me, only a few steps ahead of Sue Ellen.

"You sonofabitch. You were tryin' to trick me. No one fools John Ambrose Kracauer. I'm gonna run your ass down!"

"No, don't! You're making a mistake!"

He ran toward the van with Sue Ellen.

"It's gonna explode!"

"You think I'm gonna *buhleeve* you, you lyin' Hebrew shit?"

He climbed, and I just managed to grab the terrified Sue Ellen by the arm and yank her free before he gunned the engine, making a hard U-turn straight at me. I started running, leaping around a garbage can across the vacant lot onto the sidewalk by the curio shop, hoping to God or *someone* he wouldn't get me or a half-dozen innocent bystanders. "Get back! Get back!" I yelled as I dodged pedestrians and then ran out into the middle of the street again, barely ten feet ahead of the van. I turned a corner, gaining a little time, and caught sight of small church out of the corner of my eye. It had a tiny graveyard off to the side, and I ran straight for it, jumping a hedge. But this didn't deter John Ambrose, who crashed through right behind me, and I raced ahead of him, weaving through tombstones toward a brick wall about fifteen feet high. I didn't know what to do. I thought about turning around and trying to shoot him, but there was no time. And I thought about prayer, but I didn't believe in it, so I just dove behind the largest gravestone I saw and held my head, doubling over like a kid at an old A-bomb drill. And then I heard it—one of the loudest explosions of my life, glass, metal, bits of furniture, rock and bone flying everywhere, as John Ambrose Kracauer went to his own personal Armageddon. Its almost made me believe in divine intervention.

But I didn't delay for even a second of spiritual contemplation. The thought of Gordie on the loose with a box of plastics made me jump up and run for the main street. I kept going until I found a cab less than a block from the Damascus Gate.

"The Eastern Wall," I told the Arab driver as I climbed in.

"Western Wall—ten shekel."

"No, no, the *Eastern* Wall." He looked blank. My head was aching and my forty-year-old lungs felt as if they'd spent a two-week vacation in a Cuisinart. "You know—the Eastern Wall of the Temple Mount. The Tomb of Zechariah."

"Western Wall—ten shekel."

"Jesus. Just take me to the Eastern Wall, okay?" I took out my map and showed it to him.

"Ah, Eastern Wall . . . twenty shekel."

"Great. Go."

We were there in a minute and a half, where the four tomb excavations—among them Zechariah's—formed a half-moon at the base of the Mount of Olives. The Eastern Wall loomed in front of us, its monumental facade, illuminated with klieg lights, about as logical a method of attack on the Temple Mount as scaling Gibraltar with a pickax to invade Spain. It was almost pitch dark. A lone Arab with his donkey making his way down into the Valley of Kidron was the only human that could be seen in the dim light of a street lamp. Gordie was not in evidence anywhere. I felt a tightening in my chest and a throbbing again where Hosea had bashed me in the forehead. This was probably all a waste. And I knew that somewhere out in that night, the Israeli authorities were pursuing me; they would find me soon, their technological weaponry as advanced as anything dreamed of by the most sophisticated Talmudists.

I sat there in the cab drumming my fingers on the seat while the driver eyed me suspiciously, waiting for his twenty shekels. One thing was clear to me: Gordie had no intention of entering the Temple Mount this way and had made up his story to deceive Kracauer, and probably me as well. The rest was murky indeed. I had no idea where he would enter. And what would happen when he did—whether he would be killed, the most natural outcome, or, given his athletic skills, he could possibly elude his pursuers and destroy some Islamic holy site, with horrifyingly predictable results. It also occurred to me that if he had deceived Kracauer, he could have deceived others as well, everyone who cast the slightest doubt on his "mission." And if that was the case, then I was the sole person left to stop him, hardly a consoling thought.

"Twenty shekel," said the driver.

I handed it to him, but continued to sit there, thinking about everything Gordie had said, everything I had seen. The maps of Temple Mount. The visions. He'd said he had gone to the pass to practice. But where and for what? Something about stables and the hidden area beneath. Then I remembered. "The double gates," I said.

"Goodbye, Yankee," said the driver. "Eastern Wall. Byebye."

"No, no, the double gates. You know, with the arches. Double Gate. Noble Enclosure. Two. Two." I held up the requisite number of fingers until he got the point.

"Ah . . . Double Gate . . . Double Gate." He looked at me as if I were nuts, then said, "Fifty shekel."

"Let's go."

We made a quick turn and screeched around the other side, coming to a halt in about another thirty seconds. He put out his hand. "Double Gate, fifty shekel," he said, nodding with his head through the Dung Gate toward the archaeological excavation at the southern end of the Temple Mount. I paid him. "Is close-ed," he said. "Other gate?" but to his disappointment I got out and slammed the door behind me, walking swiftly through the entrance and stopping at the checkpoint for the usual bomb inspection. I wondered how Gordie had gotten through here, but the lower perimeter walls were long and the night was dark and he was certainly agile.

I backed off into the darkness and climbed over a barricade into the excavation area in the direction the cab driver had indicated. I stumbled around a bit, slipping on old Herodian stone, moving up and down little narrow stairways, one of which led down into what looked like a cistern illuminated by a worklight. As I came around the Southern Wall I noticed two arched doors almost directly down from the silver dome of El Aqsa Mosque—the Double Gate. They were walled up as if they had been sealed for fifteen hundred years. Not a soul seemed to be around. Then I saw it—a figure swinging just above the arches, hanging from rope grappled to a lintel of an alcove fifty feet above. It had to be Gordie.

Then I wondered where were the soldiers, the elite marksmen waiting to pick him off the moment he reached the top. Someone was giving this kid an awfully long cord, but then I remembered—Rabbi DeLeon, *hoserim teshuvah*. The authorities, Max and his pals on the Jewish Desk, had never bothered to come and stop Gordie because they were totally aware of the kind of weaponry he had, indeed they had picked it for him. And it didn't take a rocket scientist to figure out what it might be.

I had two options. I could make a ruckus, yell out to him, attracting the soldiers not more than fifty yards off, giving them no choice but to shoot him or to cause him to blow himself up at the least, or I could test my forearms on the rope and try to talk him out of it. The way I saw it, that was *his* only chance. I grabbed the rope and started pulling myself up. I hadn't gotten more than a step when he saw me coming.

"It's all right, Joshua," I whispered, just loud enough. "It's me. Why didn't you wait?"

He stared down at me strangely. "How'd you find me?"

"*Baruch ha-Shem*," I said. "I had a vision."

"Go away, Wolfe. Go, please."

"No, no. I can't. I saw something very disturbing," I said. "An augury of some sort."

He hesitated a second, giving me a chance to pull myself higher. I hung there, swinging, only a few feet below him, the lintel only a few feet beyond that.

"It's the wrong night," I said. "Inauspicious. I saw a vision of the detonator caps. They're made in a funny way. They don't explode the plastic. They just explode the person who uses it. They're a booby trap, Gordie."

"That's not possible," he said.

"Yes, it is. I promise you. Take a look."

"It's not possible," he repeated.

"Yes, it is," I insisted. "The man who sold it to you. He's not your friend. He doesn't want to liberate the Temple Mount. He wants you to die."

"This is nonsense."

"No, it's not. Gordie, I promise. That, at least, is the truth. Many people want you to die. It's terrible." I climbed up close to him, practically touching his feet. "I beg you, Gordie. Stop.

Rachel would be so sad if you died. And your mother. You don't want to hurt them. You—"

"No! No!" he shouted, shaking his head, not wanting to hear what I was saying. He grabbed a second rope and flung it above him. It made a graceful arch, landing just the other side of the short wall on top of the Mount. He pulled it backward and it caught. Then, like an experienced mountaineer, he started walking up the side with startling rapidity.

I reached for the second rope and missed it. Then, gasping for breath, I let go with my left hand and stretched out, making that last extra effort and just catching it with my fingertips. I pulled it in and started after him, but my early-middle-aged grip wouldn't take, and I slid down, almost losing hold altogether and plummeting into the excavations. I caught myself at the last second, banging hard into the wall, nearly dislocating my shoulder. Endless hours of jet lag, exhaustion and sunstroke coupled with too many years of chasing people for ambiguous purposes flashed through my brain, and for a split second I had an odd desire simply to release and forget the whole thing, everything. But I grabbed on tight and kicked outward, catching the ancient brick on the soles of my sneakers and pushing myself upward. I made some quick progress and within seconds was within a few feet of Gordie again. We were nearing the top of the wall, the black dome of the El Aqsa Mosque looming in front of us as if we were two astronauts approaching the dark side of the moon. In a few seconds he would be there.

"Stop, Gordie! Stop!" I pleaded with him again. "Please, stop!"

It was then that the giant searchlight struck, blinding us both with the power of some unseen laser. No doubt they had been hidden in the excavation the whole time, watching, hoping for the best. But with two of us together they had to stop us. It was one thing to justify the incineration of a young zealot, but another the death of an American detective working for the Arabs. That, even for such skilled professionals, would have been too difficult to explain.

Now the light began to focus more sharply in our faces. Gordie held his free arm across his eyes to block the light. I could see his expression clearly—terror, confusion, madness, tears. " 'The Lord shall become King over the whole earth, saith Zechariah,' " he shouted, his voice hoarse and plaintive. " 'On that day the Lord shall be the only one, and His name the only one.' " And then he started to sob, swinging there on the Southern Wall of the Temple Mount.

"Help me," he said. "Help me."

"It's all right, Gordie." I said. "I'll do what I can. I promise."

TWENTY-FOUR

The one called Yitzhak lit another Gauloise and shook his head. I was sitting opposite him in the same room in the Russian Compound, but this time he was not alone. He was accompanied by a fifty-year-old woman in a print dress and a stenographer.

"I want to see Max," I said.

"Mr. Hirsch is on vacation in Spain."

"How convenient."

"How inconvenient of *you* not to leave the country when you were asked."

"So that you could sacrifice that kid?"

"Mr. Wine, amateurs should not play in professional games. You have very little idea what you are talking about."

"Don't I? You wanted me to leave the country so he would go on with his cracked vision of liberating the Temple Mount and blow himself up in the process."

"And why would we want to do that?"

"Simple. He dies here in the midst of a seemingly deranged act. One that is known to have been attempted several times before. You blame *him* for the assassination of Joseph Damoor in Los Angeles. No one can question it. Or would want to."

"And why would we involve ourselves in such a bizarre plot? The assassination of Joseph Damoor is no concern of ours."

"Isn't it?"

"You are trying to tell me, Mr. Wine, that Joseph Damoor was murdered by an agent of Israeli intelligence."

"Who knows?"

"What a peculiar accusation. In the meantime you are in considerable trouble here, trespassing on a holy site, conspiring to use illegal weapons, various other crimes."

"Actually, I don't think he *was* killed by an Israeli agent, at least not directly. I imagine he was killed by someone else for an entirely different reason. But Israeli intelligence had a damn good reason to hush it up. Good enough, in fact, to be willing to sacrifice Gordie Goldenberg."

"We don't do things like that."

"*Every* intelligence agency does things like that. That's the business you're in, Yitzhak."

"Making a judgment, are we, Mr. Wine?"

"Just being factual. Anyway, if I were to make a guess, Joseph Damoor was murdered by gangsters in the employ of Menashe Kandel working on behalf of Rabbi Judah Lipsky."

"Well, this *is* getting highly baroque. First you are saying our government is involved. Now you are saying it is Judah Lipsky." He smiled. "Some of us here are well known to be enemies of Rabbi Lipsky and what he stands for."

"That's precisely the point."

"Mr. Wine, now I'm really confused. I think it's better you called yourself a lawyer. Unless you would prefer we appointed one for you."

"Yes. Maybe I should make a call. But not to a lawyer. To the *New York Times*. I have information they would find interesting, and, as Rabbi Lipsky himself indicated, the *Jerusalem Post* might be reluctant to print it. State censorship, I suppose."

"What information?"

"About Lipsky's *shiksa* problem. Remember, we discussed it before. You told me Lipsky hadn't touched another woman since he was married, and as far as I know, you were right."

"This hardly constitutes news, Mr. Wine, even in your advanced society."

"No, but information that he was formerly married to Suzi DelVecchio, a lapsed Catholic and sometime porno actress who committed suicide in 1969, might attract more attention. And that he married her under the name James Larson, a man who himself appears to have mysteriously disappeared at the time of her death."

"And you have proof this Larson and Lipsky are the same man?"

"No proof. But Lipsky was missing during those years and I overheard Kandel calling him by that name when he said he'd solved his *shiksa* problem."

Yitzhak smiled. "Americans make such marvelous conspiracy theorists. Mr. Wine, this is one of the more bizarre stories I have heard in a lifetime in a rather bizarre occupation. You are asking me to believe that Judah Lipsky married a woman under an assumed name and then hired Menashe Kandel to kill Joseph Damoor twenty years later. For what conceivable purpose?"

"To cover it up. I can't imagine anything more damning to the reputation of the ever so devoutly Orthodox Rabbi Judah Lipsky than the revelation that he, of all people, married a Gentile—whether he participated directly in her death or not. A Gentile who, incidentally, was about to have a child that would have been born, as you know, through the mother's side, a non-Jew. Judah Lipsky would have been a miscegenator."

"And how, in this world of paranoia and conspiracy that you inhabit, would Damoor have known all this?"

"That's what I've been trying to figure. I must admit it doesn't make a lot of sense." I looked over at the stenographer, who was racing to keep up with my every word. Yitzhak glanced over at the woman and lit another cigarette. "The only thing that computes is that *you* told him."

"*We* told him?" Yitzhak's sarcasm was withering.

"Yes. Damoor was supposed to come here last week, to the West Bank, for a Peace Now conference. There was sure to be a lot of media attention. It would have been a great opportunity to wreak havoc, destroy Lipsky's reputation. As you say, Lipsky is your enemy."

"Mr. Wine, you are piling absurdity on absurdity. We tell Damoor that Lipsky has this dark past, then Lipsky kills Damoor. How would Lipsky even know we had done this, unless he's psychic?"

"Or has penetrated your organization. You've certainly penetrated his. Why wouldn't he have penetrated yours? Hanna Klein was certainly very interested in the members of the Jewish Desk, I can tell you."

"And who is this . . . shall we call it double-agent? . . . this loyalist to Jewish fundamentalism in our midst who warned Lipsky of our activities?"

"My guess is that it's Irv Hurwitz. He wasn't sure which side I was on, so he let me out of the Holocaust Prevention Instituute when I broke in the other night. I imagine he told Lipsky what you were up to with Damoor and that his whole career was in jeopardy. Fortunately, Rabbi Judah had the perfect patsy. He waited for the day he knew his boy Gordie Goldenberg was heading for Israel and had Menashe Kandel's people lower the boom on poor Damoor that very day, as if they were a group of out-of-control terrorists from the JDS."

"And after this happened, we just sat by with our hands tied like good little boys . . . even, as you hint, participated."

"You had to. The last thing you'd want known is that the first fatal example of bloody Middle East terrorism to reach U.S. shores was *not* instigated by the PLO or by the Hizbullah or by the party of some other nutso fundamentalist Islamic god but, however inadvertently, by the Mossad . . . not after the Pollard affair, the arms deals with Iran, the gargantuan aid payments, etc., etc. and so forth. All the lobbyists in the world couldn't save you from *that* one. You'd be up to your nose in hearings for the next five years. Poor Gordie Goldenberg would have to go. It was the only solution."

With that I shut up. No one else said anything either.

It was Yitzhak who finally broke the silence. "But you say you have no proof."

"No. But I imagine you do. That's probably what got you started with Damoor in the first place. In any case, it doesn't matter. One word to the foreign press and you'll have two thirds of the investigative reporters from here to Honolulu down on you like starving fish at a feeding."

Yitzhak and the woman looked at each other. It seemed as if they were about to launch into an internecine discussion, but stopped with a mutual expression that read to me as resigned frustration.

"So what do you want us to do?" he said.

"The only thing you can do. Notify the U.S. authorities and extradite Kandel and Lipsky for prosecution."

"Yes. . . . But you realize, Moses, that is impossible. The moment we do that, our, as you say, inadvertent involvement in U.S.-based terrorism will be revealed. Kandel and Lipsky have us—how do you say it?—by the balls."

"So do I."

"Then you must make a choice. To whom do you owe your allegiance?"

So it had come to that after all, the old dual-national question. Where do your loyalties lie? Israel? The United States? God? In my heart, I had always thought mine lay with justice.

As if anticipating my response, Yitzhak said: "I will remind you—nothing we do will bring back Joseph Damoor. Unless, of course, you feel it necessary to exact an eye for an eye." He added that last without the slightest ironic inflection before continuing: "And I do think it would be unfair, not to say counterproductive, for our country to be punished for an action which had a positive intent, an intent I'm certain you support."

"Listen, Yitzhak, I don't support gangsters like Kandel and fanactics like Lipsky running around loose while innocent kids are either punished or killed."

"To begin with, I can promise you that at this point nothing will happen to the innocent. I know *you* wouldn't permit it, and, it may surprise you to hear, we no longer have the stomach for it."

"I'll believe *that* when I see it."

"As for Kandel, I can assure you that we have our ways to make him suffer, perhaps more than in a court of law. As you can no doubt guess, his business relationships are highly precarious and susceptible to sabotage by covert methods readily available to us. You will be able to chart his bankruptcy and ultimate ruin for yourself in the pages of the *Wall Street Journal* and *Variety*. . . . Lipsky is a different matter. I wish I could tell you he is as easy to destroy, but a demagogue with an army of true believers is a formidable opponent. We must continue our war with him by other means."

Yitzhak studied me to see if his speech had had any effect. I tried not to reveal my feelings but simply replied: "If you're not going to punish the innocent, what then do you expect me to tell my employers back in Los Angeles?"

"In Orange County, you mean."

"Yes. In Orange County."

Yitzhak glanced over at the woman again before speaking with the most minute hint of a smile. "Don't worry about that, Moses. Your friends in Orange County will be very pleased with your activities and you will be paid handsomely for your work."

"Your people too?"

"A fraternal organization."

So that was it. The cesspool was getting ever worse. I had

been part of a CIA-Mossad sting to make sure the American public would never suspect Israeli government involvement in the death of Joseph Damoor. Putting the best face on it, it wasn't very flattering professionally. Putting the worst face on it, it was disgusting.

"We have a sad history, Moses—our people. We can only ask you to cooperate."

"Cooperate? Every bone in my body wants to blow the whistle on this whole rancid business. And stop playing on the fact that I'm Jewish. First and foremost I'm a human being. The buck stops there."

"Ah, a citizen of the world, *hors de combat.* Congratulations. The human race should be honored to have you. . . . Well, go ahead. Call the *New York Times* or whoever you want." He pushed the phone toward me. "Of course, you do realize that all your accusations will be denied and that actual hard proof of the relationship of Lipsky and this woman has long ago been erased. All you will succeed in doing is undercutting us. Lipsky will be embarrassed, no more. That was all we were aiming to do in the first place, all we *could* do. In fact, an accusation of murder without specific evidence will only succeed in making a martyr out of the man you wish to dethrone. He's quite clever that way." Yetzhak looked at me. Lipsky was't the only clever one, clearly. "And right now you are in a position to help people, instead of to hurt them. Be, shall we say, the Christian God instead of the God of Wrath. Or to put it in Kabbalistic terms, help repair the world."

"You want to make a deal."

"Obviously."

"Over Gordie Goldenberg."

"Yes. He's a very sick boy, I'm sure you will agree. We will do exactly what you want to make him better, assuming, of course, that you shut up about our business."

"Of course." I looked at Yitzhak. I wasn't sure if I liked him or hated him. "All right. I'll do it. But there are other things I want as well."

"Speak."

"I want Gordie placed in the best mental hospital you can find, one with the most advanced humane techniques. I want him there until he's cured of his visions and his madness, whatever it costs, and I want you to handle his mother so that she'll let him go. You'll know people who'll be able to do that. I don't. Also, I want periodic reports of his progress from the doctors. Furthermore, I don't want him ever blamed for this crime, and I don't want any other innocent party to take the heat for it either. And if it ever comes around to you, don't expect a peep out of me in your defense and don't expect me to perjure myself one word if I'm subpoenaed. Furthermore, there's the family of Joseph Damoor. I want them recompensed at the highest level with their children's educations paid for."

"Done."

"Also, there's a girl named Ellen Greenspan presently being held by a fatboy Orthodox deprogrammer who calls himself Hosea the Prophet. I want her freed by tomorrow, and I want Hosea arrested for kidnapping."

"Also done."

"Then I want to be on the morning flight to Los Angeles. I miss my *shiksa* girl friend, Chantal Barrault. I feel like doing a little miscegenating."

"Fine. That's all?"

"One more thing. I want to go to Yad Vashem. I'm Jewish. I want to see the Holocaust Memorial."

"I'm sorry, Moses. That's impossible. You want to go to Los
Angeles tomorrow morning and it's eleven o'clock at night. Yad
Vashem is closed."

"Open it."

TWENTY-FIVE

I went to Yad Vashem that night and I saw the memorial. I
walked along the Avenue of the Righteous with its carob trees
commemorating the Gentiles who'd risked their lives to help
Jews and I visited the Hall of Names with its biographies of
three million of the victims. I thought of my children, of other
members of my family, of myself, of how lucky we were to be
alive, and I wept at the indescribable terror and suffering of
my people, the incomprehensible evil of it all. Then I went
home.

Life resumed in Los Angeles at it had been before. As Yitzhak had predicted, Terzi and Said were very much satisfied
with my efforts, even though I was not able to bring them a
culprit. At least I had eliminated Gordon Goldenberg. They
also decided it was pointless to continue and sent me a generous check. Sonya was relieved I hadn't become a religious

fanatic. Chantal had had the good sense not to sell my car, and things went well with her and then they went badly and then they went well again. Work in general was also good. I had a political case helping the El Salvadorean refugees, which I was able to do for nothing because I got several cases that came in out of nowhere with high pay for almost no work, tracing down a lost relative that took me a couple of hours for five thousand dollars, an industrial accident I handled in a day for forty-two hundred, as if someone were looking after me, or wanting to keep me friendly. I also began to receive letters from a doctor in a hospital outside of Boston, detailing Gordie's treatment, even to describing the intimate nuances of his daily life. It seemed more than one could hope. And one time I saw a flyer taped to a window on Fairfax Avenue advertising a fund-raising speech at a local synagogue by Rabbi Judah Lipsky, "Is There a Good Arab?" I chose not to go.

Then one day, three months later, I had slipped off for a quick lunch at Angeli's Café on Melrose, something I did two or three times a month when I had a moment to play hooky and indulge myself in a plate of pasta with oil and garlic, when a man walked up and asked if he could join me. I would have recognized him immediately had it not been for the lack of beard and the trendy West Hollywood jacket with rolled sleeves.

"Sit down, Max."

"The return of your double betrayer," he said with an ironically self-effacing smile, as he squeezed into the seat opposite me behind an effete-looking man in a voguish ponytail.

"Come to check up on how I'm doing? See if I have any complaints?"

"You might say that." He glanced at my plate. "I see you haven't lost your taste for pasta."

"Well, if it's any consolation to you and your pals, so far I'm reluctantly cooperative, aside from isolated moments when I feel like personally assassinating Judah Lipsky."

"You have my blessings."

"No, I don't. If I did it, they'd figure I was working for you."

"Perhaps." A waiter came over with a menu, but Max politely waved it away, asking only for a glass of water.

"You *really* are kosher?"

"Does that surprise you?"

"Well, it's hard to know what's an act and what's not."

"Sometimes for me as well." He smiled wistfully. "You know, Moses, my superiors were extremely impressed with your behavior—not just now, I mean, but back in Israel. They thought, under the circumstances, you conducted yourself very well. That you are, shall we say, gifted in the craft. They would like to . . . get to know you better."

"Is this supposed to be an invitation?"

Max fiddled with a spoon. "Only if you are interested."

"Well, forget it. As far as I'm concerned, spies are like nuclear weapons. The world would be better off without them." I sounded definite, but I had to admit on some level I was flattered, intrigued.

Max shrugged. "Sometimes they are necessary."

"I wonder."

"I see. . . . Well, I guess we don't have anything more to say to each other." The waiter arrived with his water. He mumbled a few words of prayer and downed his glass. "Goodbye, Moses. I'm sorry that I had to lie to you. It does not make me comfortable. It never does. But particularly since I considered you a friend."

"It doesn't make me happy either. For the same reasons,

and also because I fell for it. But before you go, tell me one thing—honestly."

"Of course."

"It's been disturbing me since I've been back, and I've been trying a thousand and one theories in my mind and not one of them seems to make any sense. Who killed Rabbi DeLeon?"

Max frowned and looked away, picking up his water glass again and then realizing it was empty. "I was afraid you'd ask that."

"Well, it is strange. I mean, there I am at the Dome of the Rock and this rabbi, admittedly an agent of yours, just happens to die in front of me with garbled, even mystical information that enabled me in some peculiar way to find Gordie Goldenberg and save him from killing himself."

Max seemed uncharacteristically diffident about responding, and I waited for him to speak with some impatience, oblivious to the din of the restaurant around me. "You're not going to believe the answer," he said finally. "But it is the truth."

"What is it?"

"I don't know." He let that sink in a minute before continuing. "I mean, I certainly wondered myself and made all the usual inquiries, talked to anybody who might have information, and I can assure you I have access to those people, and I still have no idea."

"No idea?"

"Well, my friend, Moses. Why don't we look at it this way? . . . The role of the detective, and perhaps sometimes even the secret agent, is to ascertain as closely as possible the reality of the physical world. But sometimes there are things that are determined in another manner, connections that are made by a different force for a more powerful purpose. If the Kabbalah itself is too overtly theistic an explanation of this for you, perhaps there are other, more or less metaphysical roads. And if you wish to understand why this happened, why this man died the way he did at the time he did, perhaps I could recommend a work on predestination by Spinoza."

He didn't specify which one.

ABOUT THE AUTHOR

Roger L. Simon's first Moses Wine detective novel, *The Big Fix*, won awards from the Mystery Writers of America and the Crime Writers of Great Britain as the best crime novel of the year, and it was later made into a film. His most recent novel, *The Straight Man*, was nominated for an Edgar Award. The series has been translated into more than a dozen languages.

Mr. Simon is also a screenwriter and the president of the North American branch of the newly formed International Association of Crime Writers.